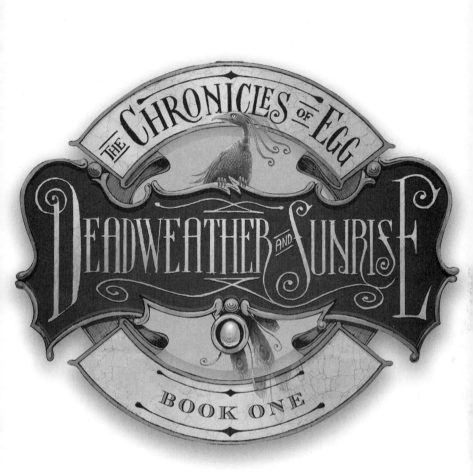

GEOFF RODKEY

G. P. PUTNAM'S SONS
AN IMPRINT OF PENGUIN GROUP (USA) INC.

G. P. PUTNAM'S SONS
A division of Penguin Young Readers Group.
Published by The Penguin Group.

Penguin Group (USA) Inc., 375 Hudson Street, New York, NY 10014, U.S.A.
Penguin Group (Canada), 90 Eglinton Avenue East, Suite 700, Toronto, Ontario M4P 2Y3, Canada
(a division of Pearson Penguin Canada Inc.).
Penguin Books Ltd, 80 Strand, London WC2R 0RL, England.
Penguin Ireland, 25 St. Stephen's Green, Dublin 2, Ireland (a division of Penguin Books Ltd).
Penguin Group (Australia), 250 Camberwell Road, Camberwell, Victoria 3124, Australia
(a division of Pearson Australia Group Pty Ltd).
Penguin Books India Pvt Ltd, 11 Community Centre, Panchsheel Park, New Delhi—110 017, India.
Penguin Group (NZ), 67 Apollo Drive, Rosedale, Auckland 0632, New Zealand
(a division of Pearson New Zealand Ltd).
Penguin Books (South Africa) (Pty) Ltd, 24 Sturdee Avenue, Rosebank, Johannesburg 2196, South Africa.
Penguin Books Ltd, Registered Offices: 80 Strand, London WC2R 0RL, England.

Published simultaneously in Canada. Printed in the United States of America.
Design by Ryan Thomann. Text set in Minister.

Library of Congress Cataloging-in-Publication Data
Rodkey, Geoff, 1970– Deadweather and Sunrise / by Geoff Rodkey.
p. cm.—(The chronicles of Egg ; bk. 1)
Summary: Thirteen-year-old Egbert, a planter's son on a pirate-infested Caribbean island chain, is on the run
from a wealthy and powerful villain trying to kill him for his connection to a hidden treasure.
[1. Adventure and adventurers—Fiction. 2. Islands—Fiction. 3. Buried treasure—Fiction. 4. Good and evil—
Fiction.] I. Title. PZ7.R61585De 2012 [Fic]—dc23 2011033411
ISBN 978-0-399-25785-8
1 3 5 7 9 10 8 6 4 2

For Ronin

DEADWEATHER

Nobody lived on Deadweather but us and the pirates. It wasn't hard to understand why. For one thing, the weather was atrocious. Eleven months out of twelve, it was brutally hot and humid, with no wind at all, so on a bad day the air felt like a hot, soggy blanket smothering you from all sides.

And the other month was September, which meant hurricanes.

Then there was the volcano. It hadn't actually blown in ages, but it belched smoke and shook the earth enough to scare away anybody who might've overlooked the pirates and the weather. The only reason it didn't scare me, even though plenty of things do, was because I'd been born and raised halfway up its slope and didn't know any different.

That's how I felt about the pirates, too. There were two kinds on Deadweather: the normal ones, who hung around down in Port Scratch, drinking and getting into knife fights whenever they weren't off raiding Cartager gold ships; and the busted-down, broken ones, who'd lost too many limbs or eyes or organs to crew a ship, but not enough to kill them outright. A few of those stayed in the Scratch, patching together a living in the taverns and the gun shops, but most of them hobbled up the mountain to work for Dad on the ugly fruit plantation.

I don't know what he paid them—it couldn't have been much, because we didn't have much. But I guess it was enough, since none of them ever staged a mutiny or tried to kill us all in our sleep.

They slept down in the barracks and mostly kept to themselves in the orchards, except for Quint the house pirate, who cooked for us and did some occasional sewing. Dad had his hands full running the plantation, so he left the rest of the housework to the kids—the kids being me, my sister Venus, and my brother Adonis. I was the youngest, which I didn't much like. Adonis whaled on me every chance he got, and even though I fought back as best I could, he had three years on me, so I usually got the short end of it—especially after he turned fifteen and shot up past six feet, with shoulders almost as wide and thick as Dad's.

Fortunately, as Adonis got bigger, he also got more lumbering, so eventually I figured out I could duck the beating by running to the orchards and climbing an ugly fruit tree, way up to where the branches got too thin to bear his weight. He knew Dad would skin him if he hurt one of those trees, so he'd just glower at me from under his heavy, black eyebrows, and shake his fist, and bellow that he could wait for me forever. Then he'd get bored and wander off.

Venus used to knock me around, too, right up until the day I got big enough to take her in a fight. She backed off for good after that, except to constantly tell me how stupid I was, and how Dad had tried to sell me but couldn't find a buyer at any price, and how someday she was going to marry a Rovian prince, and the prince would have me ground up and fed to his horses.

"They'll gobble you up, Egbert, bones and all," she'd say, sneering down her long, sharp nose at me.

At some point, I found out horses don't eat meat, but I never bothered to tell Venus. Just like I never bothered to tell her no prince of Rovia would ever marry a commoner, let alone try to find a wife by leaving the Continent and sailing thousands of miles across the Great Maw to a sweaty little pirate-infested island so unimportant it didn't even show up on the maps of the New Lands in *Geography of the World*.

There was no point in telling her any of that, because Venus ignored any fact she didn't like, and the ones she couldn't ignore, she screamed at. And whenever she screamed, Adonis would come running—not because he cared about Venus one way or another, but just for the excuse—and I'd get slugged, unless I got to a tree fast enough.

And if I did, he'd stand under it and yell the same fist-shaking curse every time: "Treat a lady like that, I'll 'ave the pirates cut yer tongue out!"

Venus was hardly a lady, except in her own mind—she belched when she ate, and picked her nose at the table—and anyway, it was an empty threat. None of the field pirates could stand Adonis, so if he'd ever ordered them to cut my tongue out, the ones who still had legs would have kicked him in the shins.

But Adonis wasn't much for facts, either. Or any kind of learning—I'm not even sure Mr. Sutch managed to teach him how to read properly.

Mr. Sutch was our first tutor, and the only good one, which was probably why he didn't last. This was years back—I was just seven when he showed up, which would have made Venus nine and Adonis ten. I guess Dad had figured out by then that we weren't going to learn to read and write by ourselves—especially since the only book in the house was a chewed-up copy of *Principles of Citrus Cultivation*—so he'd sent out a flyer with the captain of the cargo ship that hauled the ugly fruit harvest up to the Fish Islands.

When the ship came back six months later, Mr. Sutch was on it—all bony and worried-looking, and pulling out a handkerchief every two minutes to wipe the sweat-fog from his glasses. Right from the start, it was obvious he was a bad fit. The volcano and the pirates had him scared out of his pants, and on his first night, I overheard him out on the porch with Dad, complaining in his reedy voice that he'd been lured to Deadweather under false pretenses.

Dad snorted. "Stuff! Don't even 'ave one."

"One what?"

"A wot-ye-say. A faults pretenses."

"What I mean . . . is that your advertisement specifically indicated this position was on Sunrise Island."

"Nah, it didn't."

"Sir, if I may—" I was inside, listening from under the sitting room window, so I couldn't see them, but I heard a crinkling of paper as Mr. Sutch unfolded what must have been Dad's flyer. "Right here, line three—it says 'Sunrise Island.'"

"Nah, look—says '*roundabout* Sunrise Island.'"

"No, it . . . that word there? It's 'roundabout'?"

"Wot ye think it was?"

"I honestly didn't know what that word was."

"Now ye do. Says 'roundabout.'"

"That's not even remotely correct spelling!"

"Quint read it fine."

"Who's Quint?"

"House pirate. In the kitchen. Got stumps fer legs. Smart one, he is. Reads AND writes."

"Look, sir . . . spelling issues aside, this island is HARDLY 'roundabout Sunrise'!"

"Wot ye mean? Head down to the Scratch, 'op a boat, east nor'east . . . catch the wind right, be there in three hours. 'At's roundabout, seems to me."

"Well, I'd very much like to do that. And as soon as possible— I think it's the least you can do for me under the circumstances."

"Wot? Put ye on a boat? Can't. 'Aven't got one—I'm a farmer. And the cargo ship's sailed, won't be back till next season . . . Might get one o' the pirates to take ye, fer the right price. 'Ave ye got a gun?"

"What? No! I'm a man of learning."

"Wouldn't chance it, then. Man shows up in the Scratch with money in 'is pocket and no gun, not likely to go well for 'im . . . Looks like yer stuck 'ere, then. So—gonna teach me kids? Or ye gonna pick fruit? 'Cause them's the only jobs need doin' round 'ere."

Once he realized he wasn't going anywhere soon, Mr. Sutch did his best to educate us. But it was a tough job. When he started, none of us could read a word or add higher than our fingers, and when we talked, we all sounded like pirates. That particularly bothered him, because he was a very formal sort, and he couldn't abide the fact that we not only didn't speak what he called "proper Rovian," we couldn't even see the point of it.

"Ye understan' us, yeh?" said Venus. "So wha's the need fer all these *duh*s and *guh*s and *yooooooooo*s?"

"My dear young lady," he said—and kindly, too, not at all sarcastic, because it was still his first day and Venus hadn't bitten him yet—"how can you expect to grow up and marry a Rovian prince if you're not capable of speaking like a princess?"

Looking back, I do wish he hadn't put the idea in Venus's head that all she had to do to marry a prince was start saying "you" instead of "ye," because once it got lodged in between her ears, there was no getting it out, and for years afterward, we had to listen to her natter on about it. But I guess it was effective, because unlike Adonis, she actually did manage to stop talking like a pirate.

The rest of the tutoring she hated almost as much as Adonis did. As for me, I loved it—not so much for its own sake, but because Mr. Sutch was the first person I'd ever met who didn't seem likely to slug me at any second, so spending time with him was a real treat. I did my best to speak properly for him, and to read, and add and subtract and even multiply things, although the multiplying could get pretty tricky.

And when Venus and Adonis complained to Dad, I kept my mouth shut. Fortunately, they didn't get anywhere with their complaints.

"What we 'ave to learn things fer?" Adonis would gripe. "It's stupid!"

"Nah, got it backwards. Need learnin' 'CAUSE yer stupid."

"Wha's the point?"

"Good for ye!"

"Why?"

"Just is."

"Why?"

"'Cause yer mum wanted it!"

There was no arguing with that. So my brother and sister just glared daggers at me and went back to their primers, and whenever Dad was off in the orchards—which was most of the time— they made life as miserable as they could for Mr. Sutch. Not that he needed much help to be miserable on Deadweather.

I was almost through the last of his primers and starting to like reading for its own sake when he suddenly disappeared. Venus and Adonis liked to say he was murdered by a field pirate, but the fact that he vanished right around the time a cargo ship lifted anchor for the Fish Islands probably wasn't a coincidence.

Dad would have sent out another flyer, but then the Barker War got going, and for the next year or two, nothing sailed on the Blue Sea unless it had at least twenty guns on it. It was hard times—for the last few months of the war, we had nothing left to eat but ugly fruit, which gave everybody the trots.

The war was named for the Barker Islands, way down south where most of the fighting was. Like all the shooting wars in the New Lands, it was between Cartage and Rovia. They were the only two Continental powers with colonies on this side of the Great Maw, and the only kinds of people around at all except for Natives, who didn't have any guns or ships and who'd been cleared out of the islands so completely that I'd never even seen one up close. There were still tribes of them on the mainland—that's where the gold on the Cartager treasure ships came from—but that was several days' sail from us, and there was no reason to ever go there, since it was all wilderness except for a few Cartager ports like Pella Nonna.

The actual shooting only came near us once. It started as a distant rumble in the darkness, off and on, sort of like thunder but not quite, and at first it hardly seemed threatening. But Dad rousted everybody out of bed, loaded us down with all the food we could carry from the pantry, and started marching us up the hill without telling us why.

He had his pistol belt on, and he carried his rifle, along with a big rucksack stuffed with supplies. Dawn was breaking, but the fog made it hard to see.

"Where are we going?" Venus whined.

"Time fer questions later. Just haul that pack."

"I can't! It's too heavy!"

"Then make Egbert carry it."

After Dad said that, Venus and Adonis both dumped their loads on me, which weighed me down so much that my legs were shaking when I finally caught up with them at Rotting Bluff. Dad kept a single cannon there on a rough stone parapet overlooking the sea to the northwest. We helped him load it—I don't know why, because from the sound of the battle raging out in the fog, there were a lot more ships than one cannon could ever stop. But Dad wanted it loaded anyway. Then we sat and waited, as the battle got steadily louder and more frightening.

"'Oo's fightin'?" For the first time I could remember, Adonis was curious about something.

Dad was hunched over the parapet, his elbows resting on it to hold his beat-up brass spyglass steady as he squinted through the lens into the fog. "Dunno. Cartager Navy, that's certain. Not sure who's takin' 'em on, though. Might be Rovians proper . . . but I think it's the pirates."

"The Cartagers comin' 'ere?"

"'Ere or Sunrise. Could be both."

"Why 'ere? Sunrise got all the silver."

"Yeh. But them rich folks on Sunrise don't steal Cartager gold. Pirates on Deadweather been doin' that longer'n you been alive. Reckon the Short-Ears got a mind to put an end to it. Wipe out the Scratch fer good."

Ordinarily, Dad wasn't much for talking, other than to order us around—and the fact that he was bothering to explain things to us was almost as unsettling as what he was saying. Venus, for one, looked like she might cry. "Wouldn't wipe *us* out, would they?"

"Dunno why not," said Dad.

"I don't want to get eaten!" she cried. I don't know where she got the idea that Cartagers were cannibals.

Dad didn't, either. He took his eye from the spyglass to cock an eyebrow at her. "Nah, won't eat ye. Just slit yer throat."

Around midmorning, the fog lifted, and we finally got a glimpse of the battle on the horizon—two massive Cartager men-of-war and five two-decker galleons were slugging it out against just four single-deck pirate sloops, muzzle flashes blinking through the smoke that hung around their sides.

"Don't much like them numbers," muttered Dad, his face knitting into an even darker scowl than usual.

But as the hours passed, it was clear the pirates were giving better than they got. All but two of the Cartager galleons had gone under before any of the pirate sloops sank, and when the first of the big men-of-war keeled over around midafternoon,

Dad—who hadn't lowered the spyglass from his eye for hours—gave a sharp huff of surprise that almost sounded like a laugh.

By sunset, it was over. The men-of-war had burned or sunk, and the last remaining Cartager galleon had been boarded and captured and was creeping back toward Port Scratch behind the two surviving pirate sloops. As he led us back down to the house, Dad's mood was so chipper that I heard him whistling to himself.

We were all headed for bed when we started hearing gunfire from the direction of Port Scratch. Venus got panicky and ran out to the porch, where Dad had settled in with a bottle of rum.

"Is it Cartagers?! Are they coming to eat us after all?"

Dad cocked his head and listened. "Nah. No invasion, that—it's a party."

"A party? For true? Can we go?"

"Nah, girlie. Pirate party's no fun for them's not pirates."

For a week afterward, several times a day Venus would stop whatever she was doing, let out a happy little sigh, and declare, "I'm sooooo glad the Short-Ears didn't come and eat us."

"Wouldn't a' minded feedin' 'em Egbert," Adonis would chime in. Then he'd cackle—no matter how many times he said it, it never stopped being funny to him—and take another swing at me.

BY THE TIME the war ended, we were half starved—and in my case, it wasn't just for food. I'd worked up a taste for reading from Mr. Sutch's primers, but they'd all disappeared with him, and *Principles of Citrus Cultivation* was starting to get pretty tiresome, especially considering that it didn't have much of a story, and I'd read it so many times I could recite big chunks with my eyes closed.

"What ye always readin' that book fer?" Dad asked me once.

"It's the only one we've got," I said.

He just scowled at that, but it must have stuck with him, because when the cargo ships started running again and he sent out a flyer for a new tutor, he wrote "MUST ONE BOOKS" in big block letters at the bottom of it. I secretly fretted over his spelling, but I didn't dare correct it—and I guess it got the point across, because when Percy finally showed up, he brought almost a wagonload of books with him.

I can still remember the first time I saw Percy and his books lurching up toward the house on top of one of the fruit wagons, the horses all lathered from the effort and Percy's massive belly jiggling at every bump. I practically fainted with joy—I'd never seen so many books, and I instantly knew the man who'd brought them to us was going to be the most important person in my life: a teacher, friend, and savior all rolled into one big, fat, sweaty package.

It turned out I was dead wrong about Percy, except for the fat and sweaty part. As horrible people go, he was miles ahead of Venus and could practically outdo Adonis.

When he first arrived, though, we all thought he was some kind of genius. Not just because he had so many books (which we assumed he must have read), but because he acted like a genius would—all scornful and disgusted with how ignorant we were, and capable of tossing around all manner of facts, seemingly off the top of his head.

Percy could tell you everything from where the wind came from (a giant hole in the sky, somewhere west of the New Lands), to why seawater was salty (fish poop), to whether you could multiply fractions together (you couldn't, and if you tried, they'd break). And he spouted his knowledge constantly—that is, during the half hour a day when Dad was within earshot. The rest of the time, he napped. Unless he was eating, which he did so often that Quint took to hiding our pantry food in sacks out behind the woodpile. Sometimes, the rats got into them, but even when they did, they left more for us than Percy.

Percy sussed out pretty quickly how things stood in our house—that Dad wanted us educated but wasn't too clear himself on what that meant—so he struck a deal with Venus and Adonis that they'd pretend to learn while he pretended to teach them, and whatever else they did with their time was fine by him, so long as they left him alone.

At first, he ignored me and could've cared less whether I read his books. So I dug into them, and it didn't take long before I learned enough to realize Percy was a complete fraud, and none of his facts made a lick of sense.

After that, he did his best to keep me away from the books for a while—mostly with a stick, which he could swing pretty fast considering how lazy he was—but the situation was no good for either of us, because it meant I couldn't read and he couldn't nap. So eventually, we struck a deal of our own: he'd let me read the books as long as I kept my mouth shut about what was in them and didn't let on to Dad that Percy was a fake.

It was fine by me, because even though I hated Percy's guts, I figured if he left, he'd take his books with him. And I really loved his books. There were a hundred and thirty-seven of them, and eventually I read them all at least once, even the terrible ones.

The things I learned from them staggered me—and not just the immediately helpful stuff, like the eating habits of horses (no meat, especially human meat, even if it's ground up) or the real reason seawater is salty (I forget, but it's definitely not fish poop). For the first time in my life, I realized there were whole other worlds beyond mine. On the Continent alone, there were cities, and countries, and kings, and castles, all going back a thousand years or more.

And not only did Deadweather turn out to be just a ragged little flyspeck in the Blue Sea a couple hundred miles east of the vast wilderness of the New Lands, but even Sunrise Island—a place that had always seemed, during the twice-yearly trips we took there for holidays and shopping, like the rich and bustling center of the universe—only appeared in *Geography of the World* as an afterthought at the very bottom edge of the Fish Islands map, and wasn't mentioned at all in *A New History of the Rovian Kingdom and Territories.*

Once I started to learn about the larger world, I'd lie awake at night in my little windowless room off the kitchen, and imagine what it would be like to be part of it somehow—to live a life that mattered, to be and to do things worth reading about in books.

But I never thought for a moment it was possible. I wasn't highborn, or rich, or brave, or strong, or even smart—none of those things that made the characters in the novels and the people in the history books so special.

I knew the world was out there. I just didn't see a place for myself in it. And even if there might be, I had no idea how to go about finding it.

It never occurred to me that the world might come find me— and that without my lifting a finger to make it happen, one day my life would change, completely and forever.

But it did. And this is the story of it.

CHAPTER 2

LEAVING

It started with the look on Dad's face. I was in the backyard, reading a book in the little sliver of afternoon shade behind the woodpile. I'd just finished splitting logs for Quint's cooking fire, and I wanted to steal a few minutes of quiet before taking the firewood back to the house.

Dad had gone up the hill to clean the cannon on Rotting Bluff, and I didn't expect him back until evening. So when I looked up and saw him coming, I got a quick jolt of fear that he was going to crack me one for slacking off.

He did that a lot. But I didn't hold it against him like I did Adonis, because unlike my brother, Dad didn't seem to take much pleasure from whacking me—he just wanted to get the point across that there was work to do and I wasn't doing it. And he never stopped working himself, except every once in a while just before sundown, when he'd sit for a few minutes alone on the back porch, staring at the threads of smoke curling up from the volcano and looking sad. It was an aching, heartbroken kind of sad, and it made me feel awful, because I knew without asking he was thinking about our mother.

Most of the time, though, he didn't look sad—just grim and determined as he went about his work. And when he'd catch me doing something I shouldn't—like sitting and reading in the middle of the day, beside a pile of wood that needed carrying—his eyes would flash with anger, and then the cracking would come.

But this time, there was no flash of anger. He wasn't even looking at me—or at anything, really. His eyes held a puzzled, faraway look, like he'd forgotten something and was trying to remember where he'd put it.

I'd already stuffed the book halfway inside the back of my pants and was hurriedly gathering the wood in my arms when he stopped a few feet away and fixed his eyes on me for the first time.

"'Ey—got paper in there?" he asked, nodding at the book.

Coming from Dad, it was an odd question. Other than the accounting ledgers he muttered over sometimes at the long table in the den, he didn't have much use for paper, let alone books.

"What, in the book?"

"Yeh. Loose-like. Fer writin' on." He raised one of his big, rough hands and jiggled it awkwardly in the air with his fingers and thumb pinched together, like he was pretending to write something.

"Only just the book pages," I said. "I could tear some out."

He shook his head. "Percy's got paper, yeh? Fer lessons and such?"

"He's got parchment. It's in the den."

He started for the house, disappearing inside so fast that I'd barely reached the porch with the wood when he popped back out again, a sheet of parchment in one hand and a charcoal pencil in the other. Without a word, he brushed past me and headed back up the mountain.

Back inside, Percy was emerging from the den, rubbing his sleep-swollen eyes. He glowered at me, like it was my fault Dad had interrupted his afternoon nap.

"What the blaze does your father want with a pencil?"

THE SUN HAD SET and we were all sitting at the dining table, eating Quint's stew, when Dad finally came back. The pencil and parchment were gone, but the puzzled look was still there. He walked past us without a sound, went to the stove, and ladled out a bowl of stew. He ate a few spoonfuls of it, leaning against the counter and staring off into space as we all watched him curiously.

"Daddy?" Venus called to him in her whiniest voice, as she twirled a lock of her dark, stringy hair around her finger. "Are you thinking about the pony?"

A while back, I'd made the mistake of telling my sister that one of Percy's novels (*The Crisps of Upper Mattox,* which was mostly lousy except for a couple of good fight scenes and a carriage race) had a girl in it who married a prince. Venus ran squealing for the book, and while she never actually read it herself, she somehow wheedled Quint into reading it out loud to her before bed. The only details that stuck with her were that the girl in question was rich and owned a pony. Venus decided the pony was key to the whole thing—if she could get her hands on one, she'd automatically be rich, and once she was rich, the whole prince-marrying business would take care of itself.

So for the past six months, she'd been asking Dad several times a day to buy her a pony. For the life of me, I couldn't understand why he didn't smack her one and put a stop to it.

"Egbert give ye trouble? Want me to set 'im straight?" Adonis held up a fist and cocked it in my direction. I shifted in my chair, ready to dodge the blow if necessary.

Dad ignored them both. He ate another spoonful of stew, then set the bowl down and wiped his mouth on his sleeve. He scratched his chin a couple of times through his beard in a thoughtful sort of way, then announced, "Lay out yer finest. Headed to Sunrise at first light."

I COULD BARELY SLEEP that night. Partly because I was so excited about the trip—visits to Sunrise Island were rare and wonderful, and we'd never gone there on a nonholiday before. And partly because the next day was my thirteenth birthday, and for the first time I could remember, I was going to spend a birthday doing something besides trudging up the far side of the volcano with my family to pay our respects at my mother's grave.

But mostly I couldn't sleep because Adonis kept busting into my room to hit me with a stick.

This wasn't a coincidence—he was trying to make me so tired I'd oversleep, because he knew if I did, Dad would leave me behind. It had worked once before and almost worked two other times. Of course, to do it he had to stay up half the night himself, which left him so tired he was always groggy and surly the next day. You'd think that would spoil his own trip to Sunrise, but I guess for Adonis, it was worth it.

It almost worked this time, too. The moment I opened my

eyes, I could tell from the heat and the heaviness of the air that dawn had already broken. Panicking, I sprang out of bed and ran smack into the wall because I'd forgotten that I'd turned my bed sideways in the middle of the night to barricade the door.

Once I got my bearings, I managed to get the bed out of the way so I could open the door and let in enough light to see. Then I found my best, most itchy shirt and put it on as I ran for the kitchen.

No one was there except Quint. He was standing on top of the counter—Quint didn't have legs, just a couple of stumps where his upper thighs should have been, so he spent most of his time standing on top of things—and prying the last of his breakfast biscuits out of an iron tray. I could tell the biscuit had set up pretty hard from the way the thick muscles on his arm had to flex to rip it loose.

"Best ye hurry," he said, tossing me the biscuit. "Yer dad already went up to get his boots on."

I knew if I wasn't sitting in the carriage all ready to go the moment Dad came out of the house, he'd smack me one for slowing us down, so I busted out the front door at full speed, trying to work my jaws over the biscuit without cracking a tooth as I went.

The carriage was parked out front, its door wide open. Percy was standing just behind it, tying up the back of Venus's dress for her, and Stumpy—the field pirate who drives for us, and who in spite of his name actually has more of his legs left than Quint— was already up on the front seat holding the reins.

I waved to Stumpy as I jumped onto the side runner and launched myself through the open door into the backseat.

Then Adonis punched me in the mouth, launching me right back out again.

Even before I landed on my back in the dirt, I was cursing myself for not having seen that coming. The biscuit rolled away, bouncing a couple times before coming to a stop near Percy's foot.

As Adonis hawed like a donkey inside the carriage, Percy bent himself over with a grunt, somehow managing to reach past his belly and pick up my biscuit without falling over. He dusted off the dirt and crunched it down as Venus wrinkled her nose at me.

"Egbert! You filthed up your best shirt! Daddy's going to smack you for that."

I opened my mouth to answer and tasted blood. As my sister stepped over me into the carriage, I put my hand to my lip and found a pretty good cut. It was either from Adonis's fist or a shard of biscuit. I wasn't sure which.

"Bleed down the front, he'll smack you twice." Percy stood over me as he said this, and little wet gobs of my stolen breakfast sprayed from his lips onto my forehead. Then he turned, blotting out the sky over my head with his big wide butt until he squeezed himself through the carriage door and into the seat next to Venus.

I had just enough time to wipe the blood with my handkerchief, dust off as best I could, and take the seat next to Adonis before Dad showed up on the porch.

He was in his best coat—the blue velvet one with the tails—and the bulges on either hip meant he'd strapped on his pistol belt, too.

That was another sign, not like we needed any, that this was an unusual trip. When we went to Sunrise Island for holidays, he always wore the coat. When he had business to do, either there or down in Port Scratch, he wore the pistols. I'd never seen him wear both at once.

19

As I chewed this over—*why get all dressed up to shoot some-body?*—Percy pulled the door shut, and the carriage shuddered as Dad swung himself up onto the front seat. Then Stumpy must have reined the horses, because we lurched forward, pulling away from the only home I'd ever had.

If I'd known then how long it'd be until I saw it again, I might have turned for another look—at the two upstairs windows, peering out from under the eaves like the eyes of some fat, sleepy giant, and the big wraparound porch with the shark's jaws mounted over the door. It's funny, but I wound up missing those jaws over the days to come. They made me feel safe, I think. You just knew no one was going to come after you in a house with teeth like that. No one from the outside, anyway.

The road from the house took us through the lower orchard. The ugly fruit trees were fogged in pretty heavy, and as we bounced down the hill, a few pirates drifted out of the haze to watch us pass. In the misty half-light, they looked like silhouettes of ripped-up paper dolls—half a leg missing here, most of an arm there, a hunk of one skull gone.

The one missing a hunk of skull was Mung. Seeing me in the carriage window as we passed, he gave me a little wink, and I managed a kind of two-fingered wave back without the others noticing and giving me trouble. Mung had worked for Dad forever, couldn't talk (probably because of his missing slice of brain), and was nicer to me than anybody. When I was little, we played catch. We'd toss an ugly fruit back and forth, pretending it was a ball, until one day Dad caught us doing it and smacked us both for wasting time. That pretty much turned us both off sports, but I still liked Mung a lot.

Percy, jolted into action by a nasty bump in the road, announced, "Time for lessons, children."

Adonis rolled his eyes, and Venus pushed out her bottom lip in a pout. "But, Percy! We're traveling."

"Nonsense. Learning never stops, not for travel, not for nothing."

He said it with a straight face, even though we all knew the "learning" was just for Dad's benefit, in case he was listening from up in front.

"Now tell me: what makes fog?"

No one answered.

"No? Nobody? Very well. I'll tell you." Percy raised a stubby finger, then paused dramatically. He always did that when he answered his own questions. To anyone who didn't know him, the pause made it seem like he was emphasizing how important the lesson was. But the truth was he needed the pause to give himself time to make up an answer.

"Volcanic activity. The same forces that make the volcano smoke . . . seep up from the ground in the night, and—"

"Why don't it stink?" Sometimes, Percy's facts were so outlandish they even made Adonis skeptical.

"What? The fog?"

"Yeh. Volcano smoke reeks. Like rotten eggs."

"Why do you THINK it doesn't stink?" Percy asked with a little snarl of disgust. Repeating questions like that was another way he bought himself extra time. "Because the ground . . . traps all the stink. Dig a hole sometime. Get down far enough, it'll all come rushing out. Gag you fierce. Then you'll see."

BY THE TIME we rolled into Port Scratch an hour later, the morning sun had burned off the fog, it was oven-hot inside the carriage, and Percy had filled my brother and sister with dozens of new facts about science, history, and math, all of them spectacularly wrong. Not that they would bother to remember them anyway.

Port Scratch was slowly waking up as we made our way down the wide, filth-ridden main road, the carriage lurching from side to side as Stumpy snaked around the pirates who'd passed out in the street the night before. The clop of the horses' hooves stirred a few of them, and they'd stagger to their feet, shake the rum from their heads, and double over again to vomit. There are a lot of things that Blisstown, the port city of Sunrise, has going for it over Port Scratch, but one of the first ones you notice is the lack of puke on the streets.

When we stopped at the dock, Dad made us stay in the carriage while he haggled for a boat to Sunrise. He always kept us in the carriage until the boat was hired, mostly because of Venus—there weren't many females in Port Scratch, let alone fifteen-year-old ones who bathed, and even though my sister looked like a horse and had the personality of a lizard, I guess the pirates weren't too choosy about who they carried off.

It took longer than usual. Ordinarily, Dad liked to head down a day early with Stumpy to settle on a boat, but this trip was so last-minute there hadn't been time for that. So we baked inside the carriage for almost half an hour, until my good shirt was so sweat-soaked it no longer itched, while Dad rooted around on the docks, interviewing half a dozen candidates and occasionally waving his pistols when things got hot.

Eventually, he found his boat—a grimy thirty-footer with no name, a swivel gun at the fore, and a rowboat tied to the aft deck. The rowboat was critical, because pirates were banned from Sunrise, and whoever ferried us there would have to stop out of range of the shore cannons while we rowed ourselves the rest of the way in.

The two men who crewed it—one short but built like an ox, the other tall and dark-featured, with a mane of black hair that hung past his shoulders—stank of rum and man-sweat, and they both had small flames tattooed on the side of their necks. It was the mark of men who sailed with Burn Healy. Of all the captains who plundered on the Blue Sea, Healy was both the most feared and the most successful—the pirate victory over the Cartager Navy that we'd watched from Rotting Bluff during the Barker War had been all his doing, although he'd been plenty notorious even before then—and any man with a flame tattooed on his neck was guaranteed to be a cold-blooded killer.

Which was why it never made sense to me that Dad seemed to go out of his way to hire them when we needed a boat for the Sunrise run. I got up the nerve to ask him once, and he just shrugged.

"Healy men get the job done," he said.

It was true enough—we always got there quickly, and despite their reputation, no Healy pirate had ever slit our throats. But they had a habit of renegotiating their rates once we got within sight of Blisstown, and the trip always cost Dad twice as much as he'd agreed to back in Port Scratch.

We got under way, and the two pirates somehow scared enough sail out of the stagnant Deadweather air to get us out of the harbor and into the open ocean, where we caught a breeze off Sunrise. By then, Adonis and Venus were napping in the hold, Percy was sunning himself on the foredeck like a turtle, and I was lying amidships, eyes squeezed shut and trying to look seasick because I knew from experience the others would leave me alone if they thought I might puke on them.

Secretly, though, I had half an eye open to watch Dad, who was sitting aft with the same puzzled look he'd worn for the past day. He eyed the crew for a long time, watching them tack into the wind. Then, convinced no one was watching him, he reached into an inner pocket of his coat and pulled out a folded-up piece of parchment.

He stared at it awhile, chewing on the side of his lip. At one point, he looked down the deck at Percy, eyes narrowed like he was weighing something, before he finally shook his head.

He refolded the parchment carefully and hid it back inside his coat. Then he whispered to himself, just loud enough for me to make out the words, "No way around it . . . Got to find a Native."

I wondered for a while what he meant by that. I should have wondered more.

CHAPTER 3

SUNRISE

$\mathcal{S}$unrise Island was breathtaking, even prettier than the name would suggest. Most of the coastline was towering cliffs that shot straight up out of the sea, but for a mile or so on either side of Blisstown, the cliffs tapered off to a stunning white sand beach that glittered like it was made of ground-up diamonds. The better part of the island was lush, green forest that sloped gradually upward until, halfway to the sky, it suddenly gave way to Mount Majestic, a jagged, massive peak made of silver.

Literally. It was actually made of silver—most of it anyway, which was why Sunrise was so rich. Even the tiniest buildings in Blisstown had carved-wood trim and expensive glass windows looking out over streets paved in stone and so clean that when I was little I was sure the horses on Sunrise never pooped.

Sunrise was even more spectacular when I compared it to Deadweather, which was a third the size and dramatically worse in every way: its gray beach littered with the rotting skeletons of wrecked ships; its tangled forest steaming with fever bugs and crawling up the sides of a dirt-black volcano so sorry looking no one had ever bothered to name it; and its lone settlement not much more than a cluster of rotting shacks that stank to high heaven.

It seemed almost ridiculously unfair, even more so when you considered that our rottenness was all Sunrise's fault. At least, that's what one of the field pirates once told me on a particularly stifling day. According to him, the reason Deadweather was a stinking bog while Sunrise was always just the right amount of hot and sunny with a cool breeze was because Mount Majestic blocked the ocean winds from reaching us.

I don't know if it was true—Percy's one book that tackled weather, *Cuspid's Natural Science,* didn't mention the Blue Sea at all—but the idea that weather was destiny, that a beautiful and pleasant island would produce beautiful and pleasant people, while an ugly swamp would breed scum like Ripper Jones or my brother Adonis, used to give me a strange kind of comfort. If my life was lousy because of the weather, what was the point of complaining? You can't change the weather.

Of course, I'd eventually learn that the truth is much more complicated—that not everyone who lives on a pretty street is a good person, and that in even the rottenest places you might find someone you can trust with your life.

But even then, dumb as I was, I had my suspicions that Sunrise wasn't quite as bright and pure as its name.

For one thing, there were the fortresses—two big square garrisons, bristling with cannons, that loomed over the harbor from the cliffs on either side. They were a constant reminder that Blisstown was blissful mostly because it was armed to the teeth, and even Rovian ships got fired on if they entered the harbor unannounced.

Then there was the attitude of the people in Blisstown. When we'd enter their shops, with their exotic seasonings and soft linens, the owners would smile big and offer to help Dad find whatever he wanted. But more than once, I'd catch one of them making a funny grimace at his wife when Dad's back was turned, a *what's-that-smell?* wrinkle of the nose or a *can-you-believe-this-fool?* roll of the eyes. Even the shopkeepers thought they were better than us.

But the biggest thing was the silver mine. It was on the western slope of Mount Majestic—the leeward side, the Deadweather side, the darker side. If you approached Sunrise from the east (and most people did, since the only points west were Deadweather and the distant jungles of the New Lands), you'd never see it. Even coming from the west, it was hard to tell what exactly was going on up there. Far above the cliffs and the forest, it wasn't visible as much more than a long horizontal gash, like a dueling scar carved in the mountain's face halfway between the timberline and summit.

But what was obvious, even from that distance, was that it was teeming with people. They crawled around it like ants, dark against the bright surface of the rock, snaking in and out of the mine in long, wriggling columns and gathered in clumps around the open fires that flickered on either end of the gash. Most of them were the same color, a deep copper red so consistent it could've been a uniform but almost definitely wasn't—they were naked, or just about. And they were too dark to be Continentals, certainly not pale-skinned Rovians, or even swarthier Cartagers.

I was sure they were Natives, although I'd never seen one in person—I guess they were too sensible to have ever lived on Deadweather, and there was no sign of them anywhere among the Rovians of Blisstown. But there they were, up on that mine, year in and year out.

I figured they weren't there because they wanted to be. And sometimes, when I watched an especially obnoxious Blisstowner swaggering up Heavenly Road in a coat studded with jewels, I'd flash back to that distant swarm of faceless people hidden behind the mountain and wonder how much of Blisstown's riches had to do with them.

I'd be lying, though, if I said that kind of thing was always on my mind when I walked around Blisstown. Mostly, I was just in awe. Even after I'd read about all the supposedly more spectacular cities of the Continent, it was hard to imagine a finer place. And I'd wish like nothing else that I could live there instead of Deadweather.

That's how I was feeling the day of my thirteenth birthday. I'd shrugged off the Natives even before we rounded South Point and the harbor came into view, and I was so excited to be approaching Blisstown that I'd forgotten to pretend I was seasick.

This cost me a punch to the side of the throat as Adonis came up from below. As I was doubled over coughing, I heard him call out to Dad, "Can we lunch at the Peacock?"

"Too fancy. Ye can eat street meats. Stop that racket, Egbert!"

Venus had popped up behind Adonis, fresh and perky from her nap. "Can we get jelly bread, too? Oh, please, Daddy! I'm soooo hungry."

"We'll see. If ye behave yerself. Business first. And don't be underfoot while I do it."

Just then, a muffled harrumph reached us from the distant shore. I hit the deck in time to hear the first cannonball approach—a soft murmur, rising inside of a second to a low whistle that exploded in a wet thunderclap thirty yards from the bow.

The tall, long-haired pirate wrenched the wheel to starboard, and the boom swung violently over our heads as the boat veered away from shore. A second cannonball hit the water, half again as close as the first, before the ship wheeled out of range of the shore guns.

"End of the line, boss," he said to Dad, nodding at the rowboat. "Ye'll wait for us."

"Till sundown. Then we go."

"Could be overnight."

My heart jumped. Venus and Adonis went wide-eyed. Even Percy, still logy from being jolted awake by the cannon fire, lifted his chin. None of us had ever spent a night on Sunrise.

"That's extra. Twenty."

"All in, yeh."

"No. Extra. Forty total."

"That weren't the agreement."

The pirate jerked his head toward shore. "Didn't factor in hostilities."

It was a lie, but completely predictable. And so was the haggling that followed, along with some pistol-waving on both sides, before Dad and the pirates agreed on a new price for their services.

They cranked down the anchor while the five of us boarded the rowboat. Then the short pirate cast us off, and I took the oars to row us ashore.

It was tough going—with Percy on board, we were awfully low

in the water—and by the time we were halfway in, my left palm was blistering and my itchy shirt was soaked through with sweat for the second time that day. I didn't mind, though. Not only was the shirt less itchy when it was soggy, but I was distracted from the pain by the ship moored at the dock ahead.

It was a five-master, monstrous in size, easily twice as big as the freighter that shipped the ugly fruit harvest up to the Fish Islands, which I'd thought was as big as ships got until I saw this one. I counted eighty portals on its starboard side, in four rows of twenty.

The top row was a gun deck, pretty standard stuff—the portals square and open under simple wooden shutters, cannon barrels dimly visible behind them. But the lower rows were something else. Each portal was fitted with its own four-pane window of actual glass, some of them open at an angle like the hand-cranked windows of the fancier homes in Blisstown. Windows that delicate on a seagoing ship seemed almost absurd, like a diamond bracelet on a donkey's leg.

As we pulled closer, and the ship grew until it towered over us like one of the island's cliffs, I realized every part of it was similarly rich—from the carved and painted trim on its quarterdeck, to its gleaming precious metal fittings, to the crew scurrying around its rigging in crisp uniforms of navy and white with gold piping.

It was like somebody had ripped a palace from its foundations and floated it on the water.

Even Dad was impressed. As we inched past it toward an open slip, he craned his neck to study the windows, thirty feet above us, then muttered an admiring curse.

We tied up halfway between the massive ship and the

boardwalk, and as we climbed onto the dock, half a dozen soldiers and the harbormaster met us. Once they confirmed we
weren't throat slitters in disguise, the soldiers shouldered their
rifles and marched in time back to the little station house at the
foot of the next dock.

As he paid the harbormaster our slip fee, Dad jerked his head
toward the mountain of a ship behind us.

"What the deuce is that?"

"The *Earthly Pleasure*. In from Rovia. Maiden voyage."

"What's her cargo? Royal family?"

The harbormaster shook his head. "Tourists. Haven't you
heard?"

Dad looked blank, but nodded like he understood. "Yeh.
Course."

As we trailed behind him up the dock, Venus looked to Percy.
"What's tourists?"

Percy snorted, like the answer was obvious. "People from Tour."

"Where's Tour?" she asked.

"Child, please! I can't answer questions when I'm this hungry,"
said Percy.

I was pretty sure there was no country named Tour, but I didn't
have any better idea of what a tourist was than Percy. I was also just
as hungry as he was, and Dad's distant look had come back, making me worried he'd disappear on his mysterious errand without
remembering to feed us. Which is exactly what happened, almost.

We followed him as he turned off the boardwalk onto Heavenly
Road and suddenly ran into more people than I'd ever seen in
one place in my life. In the space between the boardwalk and
the Peacock Inn at the top of the hill were a few hundred richly

dressed, overfed Rovians. Unlike Dad, none of them seemed to have a destination in mind—they sort of wandered about, like livestock in a field, chatting with each other and occasionally clustering in shop windows to gawk at the items for sale.

I was half aware that these people must have been passengers on the *Earthly Pleasure,* but at that point, they (and everything else that wasn't food) were meaningless compared to the street meat shack, which Dad passed without so much as a look.

It was midday, and the big iron grill behind the vendor's open counter crackled and smoked with roasting meats. To follow Dad, we had to pass through the cloud of smoky air that surrounded the shack, and when the smell hit me, my stomach wrung itself out with wanting.

The others had a similar reaction—Percy actually whimpered—but Dad was moving fast, and we didn't dare pipe up to complain. He zigzagged through the cowlike crowd, weaving into the road where necessary, until he reached the lawyer's office.

It was a tiny two-story building with JULIUS ARCHIBALD— LEGAL SERVICES painted on a wooden sign above the porch. Dad climbed the low stairs and rapped on the door as the rest of us waited at the edge of the street.

A little man opened the door. He was so short that he found himself staring through his spectacles right into Dad's chest. His eyes moved up until they reached my father's.

"Masterson. Quite early in the season for you. Did the crop fail?"

Dad shook his head. "I've need fer consultation. Plainspoken and private."

"Of course. For a modest consideration."

Dad lowered five coins one at a time into the tiny man's hand. "There's two fer honesty. Three fer privacy."

The coins disappeared into the lawyer's vest pocket. "Please. Come in."

Dad was halfway inside when Venus saved us. "Dad! We're starving!"

"Right." He stepped back out and dug for a few smaller coins, which he gave to Percy. "No jelly bread. And don't stray."

The four of us were gone before he finished the sentence.

There were two customers ahead of us for street meat, and the minute it took them to complete their order seemed more like an hour. Percy scowled at the backs of their heads while Adonis jiggled his leg and Venus chewed her knuckle.

"I want bird. Two of them."

"Me as well."

"Anything's fine for me." Which was true. I was so hungry I could've gnawed the charred bits off the grill without waiting for it to cool. Besides, direct requests tended to backfire on me.

The customer in front of us had barely gotten his skewer when Percy elbowed him aside, jammed his fists onto the counter, and leaned in so hard that the vendor nearly fell backward into his grill. "Give me double mutton fancy, four redbirds on the bone, and . . ." Percy turned his head to look at me. I tried to seem bored, because I knew the hungrier I looked, the crueler his order would be.

"Got any pickled rat?"

I must have looked like I was starving to death.

"Sir, this is a reputable establishment. We serve no rat."

"What's your bottom shelf?"

"Innards."

"What kind?"

"It's a mix. Brains, pancreas, bit of spleen—"

"Give us that."

"Comes on a bun."

"Skip the bun."

The innards actually weren't bad, although they would have tasted better if I hadn't known what they were. I finished first, because my portion was smaller and I wasn't much interested in chewing it, and spent a few minutes watching the crowd.

On the surface, they were like most of Sunrise Island's permanent residents—Rovian looking, elaborately dressed, and clearly disgusted by us. But there were small differences. Their skin was paler, except for the ones whose faces and necks were red with sunburn. Their clothes—three-button coats, cravats, bustled skirts—were both more fancy and less appropriate for the weather than a Sunriser's usual cotton and silk. They suffered for it in the midday heat, beads of sweat creeping down the men's brows under their top hats, the women holding parasols and fanning themselves.

In spite of the heat, they all smelled unusually pleasant, like they'd rubbed themselves with lavender.

And the looks they gave us as we stood by the meat shack, my siblings and Percy still gnawing their food with both hands to their mouths, were as much confusion as anything, like they couldn't figure out how we'd gotten there. They gave us a wide berth as they strolled past, heads turning slightly to keep us in their line of sight for a few extra feet, as if we were unpredictable wild animals that might lash out at any second.

A family of five passed us, the youngest son staring at me with saucer eyes, and I was about to bare my teeth at him just for fun when Dad's voice made me jump.

"That's done, then."

Over Dad's shoulder, I caught a glimpse of Archibald the lawyer running across the road, then vaulting up the steps of the Peacock Inn and disappearing inside.

"'Ave to wait a bit now." Watching Adonis lick sauce from his fingers, Dad rubbed his mouth. "Could use a bite meself."

He eyed the street meat vendor a moment, then turned away. "Let's head to the Peacock."

THE DINING ROOM of the Peacock Inn was as crowded with the new arrivals as Heavenly Road had been. Dad paused inside the door, and I think he would have gone back for street meat if a dozen heads hadn't turned to stare at him. At that point, plunging forward was a matter of pride.

The sour-mouthed man who seated guests from a little standing desk at the dining room entrance did his best not to notice us, staring down at the desk like there was something absolutely fascinating on it, until the level of Dad's voice threatened to stop all conversation in the room.

"S'cuse me . . . pardon . . . 'Ey! Server!"

"May I help you?" As he grudgingly locked eyes with Dad, the middle of his face puckered like he'd just smelled something revolting. Which, to be fair, he probably had.

"Need a table. Spot o' lunch."

"Yes, well . . ." The sour man made a show of reviewing a page of scribbled names. "I'm terribly sorry, but we're rather overbooked at the moment. What with the boat in, you know. Afraid you'd have to wait."

"How long?"

"Perhaps Thursday."

Dad's head reared back, up and off his shoulders. It was a move that, if I were standing in front of him, would have meant an incoming fist.

"Ye know I'm a regular?"

The sour man's blank look said, no, he was not aware of this.

"Savior's Day and Resurrection Sunday. Regular as clockwork."

"Oh. I see."

"Take my business elsewhere if I'm not well served."

"Certainly wouldn't want that . . . There is one other option. For our favored guests."

"Which is?"

"A private dining room. Just let me . . . yes! One's available now. For a modest surcharge."

"How much?"

"Three hundred." The sour man's mouth stayed frozen, but his eyes warmed with pleasure as Dad's head sank back into his shoulders. Short of an explosion—unlikely but possible, because Dad's fuse got short when he was hungry—the battle was over.

As Dad stewed over the least embarrassing way to exit the room, a door at the back of the hallway opened and a man stepped out. He was middle aged, handsome, and almost as tall as Dad. He walked in a way that immediately reminded me of a book I'd read about Lord Calverstop, the hero of the Battle of Olstom. It was the kind of confident swagger that could convince men to follow him off a cliff without so much as looking down.

As two other men—both older, fatter, and not nearly the type you'd follow off a cliff, even though one of them was in Rovian military dress—emerged behind him, he moved toward the exit, only to stop at the sight of Dad.

"Pardon my interruption, but . . . are you by any chance Hoke Masterson?"

"That'd be me."

The handsome man smiled, showing a full set of teeth. "The agrarian wizard of Deadweather Island! My dear sir, it is an honor!" He said this so sincerely that Dad, in spite of his natural suspiciousness, was obliged to shake the man's outstretched hand.

"Allow me to introduce myself. Roger Pembroke, local businessman. I've heard of your legend for years, and have long desired to meet the man who could build a thriving enterprise in such an unlikely environment. Truly, sir, I stand in awe of you."

The sight of an apparently upstanding and well-respected Sunriser showering Dad with compliments stunned us all, Dad especially. As Dad's mouth hung open in shock, Pembroke introduced his companions. The soldier was Colonel Something-or-other, and Pembroke referred to the second man as "Governor Burns," making me briefly consider the dizzying possibility that the jowly, balding fellow shaking my father's hand was the actual, king-appointed governor of Sunrise Island.

Both men left in a polite hurry, and when they were gone, Pembroke drilled back into Dad.

"I'd relish the opportunity to speak with you about your experience in business. Are you coming or going?"

"We was, ah . . . undecided."

"Are you hungry?"

"Bit peckish, yeh."

"Then please! Join me! As my guest. It would be an honor." He turned to the server. "Honus, could you procure a private dining room for us? On my account, of course."

The server gripped the side of his desk, like he was trying to avoid a sudden faint. "Right away, Mr. Pembroke."

CHAPTER 4

MILLICENT

An hour later, a white-shirted waiter was clearing the remains of the greatest meal I'd ever seen, made all the greater by the fact that I'd actually gotten to eat some of it.

Unclear on the ground rules for tormenting me in front of Roger Pembroke, Percy and my siblings had decided to ignore me and focus their attention on stuffing themselves sick with a massive second lunch of smoked pork, swordfish, bittersweet greens, and mashed potatoes soaked in butter and herb. By now, their bellies were so swollen that Adonis was staring slack-jawed into space, Venus's eyes kept flitting shut, and Percy was quietly squirming as he tried to loosen his belt without anybody noticing.

Dad hadn't so much as glanced at us since we'd taken our seats, his attention absorbed by Pembroke's bottomless thirst for even the smallest details of the ugly fruit business. At first, Dad had limited himself to one-word grunts and the odd short sentence.

But Pembroke was so charming, and he refilled Dad's wine glass so eagerly, that Dad had been won over to the point where his answers ran to paragraphs, some of them containing more words than I'd normally hear him use in a week.

"Do you export to the Continent?"

"Nah, it's all oranges with 'em—they're 'orribly stuck up about it, like fer fruit to be worthy it needs be pleasant to look at and sickly sweet. Plus in the forty days it takes crossin' the Maw, 'alf the cargo rots." Dad scowled. "Nah—most o' my trade's to the Fish Islands. That, and . . . well, ever since the war, they can't get Barker oranges on the mainland . . . so I been runnin' the occasional boat to Pella Nonna."

Pembroke raised an eyebrow. "Trading with Cartagers—that's politically adventurous."

"Don't care fer politics. I'm a businessman. And Cartager gold spends the same as Rovian silver . . ."

Dad droned on, but I stopped hearing anything just then, because the waiter had reappeared with a tray of sugar-glazed jelly bread still steaming from the oven. At the sight of it, Adonis snapped out of his daze, Venus gave an achy moan, and Percy dropped his chin and tried to force a belch that might clear enough room in his gut to cram in more food.

I sat bolt upright—since I started the meal still hungry, I not only had room for dessert, but this would be my first taste of jelly bread. In all our trips to Sunrise, I'd never once had any. Denying me jelly bread wasn't official family policy or anything. It just always seemed to work out that way.

So when the waiter set the tray down in the middle of the

table, I had to force myself to remember my manners and wait a polite second before reaching out for a piece.

Waiting turned out to be a terrible idea, because in that second Adonis slid the tray in his direction, leaving it just out of my reach.

As the greedy hands of Percy and my siblings tore through the bread, I made a second effort, stretching myself across the table so desperately that Dad noticed the movement out of the corner of his eye and glanced my way.

I quickly sank back into my seat. When Dad turned back to Pembroke, I locked eyes with Adonis.

Please, my eyes said. *Just one piece.*

Not in a million years, said Adonis's eyes.

By the way, his eyes added, *I'm enjoying this.*

To take my mind off the disappointment, I forced myself to listen to Dad and Pembroke. Dad was leaning forward, his voice low and tentative.

"Say, ah . . . ye got any pull with them what provisions the silver mine?"

Pembroke smiled. "A bit. Why do you ask?"

"Just wonderin' if them slaves ever get scurvy. In case o' which—bit o' ugly fruit in the diet might do 'em right."

Pembroke's smile disappeared—and when he spoke, his voice had gone suddenly cold and formal. "Sir, I assure you—the Natives in that mine are paid an honest wage. Slavery is an abomination and a crime—not just by the laws of King Frederick, but in the eyes of our Savior."

He said it quietly, but with such a steely tone that Percy and my siblings all stopped chewing and turned to stare across the table. Everyone suddenly looked worried, Dad especially.

His eyes widened, and he had trouble keeping his words untangled. "Nah—course, it's—weren't—didn't intend . . ."

Pembroke broke into a wide smile, sweeping away the tension with a pleasant wave of his hand.

"Not at all! It's an understandable mistake. After all, it's not exactly a plum appointment up there. But these Natives are quite grateful for the opportunity. And you've got to hand it to them, they've got some pluck, leaving the primitive comforts of their tribe to come here in search of a more civilized life. We do our best to give them that, along with honest pay for honest work . . . But it's a very sage point you make about the ugly fruit." Pembroke nodded solemnly. "I'll see to it that it's raised with the proper authority."

"Be much obliged," said Dad, practically sighing with relief.

"Not at all. My pleasure!"

There was a moment of silence that was just starting to feel awkward when Pembroke leaned in toward Dad with a twinkle in his eye and a little thrill in his voice.

"Know what I'd like to get your take on as a businessman? This tourism initiative. Think we're on to something?"

Dad sat back, tapping his front teeth with a fingernail and trying to look thoughtful, even though I was pretty sure he had no idea what tourism was. "S'pose I'd need a bit more information."

"Here's the general idea: for years, every Rovian silver trader who's dropped anchor here has gone batty for the place. Which I completely understand—I mean, Rovia, it's the Motherland, much to be admired and all that—but do you realize what the climate's like back there? Abysmal! Cold, wet, the sun never shines—there's something to be said for the argument that we wouldn't have overseas colonies in the first place if men of ambition hadn't been desperate for some half-decent weather.

"And Sunrise, well, it's . . . paradise. So a few of us got to thinking—maybe the island's an asset in itself. Can't exactly bottle it and sell it . . . but what if . . . given the average Rovian merchant's got more money than places to spend it . . . I mean, how many half shares in Wartshire cattle farms can a man buy, really . . . ? So what if . . . we could sell the experience of being here? Not permanently, 'cause that'd cause no end of problems. But temporarily?"

Pembroke paused. My father slowly nodded, doing a decent job of looking thoughtful.

"So we pooled our resources, commissioned the *Earthly Pleasure*—which we built from the timbers up as sort of a floating estate, pleasant to live in as a Pinceford castle—and sold tickets for a four-month journey here and back. Advertised it as a 'Grand Tour of Sunrise.' Which is how we took to calling it 'tourism.'"

I glanced at Percy. His cheek bulged with the wiggling outline of his tongue as it searched his mouth for unchewed bits of jelly bread. If he'd been paying enough attention to know he'd just been proven ignorant, he didn't show it.

"And they went for it?" asked Dad.

"Like lemmings! Booked to capacity, four hundred passengers. And among them, some VERY influential names. I daresay this will raise our stature at court. Which, frankly, is more than a little overdue—for all the silver this island's put in the royal coffers, one might expect King Frederick to show a bit more appreciation of us . . . Still, I think that'll be put right once the ship returns, especially since this bunch are so over the moon—apart from some minor gripes about sunburn. A few of them even swear they'll be back next season! And we've practically sold out a second voyage already."

"How much ye chargin' a head?"

"Six thousand."

Dad was aghast. "Madness!"

"Exactly. So what do you think? Have we got a winner?"

Dad was quiet for a moment, puzzling something out. "Just one problem."

"What's that?"

"What 'appens when the pirates get wind? Boatload o' rich Rovians is a fat prize."

Pembroke smiled. "Let's just say we've taken an excess of precaution in that department."

Dad shrugged. "Hats off, then. Sounds like a winner."

"You think so? So glad to hear it! Means a great deal to me to get the approval of a such a keen business mind as your own."

Dad pressed his lips together, making an odd kind of grimace. It took me a second to realize he was trying not to smile.

Pembroke started to reach for the plate of jelly bread, only to find it stripped bare. I was about to blurt out that I hadn't eaten any myself when he gave our end of the table a faintly amused look and turned back to Dad.

"Of course, to really make it pay, we need to get whole families on board—that way, instead of one ticket per customer, we sell five or six. Speaking as a family man—if you lived in Rovia, would you take your own children on such a voyage?"

Dad looked down the table, like he was surprised we were still there. Venus sat up straight, wiping jelly from her lip and trying to look sweet. Adonis smirked in his usual pleased-with-himself way.

"Some of 'em," Dad said.

Pembroke took the comment as a joke. "There's another thing I admire you for. Must be a real challenge, being a single father."

Dad nodded. "Yeh. Hard goin'. Wife's gone thirteen years to the day."

I looked down at my hands. Pembroke's voice went soft.

"I'm so sorry. How did she—?"

A knock at the door interrupted the question. Archibald the lawyer entered.

"Arch! Pleasant surprise. Have you met Hoke Masterson?"

Archibald nodded. "He's a client. Actually." He turned to Dad. "Sorry to interrupt . . ."

"Yeh, yeh." Dad lumbered to his feet. He and Archibald disappeared into the hallway. A moment later, Dad came back alone.

"You use Archibald? Excellent choice. I do a bit of business with him myself."

"Yeh. He's not bad." Dad turned to us. "Well, children, looks like we'll be here till mornin'."

After we all chirped with excitement, Pembroke asked, "Do you have accommodation on the island?"

"Reckoned we'd board at the Peacock."

Pembroke looked almost offended. "Why, I wouldn't hear of such a thing! You absolutely MUST stay the night in my home."

DAD TRIED A FEW mild protests, all of which Pembroke waved off. Then he murmured some instructions to the waiter, and by the time we stepped out onto the Peacock's crowded front porch, a large coach stood waiting for us, with four of the whitest horses I'd ever seen harnessed to it.

The uniformed driver opened the coach door, and Pembroke beckoned for us to climb in. As we walked over to it, I felt the bystanders staring at us, and for a second, I had the odd feeling of being in a fairy tale, like some poor scut-work orphan girl who'd been plucked from the crowd and turned into a princess. The feeling went away in a hurry when I put my foot on the coach step and remembered that Adonis had climbed in before me. I jerked my head down and to the side as I entered, but I didn't have to worry—he was too busy gawking at the velvet inner walls to bother slugging me.

Pembroke sat in the coach with us, quietly enjoying the sight of us gaping at everything like awestruck monkeys. The ride was so smooth it was almost eerie—we glided down Heavenly Road with hardly a bump, and when we reached the bottom and turned up the unpaved shore road, I could barely feel the difference in grade.

After we passed the beach, the road quickly turned steep as it followed the rising cliff toward South Point. In maybe twenty trips to Sunrise, we'd only come this far once, on a balmy Savior's Day when Dad took us on a two-mile hike to see the view from the point. Two-thirds of the way there, we'd passed a wide road snaking up into the wooded hills, fronted by a gate, a sentry box, and a pair of garrison soldiers who stood frozen in place, staring straight ahead as we passed. Back then, I'd had fun fantasizing about the secrets they were protecting behind that gate—the top three being a castle of gold, a prison for magic elves with a taste for violent crime, and the world's largest jelly bread loaf—and I could feel my blood stir up when we turned off the main road and the sentries opened the gate to admit us.

The road turned even steeper, the woods on either side thick with trees. Occasionally, a road branched off, and as we passed one of them, I caught a glimpse of what looked like the corner of a building a quarter mile distant at the top of a hill.

A mile farther, we turned up a side road into a thick woods. The road wound sharply before the woods suddenly gave way to a massive, perfectly groomed lawn. It sloped upward for several hundred yards before it flattened onto a hilltop crowned by a gleaming yellow mansion that, had it been a little smaller, could've passed for the golden castle in my fantasy.

When we reached the drive in front of the massive columned doors, a woman appeared. She was tall, blond, and clad in a blue dress so elegant that at first I figured she must be headed to a ball, or maybe a wedding. She came out to greet us, trailed by a handful of servants.

"Welcome back, darling!" She kissed Pembroke on the lips before turning to us with a big smile. "And you must be the Mastersons!"

"Indeed they are." Pembroke led her by the arm to my father, and she held out a slender hand to him. "Hoke Masterson, my wife, Edith."

"Pleased to meet ye." Dad took her hand but didn't know what to do with it. He started to lift it up like he was going to kiss the back of it, but then must have lost faith in the idea, because he quickly dropped it with a pained look.

"The pleasure is mine! And these are . . . ?"

"Oh. Yeh. This is Adonis. Me oldest." I think Adonis probably tried to smile, but he only managed to smirk.

"Venus, me daughter." Venus gave a flouncing sort of curtsy.

"Percy, the children's tutor." Percy bowed as far as his belly would let him.

"And, aah, that's Egbert." Dad muttered, his voice trailing off. I did my best to bow, although I'm not sure it looked like a bow so much as a chicken pecking at feed.

None of us had much practice with manners. But Edith Pembroke smiled at us like we were the royal family. "We're so thrilled to have you! I do apologize, but the messenger Roger sent to tell us of your visit only just arrived, so your rooms aren't quite ready. Perhaps in the meantime we could enjoy a drink on the veranda? Our daughter Millicent's just finishing her lessons. She might like to show the children around."

She turned to the house and called out, "Millicent!" in an almost musical tone.

Nobody answered. Mrs. Pembroke called out again. "Millicent?!" It was still musical, but this time there was an edge of threat to it.

"Coming, Mother . . . ," came a voice from inside, every bit as musical, but in a way that seemed to be making fun of Mrs. Pembroke.

Then she stepped into the sunlight, and I went weak all over.

Millicent Pembroke had a thick mane of honey-gold hair and long, sleek limbs that swung, careless but smooth, as she walked toward us. There was something dangerous about the way she moved—it reminded me of certain pirates back on Deadweather, the ones who called the shots, who had a wicked smile that said it was all great fun for them and might be for you too, so long as you didn't cross them, and if you did, what happened next would be quick and brutal.

The rest of her didn't remind me of a pirate at all. Other than Venus, I'd practically never seen a girl near my own age, and the few I had laid eyes on—in or around the shops on Heavenly Road—looked prim, and curt, and no fun at all. Millicent was dressed like them, in a blue-and-white checked dress, but somehow it hung differently on her, like her wearing it had turned the dress into something not at all prim, and a little wild.

Seeing us, she cocked her head with an amused smile. "Oh, hel-lo. I'm Millicent. Do you play croquet?"

My brain had suddenly gone thick and slow, and I was still sorting out the words of her question when Adonis blurted out, "Yeh! Definitely."

"All the time," chirped Venus.

"I'm mad for it. Let's have a go!" She turned and loped across the lawn toward the side of the house. My brother and sister ran after her, and I followed like I was in a trance.

MILLICENT LED US to the backyard, where a croquet game was set up—or what I guessed was one. I'd never so much as seen a

49

croquet ball, let alone wickets and mallets and posts, and I'd only heard of the game from a book I'd read, *Quimby Goes to College*.

I was sure Venus and Adonis were even more ignorant than I was. But they both pretended to know exactly what they were doing, copying Millicent as she picked up a mallet and ball from a rack.

"Girls against boys. No swearing when you lose. That's the wrong mallet."

"Nah, it ain't." Adonis stuck his chest out like he was running the game.

"Yes, it is. That or the ball—they've got to match. Look, here—" She snatched Adonis's ball from his hands and replaced it with another before he could complain. Then she handed mallets and color-matched balls to Venus and me.

She put her ball in front of the stake and whacked it through a pair of wickets.

"Bonus!" She hit the ball two more times, sending it through another wicket, then hit it a fourth time before turning to Adonis. "You're next."

After a moment's hesitation, Adonis put his ball near where she'd started and cracked it hard, hitting it around the wickets and most of the way to her ball.

"That was stupid. You trying to play spoiler? Here, your turn."

She pointed at Venus. As my sister tried to copy what she'd done, Millicent looked at me and Adonis.

"So you're from Deadweather? Are you pirates?"

"Not all o' Deadweather's pirates," Adonis informed her.

"Well, who else would live there?"

"Us. Me dad's a rich plantation owner. And I'm 'is inheritance—means I get it all someday. Makes me rich, too."

"Well, good for you. Must be smashing. His turn." She pointed to me.

I'd been debating whether to correct Adonis—if Dad was rich, I didn't know what rich meant—but the thought of talking made me nervous, so I was grateful for the distraction. I put my ball down and managed to hit it through the first two wickets.

"Bonus! Twice more."

"Why's *he* get to go again?"

"You play all the time, so I don't need to answer that, do I? Or do you play alternate rules? That would explain a lot. Does the loser actually win in your version? Say, what's your name?"

"Wot? Adonis." Adonis was having a hard time keeping up his I'm-in-charge act under Millicent's flood of words. She turned to Venus.

"And what do they call you?"

"Venus. I'm rich, too. I've almost got a pony. And I have LOADS of dresses. They're all made special for me."

By a legless pirate, I thought to myself.

"Mm. Well, the one you've got on certainly looks special."

As Venus stared at her, trying to decide whether it was a compliment or an insult, Millicent turned to me.

"You don't talk much, do you? What's your name?"

I tried to answer, but my brain was still thick and sluggish. Finally, Adonis answered for me with a sneer.

"He's Egbert."

"I'm Egbert," I repeated, sounding like a fool.

Millicent screwed up her face. "Why?"

The question hit my brain like a rod thrown into a spoked wheel, shutting it down completely. As I gaped at her like an idiot, she laughed and pointed to my siblings.

"I mean, look—he's Adonis, she's Venus. Why aren't you Apollo? Or Mars?"

Venus looked confused. "Why would he be?"

"Yeh, why?" Adonis wanted to know.

"Don't you get it?"

Her eyes went to each of us in turn as she shook her head, like it was funny but sad to her how hopeless we were. My heart started to thump with fear at the idea she might lump me in with my brother and sister. Their brains hadn't just shut down like mine—they'd never been running in the first place. But to Millicent, the results were the same: we all looked equally stupid.

I gulped hard, somehow willing my brain to lurch into gear and move my tongue.

"It's like . . . why isn't . . . our dad named Jupiter?"

"Exactly!" She wheeled back to me. "You get it. Why don't they?"

I shrugged. "I read books."

Her face lit up. "I love books! What's your favorite?"

"*Basingstroke*." It was such an easy question even my half-busted brain could handle it.

"Oh, that's a great one! The bit with the lion's genius! Who's your favorite character?"

This was harder. I thought for a moment. "I guess it *should* be James . . . but it's not—it's more Cecil."

"Right on! Because he's such a laugh!"

"Yeah!" My brain was chugging to life now. "It's like, he really wants to be good, but he just keeps getting in his own way. Saying the exactly wrong thing—"

"Like at that dinner with the countess!"

Venus and Adonis were staring dumbly at each other, like Millicent and I had started speaking a foreign language. This should have warned me to back off, because they were at their worst when they felt threatened. But Millicent was nodding and smiling, and I couldn't help myself.

"Or when they're on the road to Hexton, and they meet that soldier, and—"

"He killed our mother!" Venus heaved the words like a giant rock that thudded at my feet.

Millicent looked bewildered. "What?"

My face went hot. "It's not true!"

"Yeh, it is!" Adonis chimed in. "Killed her this very day. Thirteen years ago."

"I didn't! It's just—she—" I suddenly felt quivery and weak, like my stomach was a whirlpool sucking up all the energy in my body. But Millicent was staring at me, and I had to get the words out.

"I was just being born. And she died in the middle. Having me. Wasn't my fault."

"Yes it was! You're a murderer!" Venus was baring her teeth like a wild animal.

"I was a baby! All I did was get born!"

"Yer evil," Adonis hissed.

"I'm not!"

I turned my head away from the others, because I could feel tears starting to build in my eyes, and I didn't want any of them to see that.

It was quiet for a moment as we all hung on Millicent's reaction, like she was the judge who would either hang me or set me free. Finally, she spoke up in a quiet voice.

"That's not murder. It's just something that happens."

I turned back to look at her. She was staring at me. Not smiling, but not unkind, either. As the whirlpool in my stomach slowed, her eyes narrowed.

"Wait—if it happened while she was having you . . . doesn't that make today your birthday?"

As I nodded, Pembroke came around the corner, clapping his hands for our attention.

"Millicent! I thought I'd treat our guests to a balloon ride. What do you think?"

"Oh, brilliant, Daddy! They'll love it!"

CHAPTER 5

FLOATING AWAY

I thought I knew what a balloon was. One of the worst novels in Percy's collection was called *The Savages of Urluk*, about a wandering tribe of cavemen. Somewhere in it, the tribe hunts down a mountain ram, and after they eat most of it raw, the father rips out a section of the ram's intestine and ties the ends of it together, making a balloon for his kid to play with.

Pembroke's balloon was a whole other thing, and not only because it was made of red silk and not intestines. It was as big as a house—just the opening at its base, a tiny part of the whole, was thirty feet in diameter. Four servants were pumping air into it using a pair of giant bellows the size of draft horses. They'd been working them pretty hard for most of an hour, and the balloon was starting to take shape, expanding across Pembroke's lower lawn like some humongous, flabby monster.

A few feet away, more servants were tending a good-sized fire over which they'd straddled a tall, four-legged metal frame. Fixed to the top of the frame was the open end of a long cylinder made of canvas stretched over barrel hoops that snaked across the lawn into the open end of the balloon, sending a steady stream of hot, smoky air inside along with what the bellows were pumping.

Finally, there was the basket—made of wicker, four feet high, six feet long, and half again as wide. The top of the basket was attached by slack ropes to the mouth of the balloon. At the bottom corners of the basket, much longer ropes snaked across the lawn in four long tails that each disappeared into a coil of rope next to a heavy stake driven into the ground.

According to Millicent and Pembroke, what was going to happen was that we were all going to get into the basket, and the balloon was going to rise up and take us into the air like birds. But none of us really believed it, and although Millicent and Pembroke were selling us pretty hard on the idea, I couldn't help suspecting they were playing some kind of elaborate practical joke on us.

Judging by the look on his face, so did Dad. And it didn't help matters that Pembroke couldn't explain to him how the whole thing worked.

"The smoke is critical. As I understand it, smoke contains certain properties, possibly electrical, that propel it upward. When the quantity of smoke in the balloon is sufficient, it rises in the air, held aloft until . . . whatever it is . . . sort of . . . dissipates."

Seeing this explanation fall over dead, Pembroke turned to Percy for help.

"Mr. Percy, you're a man of learning. Can you explain the science behind this?"

Percy cocked his eye doubtfully. Any interest he had in impressing Pembroke must have been outweighed by the fact that Dad paid his wages.

"Only birds fly," he said.

"Then you'll all be birds in no time," said Pembroke with a grin. A moment later, the balloon, which until now had been expanding out as much as up, started to waft skyward with real purpose.

The basket's upper ropes stirred awake, pulled up by the force of the giant mass.

"Quickly! Into the basket!" Pembroke opened a little door in the side and beckoned us in. We climbed aboard, suspicious but game.

"Aren't ye coming?" Dad asked Pembroke.

"Love to. But there's a weight limit. Even the five of you might be too much. Besides, it's old hat for Millicent and myself."

"I've been up at least a dozen times," said Millicent. "It's smashing! You won't believe the view! You can see all the way to Blisstown!"

The balloon was fully expanded now, and the servants at the bellows picked up the canvas cylinder, holding it over their heads to direct the smoke up into the balloon. Pembroke clapped enthusiastically as the ropes snapped taut against their stays.

There was a short lurch, and the ropes creaked—but that was it. I looked up. The balloon loomed directly over us, swaying like it was unsure of itself.

Pembroke urged his servants to stoke the fire, and the column of smoke rising into the balloon thickened. But our basket stayed earthbound.

"Blast! It's too much weight." Pembroke stewed a moment, his look darkening. He seemed almost angry, as if the balloon's failure to launch was a personal insult.

Finally, he sighed and stepped forward to reopen the basket door. "Mr. Percy, would you be so kind as to step off? We'll take you on the next go-round."

Percy shrugged and stepped off, losing his balance and falling over when the balloon suddenly jerked upward.

Pembroke slammed the door and jumped back as we rose into the air. I sucked in my breath as I felt a brief, intense thrill— *flying! We were flying!*—that quickly leaked away when I realized the balloon had stopped rising ten feet off the ground.

We hovered there, coughing as we peered down at Pembroke through the thick smoke the servants kept directing past us into the balloon.

"Blast!" He really looked angry now, so much so that I wanted to call out and reassure him that even if we were only ten feet in the air, it was ten feet farther than we'd ever flown.

Millicent stepped over to join him, her perfect face gazing up at us through the dirty haze. She met my eye, and I looked away quickly.

Then Adonis had a brilliant idea. "Dad!" he barked. "It's still too heavy! Let's throw Egbert over."

I started to protest, but suddenly realized that if they were in the air and I was on the ground, I'd be with Millicent and not them. In an instant, the chance to fly seemed worth skipping.

"Don't bother," I said as I vaulted over the side.

I hit the ground at an angle, falling over as pain shot up one ankle. But it was only pain. I jumped to my feet, and my heart sank when I saw Millicent looking at me not with pleasure but anger.

Fortunately, she was angry *for* me, not *at* me. As Pembroke watched the balloon shoot into the sky, the four coils of rope whirring as the basket played out its tethers, Millicent tugged his arm, then pointed to me.

"But, Dad, it's his birthday!"

"I don't mind," I said quickly. "Really. I'm not much for heights."

"Are you sure?" Millicent asked. "We can do another."

"Either way. It's all right."

"But it's your birthday!"

"It's okay. Really."

Pembroke studied me for a moment, frowning. Then he sighed and patted me on the shoulder. "Don't worry. We'll figure out what to do with you."

The tethers snapped taut. We all looked up. The balloon was so high in the air that when a head popped over the side of the basket to look down at us, it took me a moment to figure out which family member it belonged to.

It was Venus. She waved at us, excited. Pembroke and Millicent waved back. We watched the balloon hover overhead for a while, then Pembroke nodded to a pair of nearby servants and turned back toward the house.

"They'll be up there a good while. Now, son—what can we do to give you a happy birthday?"

My cheeks flushed at the question. No one had ever asked me something like that before. But I figured out an answer pretty quickly.

"Wouldn't mind another game of croquet."

"All right," Millicent said brightly. "But I'll most likely trounce you silly."

"I don't mind."

"Mr. Percy, why don't you accompany us back to the house?" asked Pembroke. "I'm sure Millicent's tutor would be delighted to exchange professional wisdom with you."

"Wonderful," said Percy, his eyes showing dread. Unless Millicent's tutor was a complete fraud as well, this probably wasn't going to go well for him.

As we all started back toward the house, I turned around for one last look at the balloon, swaying on its tethers hundreds of feet in the sky.

Don't come down, I thought to myself.

MILLICENT AND I went back to the croquet pitch. We began a new game, and she quickly started trouncing me.

Worse, without Adonis and Venus to knock heads against, our conversation turned stiff and awkward. My brain had gone back into a cramp, and I struggled to put together even the stupidest answer to her stream of questions.

"So your father's got a plantation? Does that make him a farmer? Or a planter? Is there a difference? What do you plant?"

"Don't . . . plant . . . anything."

"How's that possible? You must plant something. It's a planta-tion! Or perhaps it's just a ruse. Are you really engaged in some-thing else? Something secret and dastardly? Are you pirates after all?"

"No, no . . ." I was getting all flustered, not just because of my brain cramp but because I couldn't figure out how to stand between turns—whether to prop my mallet over my shoulder, or set it down and lean against it, or cross my arms with the head sticking up over the crook of one elbow.

I tried all three. None of them felt right. Trying to find a fourth option, I dropped the mallet on my foot. Millicent watched me with a kind of amused suspicion.

"I think you are. Look at you—you're hiding something. I'm going to have Daddy take this up with the garrison commander. They'll get to the bottom of it. Torture you if they have to. We'll flush you out, you dirty criminals."

"No, look . . . it's already planted. You just pick the fruit."

"Now we're getting somewhere! What kind of fruit?"

I sighed. "Ugly fruit."

"Eeew. What's that?"

"Just a fruit."

"Strange name. Who wants to eat something called ugly fruit? What's it like? Tell me. Is it reeeeeally ugly?"

"I guess so. It's sort of big and lumpy."

"How's it taste?"

"I don't know. Like a . . . boring orange."

"That's funny. Do you pick it yourselves? You and your brother and sister?"

"No. Well, they don't. I do, a bit. Mostly we've got field hands. Just . . . well, they don't all have hands."

She looked at me curiously, leaning lightly on her mallet. I made a note to stand that way myself the next time.

"The field hands don't have hands?"

"Some of them. It's complicated."

"You're not like them, are you?"

"The field hands?"

"No. Your brother and sister. You don't even look like them. Your hair's lighter. It's curly, too. And you're missing that big horse nose they all have. And your name! How did *that* happen?"

"I don't know. It's not my fault." I suddenly felt like pushing her over.

"Don't get mad. I didn't say it was."

"I don't like my name."

"So what do people call you?"

"Egbert."

"But you don't like it."

"So?"

"You should come up with something you like."

"You can't change your name."

"Course you can. Give yourself a nickname. Like Egg. Or Bert. Or Grumpy."

I passed her as she said this, on my way to my ball, and she gave me a playful shove on the shoulder. Her touch made my stomach flutter—I both liked it and didn't like it at the same time.

"Do you fancy any of those? I mean, not Grumpy. Obviously."

"Egg's all right."

"All right, then. You're Egg. 'Hello, Egg!' How's that sound?"

My ball was in a tough spot. To reach the next wicket, I'd somehow have to get around hers. Between working out all the angles of the shot and choosing a new name, I was starting to feel overwhelmed.

I shut my eyes for a moment. That made me dizzy, so I opened them again.

"'Morning, Egg!' 'What's Egg think about that?' 'Could you pass the salt please, Egg?' Well? What do you think?"

"It's all right."

"Loads better than Egbert. All right, then! It's settled. When the others come back, we'll tell 'em that's your name from now on."

"They won't care."

She considered this for a moment. "No, I suppose not. You don't get on much with them, do you?"

"Not much."

"You know why? Because they're horrid. And you're not. Don't you think?"

"Maybe." Hearing her say I wasn't horrid set my stomach fluttering again.

She dropped her voice a notch, taking the sparkle out of it. "That's completely daft about your mum, you know. They're absolutely wrong. And anyway, I think you're lucky you don't have a mother."

"What?"

She looked over her shoulder at the big yellow mansion. "I've got one. And she's beastly."

"She doesn't look beastly."

"Of course, she's quite beautiful. But the worst ones always are."

I was confused, and I must have looked it, because she made an exaggerated show of disbelief. "Don't you know? Come now, Egg. All the books you've read, and you don't know beautiful women are evil?"

"They're not always. You're beautiful, and you're not evil."

I hadn't meant to say that—it just sort of fell out of my mouth before I could stop it. Millicent blushed, which until then I wouldn't have thought was possible.

"Are you courting me?"

"No—I—sorry! I didn't mean . . . well, I did, just not . . . I shouldn't have said it."

I quickly turned away and gave my ball a whack. It struck hers hard, carrying it a good twenty feet off the wicket.

"And now you've knocked me out of position! Of all the nerve!"

"Sorry!"

Panicky that I'd ruined everything, I rushed over and picked up her ball. As I ran back to return it to its original spot, she began to laugh.

"That's against the rules! You're making a complete hash of things!"

"I'm sorry! Here—" I handed her the ball. "Put it wherever you like. I don't mind."

As she took the ball, she smiled at me.

It wasn't a big smile—no teeth, just the mouth turned up at the corners, with a little crinkle of warmth around her eyes.

But it conquered me completely. As time went on, that smile became the thing that I lived for—the answer to every question, the solution to every problem, the image that during even the worst moments I could call up in my mind to remind me that this was what was worth the struggle and the pain.

Even now, I can still see it as clearly as if she's standing in front of me, eyes locked on mine, filling me with bliss.

I stood drowning in that smile, so lost to the world that even after Millicent broke away with a look of alarm, it took a few seconds for me to register the sound of voices shouting on the lower lawn.

I followed her dumbly as she started off toward the voices, then pulled up short, her head tilting upward.

The red balloon was floating through the sky toward us, rising and gathering speed as it went, the four tethers twisting in the breeze beneath it.

Then it was past us, and I saw the dark outlines of heads poking out over the basket. They were calling to us, but I couldn't hear the words.

Then we were running after it, Millicent yelling as her father and Percy emerged from the veranda and joined the pursuit, running until we ran out of lawn and had to back off to keep it in view over the trees.

I heard Percy curse with astonishment. Then I felt a strong hand on my shoulder. Roger Pembroke's face was grave.

"I'm sorry, son. There must have been an accident. We'll fix it."

He squeezed my shoulder and gave me a confident nod, and whatever fear was rising beneath the fog of confusion in my head instantly melted away—somehow, his look and touch had the magical effect of convincing me that he was in charge, and as long as I trusted him, everything would be okay.

Then he turned and ran toward the lower lawn, where the servants' shouting was dying down. I turned my attention back to the sky. Within a minute, the balloon had shrunk to a thumbnail over the shoulder of Mount Majestic, blurring into the reddish light of the setting sun.

A minute after that, it was gone for good.

CHAPTER 6

IN THE CLOUDS

Tell me, Egg—what do you know about the Fire King?"

It was ninety minutes after my family had disappeared, and I was sitting with the Pembrokes at a giant slab of a table in the formal dining room of Cloud Manor, which I'd just learned was the name of their mansion.

It was strange—I'd never heard of a house with its own name—but so were a lot of things, all at once: I was wearing a silk shirt, and I'd just had a hot bath, and upstairs was a feather bed in a big room with huge windows that I'd been told was mine to sleep in, and all through dinner the Pembrokes had treated me as an honored guest, offering me first helpings of everything and calling me Egg, which no one had ever called me before.

And of course I'd just watched my family sail away over the horizon in a giant runaway balloon. That was shock enough all on its own, and to suddenly find myself living like a grand duke right on top of it was so disorienting that I'd started to feel like I'd slipped loose from reality and was floating in some kind of dream world, where any second the room might fill up with flying dragons and unicorns.

So I guess it's understandable that when Roger Pembroke asked me about some king I'd never heard of, I wasn't levelheaded enough to wonder why he was asking, or to answer with anything smarter than "The what king?"

Millicent piped up. "The Fire King! Hutmatozal. Don't you know the legend?"

"No. Sorry. Is he Rovian?"

Pembroke chuckled. "Oh, heavens, no. He was a savage. Ruled the Natives in this area about a hundred years ago. Your father and I—"

"You don't know about the Fire King's treasure? Or the Fist of Ka? It's absolutely—"

"Millicent." Pembroke stopped her with a little wave of his fingers. Then he turned back to me. "Your father and I were speaking. He showed me a parchment he had with him. In Native writing. Do you know where it came from?"

"Not exactly."

"What do you mean?"

He leaned forward, his ice-blue eyes watching me closely. I thought very hard. If this was some kind of test, I wanted to make him happy by passing it.

"I think he copied it. From something he'd found. There's a cliff up above our house, called Rotting Bluff. Looks out over the sea. We keep a cannon there, just in case. Every so often, Dad goes up to clean it. He went up yesterday. Came back sort of . . . distant. Like he was thinking hard about something. Went out again, same direction. Only that time, he took a parchment and pencil. Then this morning, he brought us here. To talk to the lawyer about it, I think."

"Did he tell anyone else about it?"

"I can't imagine. He doesn't talk very much. Not to anybody."

"Not business associates? Or friends . . . ?"

"Don't think he has any of those."

"Which?"

"Either."

Pembroke was sitting back in his chair now, his eyes still fixed on me. His look made me nervous. I couldn't tell if I'd said too much, or not enough.

Millicent jumped in again. "Daddy's an expert on the Fire King. He's got loads of books about Natives, and he's searched all over Sunrise for the Fist." She turned to him. "What was in the parchment, Daddy? Was it a clue to—"

He cut her off. "It was nothing, Millicent. Native gibberish."

Then he smiled at me, which was a huge relief. "Thank you, Egg. It makes sense now. Millicent's right—I'm fascinated by Native history. It's quite a challenge, trying to separate what's actually true from all the wild legends about magic trinkets that don't exist."

"Since when don't you think it exists?" asked Millicent, scrunching up her nose.

"Since my thinking's matured, sweetheart. It's good fun, but it's nonsense. A tale for schoolchildren." He smiled at me again, with a kind look. "I had the impression your father was keen on the subject as well. Now I see it was just a coincidence."

"Why don't we serve dessert?" suggested Mrs. Pembroke.

"Yes, let's!" Millicent leaned across the table. "Close your eyes, Egg—you'll love this."

"Precious, he doesn't need to close his eyes—"

"Of course he does, Daddy! It's a birthday surprise! Don't be stupid."

"Millicent," said her mother, in a tone that gave that one word a whole sentence of meaning: *don't-call-your-father-stupid-or-there's-going-to-be-trouble.*

"Mo-ther," replied Millicent, meaning *I'll-say-what-I-want-just-try-and-stop-me.*

In my house, there would have been a smacking for that. But Mr. Pembroke just smiled at his daughter like he was amused, while Mrs. Pembroke bunched her eyebrows together but said nothing.

"Come on, Egg! Be a sport."

I squeezed my eyes shut. In a moment, I heard the kitchen door open. Then came footsteps, along with the unmistakable smell of jelly bread. A tray clanked onto the table.

"All right, then—open them!"

A steaming loaf of fresh jelly bread lay before me. The words "Happy Birthday, Egg!" were written in white frosting across the top.

As I stared at it, stunned, the Pembrokes—along with the three servants who were in the room—all cried out, "Happy Birthday!"

I started to cry.

It was horribly embarrassing, and from the looks on the Pembrokes' faces, it was more than a little awkward for them, but I just couldn't help it. No one had ever been nice to me like that before. And I'd long since learned never to cry over pain or cruelty, but I didn't know what to do with kindness. I was pretty sure you weren't supposed to cry about it, but the tears just started leaking out and I didn't know how to stop them.

Mrs. Pembroke must have gotten the wrong idea, because she got up and came over to kneel beside my chair, her soft hand on my arm.

"Don't you worry about a thing," she said. "Mr. Pembroke is a very resourceful man, and he's going to do everything in his power to make sure your family comes back safely to you. All right, darling?"

I nodded. Just the mention of my family did a decent job of stopping the tears.

"Thank you," I said, wiping my eyes. "Can we eat this now?"

I'll say this for jelly bread: it was worth the thirteen years I'd waited to taste it. And when she saw how much I liked it, Mrs. Pembroke made sure we ate it every night, for the entire time I stayed at Cloud Manor.

IN THE END, I was there three full weeks—the happiest, most carefree weeks of my life, so different from everything that came before and after that when I look back, they almost seem to have belonged to someone else. I spent the days tagging along after Millicent like a puppy, going from lessons with her tutor to croquet games to horseback rides in the hills below Mount Majestic to long, lazy hours reading in the library.

The library was my favorite—it was enormous, lined with bookshelves so tall you needed a ladder to reach the upper rows. Early on, I found the Native books Millicent had mentioned—there were a dozen of them, up on a high shelf, and although they were written mostly in Cartager, there were a few titles in Rovian, like *Savage Tribes and Customs* and *Across the Maw: Cartager Conquests in the New Lands*. I tried to look at them because I thought it might impress Mr. Pembroke if I could discuss one of his interests with him, but the ladder to reach the shelf had gone missing, and no matter how often I asked, the servants never could seem to find it.

I'm not quite sure where Percy went during these weeks. There were loads of servants at Cloud Manor—between the mansion, stables, grounds, and greenhouse, there must have been dozens—but they kept out of sight, scurrying around the edges of wherever we were but otherwise in their own secret world. Once my family disappeared, Pembroke must have shuffled Percy off into this world so deftly that I barely noticed he was gone.

So it came as a shock when he appeared at my elbow one afternoon in the stables. He was in a servant's uniform, holding a currycomb and wearing a furtive look.

"Master Egbert! You look well. Food's good, eh?"

I was too stunned to answer—not just by his sudden reappearance but by the fact that he'd called me Master. And rather than sneering, he seemed to want to impress me.

As I stared at him, one of the other servants exited a distant stall and, seeing us talking, began to stride toward us. Percy lowered his voice and quickened his speech.

"Want you to know I've always felt you got a bit of a raw deal with the old family, rather too hard on you, never MY idea certainly—"

"Ch-ch!" The other servant uttered something that sounded like a bird call but must have had some meaning specific to their business, because Percy broke away from me, pleading as he went.

"Don't forget your old Percy—put in a good word—wouldn't mind tutoring!"

Then he was gone, and within an hour, I'd managed to put him out of my mind again.

Just like, I'm embarrassed to admit, I'd mostly put my family out of my mind. And not accidentally, but intentionally—because thinking about them forced me to think about how living with the Pembrokes might only be temporary, and it was so wonderful, and life with my own family had been so lousy, that I never wanted to leave.

But sometimes the thought of Dad would creep in, and I'd get a little gnawing pang of guilt, thinking about how hard he used to work, and how he'd never had the chance to live, even for a day, as richly as I was living at the Pembrokes'.

Then I'd force myself to remember all the times he cracked me for lazing around, and how he never seemed to crack Adonis nearly as much even though Adonis was easily twice as lazy as me. Or how he never said a word or lifted a finger when Venus or Adonis went at me.

That made it easy to forget again. And when Mr. Pembroke updated me on the search, with vague but confident promises of search parties "leaving no stone unturned" or "scouring every corner of the map," I'd nod and smile and quickly change the subject.

This seemed to be fine with the Pembrokes. Everything seemed to be fine with them—fine and rich and effortlessly happy.

Except for Millicent and her mother. They fought constantly, not in the normal way, but in their own odd style—with words that seemed pleasant on the surface, but had ugly meanings stuck to their undersides.

"I'll be at the stables, Mother," Millicent would say as we went out, but the way she said it made the words mean something more like *leave-me-alone-you-shrew*.

"You've finished your lessons, then?" Edith would reply. Meaning *don't-you-dare-leave-without-doing-your-work*.

"In spec-tacular fashion," Millicent would say, or really, *haven't-done-a-bit-of-it-but-just-try-to-stop-me*.

I couldn't understand why they didn't get along, because Mrs. Pembroke seemed like the nicest person I'd ever met, and even though Millicent had a wicked streak, she was smart and funny and beautiful, and what more could a mother want in a daughter?

Eventually, I got up the courage to ask Millicent about it. We were in the library reading, and Mrs. Pembroke had just paused at the entry to call out Millicent's name, in a way that meant *don't-sit-with-your-legs-over-the-side-of-the-chair-because-it's-not-ladylike*. Millicent grudgingly sat up straight, but as soon as her mother was gone, she swung her legs right back over the chair again.

"How come . . . you and your mother . . . ?"

"Why is she such a hectoring shrew? Is that what you're asking?"

"She doesn't seem like a shrew."

"Because you're not her daughter."

"No, but . . . I mean, she doesn't even smack you—"

"Like to see her try." Then Millicent sat up and turned in her chair, leaning in toward me like she was telling a secret.

"Know what her problem is? She's insanely jealous. Because I'm going to run Daddy's business one day—he already lets me sit in on meetings, and he tells me absolutely EVERYTHING about what's going on. Things he'd never tell her, because she doesn't understand business in the slightest. And it drives her mad with envy, and all she wants to do is keep me from it.

"But of course she can't contradict Daddy, so she crosses her arms and clucks like a hen, and makes silly comments, like"— Millicent's voice rose to a mimicking, high-pitched whine, which didn't actually sound like her mother at all—"'Dah-ling, you don't know WHAT you're getting yourself into!' Or 'I just want you to be happy, sweetheart.' Like she even knows what'd make me happy! Sometimes, she even convinces Daddy to keep me out of his meetings. He has to shoo me out of his office, and when I complain, he says, 'Love to have you, princess, but we don't want to upset your mother.' And then of course, when I confront her, she denies the whole thing. Pfft!" She let out a little huff of disgust.

"What WOULD make you happy?" I asked.

"Running Daddy's empire! Certainly not skulking off to Rovia to marry some boring old twit and live in some moldy castle like SHE wants for me."

"I thought only kingdoms had empires."

"Oh, Egg . . ." Millicent looked at me with a sort of amused impatience. "Daddy IS the kingdom around here. He runs EVERYTHING."

"Doesn't the governor do that?"

"Who, Burns? That sorry old man? He's just a puppet."

"What's a puppet?"

"You know." She raised a hand and fluttered her fingers, like she was operating a marionette. "He moves whichever way Daddy tells him to. It's the same way with the soldiers."

"What, is your dad a general or something?"

"He doesn't have to be—he pays all their salaries. Right down to the garrison commander."

"And he runs the silver mine, too?" I'd gathered that much just from overhearing Mr. Pembroke's conversations in the entrance hall with the men who were continually coming to visit him in his office.

"He doesn't just run it—he *owns* it. It was all his idea, you know. The mine didn't even exist before Daddy. And he's got plans to expand way beyond it. In fact, he's working on something now that he says will make the silver mine look like a street meat shack."

"What's that?"

"It's business—you wouldn't understand," she said, more than a little haughty. Which annoyed me, because I got the impression she didn't really understand, either. I was about to tell her as much when she lowered her voice and said, "He controls the pirates, too."

That was so preposterous that I had to laugh. "No one controls the pirates!"

"That's what they want people to think. But it's not true—or anyway, Daddy's got an understanding with them. Nothing happens on the Blue Sea without his say-so."

She looked so sure of herself I couldn't quite muster the confidence to tell her she was crazy.

"So that'll be you someday—ordering pirates around, telling the governor what to do?"

I meant it as a joke, but I had to admit it was surprisingly easy to imagine Millicent at the big mahogany desk in her father's study, yelling at the governor to do her bidding.

"Don't tease me, Egg. I'll have you killed. I could do it, too."

"I'll be sure not to beat you at croquet, then." I'd almost won a game the day before, and she'd gotten so mad she broke a mallet and wouldn't talk to me until dinner.

"Like to see you try," she said with a smile, standing up and smacking my leg as she headed for the door. "Let's have a go."

Something about that conversation upset me badly. I had no idea why at first, but all the way through the croquet game that followed and the horseback ride after it up to the big meadow in the foothills, I was glum and snappish with Millicent.

At first, she didn't notice. Then she noticed and teased me about it. Then, when the teasing just made me more short-tempered, she resorted to pleading.

We'd tied the horses up and were walking through the meadow when she saw a mountain gopher and took off after it, yelling for me to help her run it down. I didn't bother, because it seemed stupid and pointless—she chased them every time we went to the meadow, and no matter how often she failed to even gain ground on one, let alone catch it, she never seemed to lose faith that she'd eventually outrun one of them.

She gave up after about fifty yards and sauntered back toward me. As I watched her approach, her eyes bright and laughing, her golden hair shining in the sun, I felt an ache building in my chest. Like my glum mood, I didn't know what it was at first.

"Stop that infernal frowning!" she called out. "It doesn't suit you at all! Bring back the real Egg! I don't like this surly one! Not one bit."

She closed the distance between us, reached out, and took my hands in hers. "Come on—tell me what I need to do to bring you back."

The answer jumped into my head so quickly it almost slipped out of my mouth before I could stop it.

Marry me.

There were a hundred reasons why thinking that was crazy, starting with the fact that we were only thirteen. But there it was. I couldn't unthink it. And right away, I realized what the ache in my chest must be.

She was still holding my hands, waiting for me to answer.

"I haven't gone anywhere," I said finally. "And I don't want to."

"Well, who says you have to?" she replied, her smile widening as she let go of my hands. "Come on. Race you down the mountain."

It wasn't until late that night, as I lay awake in the big feather bed, that I realized why Millicent's telling me about her father's empire—and her plans to inherit it—had put me in such a dark mood.

I'd always known Roger Pembroke was rich and powerful, but until then I hadn't really grasped just how exceptional he was. And the moment Millicent laid it all out for me, I knew—deep down, in the place where you feel things before you understand them or even realize they're there—that this meant I couldn't marry Millicent.

Never mind the fact that no one got married at thirteen— King Frederick might have been paired off at twelve with the Umbergian princess who became Queen Madeleine, but for commoners, it wasn't even a theoretical possibility until you were north of seventeen.

And never mind the fact that I had no idea if Millicent liked me that way. She did on some level, clearly—it never seemed to bother her that I was always following her around, we never lacked for things to talk about or do together, and since that first smile out on the lawn, I'd gotten dozens more from her, both big and little.

But whether she liked me the way I liked her, with the kind of feeling that put an ache in my chest—that was a mystery. And no matter how carefully I picked over every one of her smiles, gestures, and offhand comments, rerunning them in my head for hours afterward, I couldn't solve it one way or another.

Never mind all that—because I'd read enough novels about rich and powerful people to know it didn't matter. If her father was that important, he'd never consent to her marrying someone like me. And as his heir, she'd be duty bound to agree.

Unless . . .

Unless I could prove myself somehow.

So from that point on, I spent hours every day fantasizing about how I could accomplish something so spectacular that both Millicent and her parents would realize I was worthy of her.

At first, the fantasies were grand and world-shaking—leading an army, conquering a new land, building an empire of my own.

But those all seemed to take an awfully long time and require endless levels of planning. So eventually they went out the window, replaced by feats of bravery and daring—saving Millicent from a burning building, or pulling her from raging floodwaters, or single-handedly fighting off a band of ruthless savages intent on murdering her.

At first, the savages seemed more promising than the other options. After all, I could wait around forever before a building caught fire with Millicent in it. And Cloud Manor was on awfully high ground, so a flood seemed just as unlikely. But the Natives in the silver mine were not only foreign and mysterious, they were close at hand, and if they ever descended from the mine to Cloud Manor, they might create useful peril in all kinds of ways.

But something felt wrong about making villains of those tiny, hardworking specks I'd glimpsed from the sea as they toiled away on the far side of the mountain. They didn't seem ruthless so much as put-upon, and I couldn't imagine they had much in the way of weapons, so vanquishing them, even in my head, felt less thrilling than sad.

Then I hit on the idea of swapping them out for pirates, who were not only reliably well-armed, but villainous by occupation.

It was a little trickier to work out the specifics—Millicent had said her father controlled the pirates, which I only half believed, but if true, it complicated things immensely. Eventually, I put together an elaborate fantasy in which the pirates, seeking bloody satisfaction from an unpaid gambling debt, infiltrated Sunrise dressed as Rovian businessmen and stormed Cloud Manor, taking the entire family hostage. Armed at first with only my wits, then a length of rope, then a succession of knives, followed by a brace of pistols, a rack of muskets, and finally a sword from the scabbard of Burn Healy himself, I slaughtered a truly staggering number of pirates, until their corpses had piled up like cordwood in the hallways of Cloud Manor and earned me such tearful gratitude from Millicent and her parents that our eventual marriage was decided upon within minutes of Healy's body hitting the floor.

It sounds crazy now. But that's how much I loved Millicent—enough to kill pirates for her. And not just a few pirates. A lot of them.

And that was the state of my mind three weeks into my stay, when Mr. Pembroke stopped Millicent and me in the entry hall on our way out for an afternoon ride. He'd left before breakfast that morning on an errand to Blisstown and was just coming back in the door with a sheaf of papers.

"Precious, why don't you go out alone today? I have some matters I need to discuss with Egg."

"Make it quick, Daddy. It's no fun riding alone." Millicent stuck her tongue out at him. Then she turned to me. "I'll take the meadow path. Catch up when you can."

We both watched her go. Then Roger Pembroke placed a hand on my shoulder.

"Come into my study. We'll be more comfortable."

COMING DOWN

By the time I sat down in one of the big leather chairs facing Mr. Pembroke's desk, my stomach was hollow and fluttery, and my whole body felt weak. Something was clearly about to change for me, and for the first time in my life I didn't WANT anything to change.

Pembroke stood a few feet in front of me, leaning back against his desk with his arms folded.

"It's been three weeks now since your family disappeared. The last of the search teams I dispatched has returned. Like the others, they found no trace. And . . ."

He took a deep breath. "Given what we know of wind conditions, and the extent of ocean to our west, I believe . . . and I want to be completely honest, because as painful as it is, you're a very intelligent young man, and you deserve the truth . . . I believe the odds of survival are so small as to be—"

He went on, but I stopped hearing him, because an image had

just flashed in my mind—of my family in the balloon, coming down in a dark and empty sea in the middle of the night, a hundred miles from shore—and suddenly I felt dizzy and scared and sick and I knew I had to force that image from my head and not think about it again or I might break down completely.

Fortunately, Pembroke was still talking, and I was able to distract myself by listening very hard to every word that came out of his mouth, even though they'd stopped adding up to sentences and for a moment I couldn't understand a thing.

"—leaving you an orphan. I'm sorry . . . But I want you to know you'll be taken care of. More than that—given that I feel some responsibility for what happened, and because we've all grown to have such affection for you these past weeks—Edith and I have been talking. And I've just been down to see Mr. Archibald, the lawyer. And . . ."

He pulled a document from the sheaf of papers he'd brought back from Blisstown and handed it to me. "We're hoping you'll join our family."

It was a single page of thick, tiny writing, titled CERTIFICATE OF LEGAL ADOPTION. There were two lines at the bottom for both of our signatures. Pembroke's space was already signed.

I stared at the words, but my head was still so addled I couldn't comprehend them. And I must have looked as confused as I felt, because he repeated the offer, more clearly this time.

"We want to adopt you, Egg. If you sign this document, I'll be your lawful father."

All I could do was stare at him. This was too much to handle.

I'm not sure how long the silence lasted, but finally Pembroke moved to take back the document.

"It's too soon. I'm sorry."

"No, it's—" I hung on to it, because I could tell he was disappointed, and even though my thoughts were a complete muddle and I couldn't think straight at all, I knew I didn't want to disappoint him.

I forced myself to talk. My voice was all quivery. "You've been so nice, and you're all so kind and"—I just barely stopped myself from saying "rich" here—"nice. And . . ."

The meaning of this was starting to drift into focus. *I would be Roger Pembroke's son. I could stay here forever . . .*

I stared up at him in disbelief. "Are you sure?"

"Yes, Egg. I'm sure. I want you to be my son."

"Mrs. Pembroke—?"

"Wants to be your mother. She cares about you very much."

That got the tears rolling. It was madness how easily the Pembrokes made me cry. Before I'd met them, I hadn't cried in years, not even the time Adonis dislocated my shoulder and Quint the house pirate had to pop it back in its socket using two blocks of wood.

Eventually, I got hold of myself again. "Thank you."

"There's no need to thank me."

"I don't know what else to say."

"Say yes."

I nodded, wiping my eyes. "Yes."

He smiled. Then he dipped a quill pen in ink and offered it to me. I took the pen and tried to sign the document against my leg, almost breaking through the paper.

"Here—use the desk."

He stepped aside, making room for me. I stood up and

immediately felt the room start to spin. I think I'd forgotten to breathe for a while.

Pembroke looked amused. "Deep breath, Egg. There you go."

I gulped some air and managed a chuckle at myself. Pembroke gave me a warm smile. I stepped up to the desk to sign my name.

"I can't wait to tell Millicent she's got a brother."

The pen froze in my hand, an inch from the paper.

You can't marry your sister. It just wasn't done. Not even in books.

In an instant, all the new fantasies that had been forming in my head went poof, gone when I realized that I couldn't have them and still hold on to my other, bigger fantasy. I set the pen down and stepped back from the desk.

"What's the matter?" Pembroke's mouth was turning down at the sides.

"I'm sorry."

"For what?"

"I can't."

"Take some time. I'm sure this all seems very sudden."

"I'm sorry, but—"

Pembroke was no fool. "If you're thinking of Millicent, trust me. This is best for you both."

I shook my head and stared at the floor. "I'm sorry."

His voice was turning hard and chilly. "What do you think? That you'll grow up and marry her? That's not possible. In fact, it's completely impossible. Now, be sensible."

"I'm sorry—"

"Stop saying that!"

He paused for a breath. When he continued, his voice was

quieter but just as hard. "Egg, you're a wonderful young boy with a very bright future. But whether you're her brother or not, you will never—NEVER—marry my daughter. So why don't you—"

"What if it's not up to you?" The words flew out before I could stop them.

"EVERYTHING IS UP TO ME!"

The question had hit some nerve deep inside him, and he exploded in a red-faced fury.

"IT WILL NOT HAPPEN! What the devil is the matter with you? Don't you see what you're being offered? And after everything we've done for you?"

"I'm sor—I—won't be any more of a bother. I'll leave immediately."

"YOU'RE NOT GOING ANYWHERE!"

We both fell silent as Pembroke slowly pulled his anger back in. He pressed his lips together, his nostrils flaring as he forced himself to breathe deeply. When he spoke again, his voice was carefully measured, but the burning look never left his eyes.

"Why don't you go upstairs to your room? We could both stand to do some thinking. Stay there until you're called."

A butler was at the door, attracted by the shouting. Pembroke motioned for me to leave. I was almost out of the room when he called to me again.

"And, Egg—this is between you and me. If you speak so much as a word of it to Millicent—or to Edith—you'll regret it."

I nodded and followed the butler out.

I spent the rest of the afternoon in my room. At first, I just lay on the bed, curled up in a ball while that horrible image of the balloon coming down in a dark sea ran over and over in my head. It made me sick beyond words, and I hated myself for having spent the past three weeks living like a careless prince, not once stopping to think about how my family must have suffered. Somehow, it felt like it was my fault—like if I hadn't enjoyed myself so much, maybe they wouldn't be dead.

And for the first time, I wished they weren't gone, even my lousy siblings. But especially Dad. I'd never known quite where I stood with him—he wasn't intentionally cruel like Venus and Adonis, but I couldn't exactly say he loved me, either. Even so, he took care of things. He was my father. And now he was gone. There was nobody left to take care of things.

I cried over it some. But eventually, I realized I was in a fix, and no amount of feeling awful, either for my family or myself, was going to change that. The only person who could get me out of it was me.

So I made myself get up, and I tried to think the situation through as I paced back and forth across the room.

It seemed impossible. I couldn't imagine getting right with Pembroke by doing anything short of giving up my hopes for Millicent. And I just couldn't do that.

So I figured I'd be kicked out of Cloud Manor, which terrified me, because I didn't know where I'd go. Back to Deadweather, probably. But I didn't have any money to hire a boat, and anyway, what was I going to do when I got there? Run the plantation by myself?

I was being crazy. I didn't have to be alone in the world—Roger Pembroke, the richest and most powerful man I'd ever known, had just offered to adopt me. He'd more than take care of me— he'd make me rich! And I turned him down? Ridiculous!

I decided to accept the offer immediately. It was the only sane thing to do.

Except I couldn't do it. Every time I contemplated signing that adoption certificate, Millicent popped back into my head. The thought of living with her, spending all our days together . . . and having to think of her as my *sister,* and me her *brother* . . . it was unbearable.

There was no way out, so I eventually gave up and went back to fantasies of killing pirates. It was the only option that seemed to have a happy ending. If I saved Millicent's life from a pack of bloodthirsty killers, all bets were off. So when it got on toward evening and I heard distant shouting downstairs, I dared to hope my dreams had come true. But the shouts never turned to screams, and eventually they died away completely.

A little while after that, a butler came to fetch me for dinner. When I got to the dining room, Pembroke was gone, Millicent's eyes were red with tears, and Mrs. Pembroke wouldn't look at either one of us.

We ate in silence, broken only by the clink of silverware and an occasional sniffle from Millicent. The gloom was so heavy I could barely get up an appetite for even the jelly bread. Whatever was happening, I was sure it was my fault.

Finally, Mrs. Pembroke excused herself from the table. Millicent watched her go.

"Beast," she hissed as her mother disappeared through the door.

"What happened?" I whispered.

"They had a huge fight—I'm sure she started it, she always does—then Daddy went out to a meeting, and he not only didn't invite me, she wouldn't even let him tell me what it was about! It's ALL her fault."

"No—it's my fault. I'm sorry." I'd meant to follow Pembroke's order not to say anything to Millicent, but I couldn't stand seeing her blame her mother.

"Don't be ridiculous, Egg. It's got nothing to do with you."

"Are you sure?"

"Of course. Why would it?"

"Your father . . . got angry with me today."

"Pffft." Millicent waved the idea away with her hand. "Daddy gets mad. Then he calms down. I'm sure it was nothing. He thinks the world of you."

I was desperate to believe this, and hearing it gave me enough hope to finish my jelly bread. I stayed up late that night, reading in the library while I waited for Pembroke to come home so I could confirm for myself that his anger that afternoon was short-lived.

But he never did, and around midnight I finally went up to my room, holding tightly to Millicent's last words. If Pembroke really did think the world of me, then maybe I hadn't ruined everything after all.

I'd just gotten into bed when there was a soft knock at my door.

It was Mrs. Pembroke. She wore a long silk nightgown and held a candle in an iron holder.

"Egg . . . may I speak with you?" Her voice was barely more than a whisper.

"Yes."

She came over to sit on the edge of my bed. Her hand trembled a bit, which made the candle flicker, so she set it on the nightstand.

Then she reached out and brushed a wisp of hair from my eyes. "You're a very sweet boy, and I think the world of you."

I was starting to well up, not just from the words, but from the gentle touch of her fingers on my forehead, when her next sentence made all the emotion stick in my throat like a rock.

"But you need to leave here. Immediately."

She went on, her voice turning cold and pointed.

"Do you have any family besides your father and siblings?"

"No."

"Any friends? Older ones who could take you in?"

"No."

She drew in a deep breath, and for a moment, her eyes looked like they might take pity on me. Then she exhaled, and the coldness returned.

"Then I think what's best . . . is for you to go back where you came from. I'll make arrangements first thing in the morning."

I opened my mouth, wanting to say something, but I couldn't find any words. Just then, the heavy creak of the front door echoed up to us from the entrance hall downstairs. Mrs. Pembroke startled, rising quickly to her feet.

"I'm sorry, Egg. It's what's best for you."

She shut the door behind her, quickly and silently, and it wasn't until she'd been gone awhile—and the meaning of her words had settled heavily into the pit of my stomach—that I realized she'd left the candle behind.

I stared at the light until it guttered out and died. Then I lay in the darkness, and tried hard not to think or feel anything at all.

I woke up the next morning to the sound of the front door again, slamming hard like a thunderclap. I dressed slowly—I figured I'd be leaving for good within the hour, and while the sensible thing would be to wear my old, itchy clothes from Deadweather, I put on one of the silk shirts the Pembrokes had given me instead. I wanted to feel the luxuriousness of the fabric against my skin one last time.

Then I tiptoed down to breakfast, taking the time to appreciate every detail of the grand staircase and sumptuous entrance hall. When I reached the dining room, I was surprised to find Roger Pembroke—who was usually up and out by this hour—chatting away with a big, rough-looking man who sat at Millicent's usual place.

Seeing me, Pembroke smiled—his best, most charming smile, the one that made me feel both special and desperate to live up to whatever he expected of me.

"Morning, Egg. Come join us." I sat down. The rough-looking man nodded at me. He didn't look like the type to smile.

"Millicent and Edith have gone to visit some friends north of Blisstown," Pembroke continued. "I thought this would be a good time for you to meet Mr. Birch. One of my most trusted and capable associates."

"Hello," I said, guessing that Mr. Birch would be taking me down to the port, and wondering if they expected me to hire my own boat back to Deadweather.

Birch nodded in reply. A butler put breakfast in front of me. Pembroke and Birch had already finished theirs. I started to eat quickly, eyes focused on my food.

"Egg, I want to apologize for my behavior yesterday."

I'd imagined a lot of different versions of this conversation, but none of them started with an apology from Pembroke.

"You don't need—"

"I do, actually. I think I'm perhaps a bit too used to getting my own way. So much so that I sometimes forget to see things from the point of view of others. Even those for whom I have only the best intentions."

The special smile returned. "I understand why you couldn't accept my offer. And the more I think about it, the more respect I have for your integrity. I remember what I was like at your age. In many ways, you're miles ahead of where I was."

It was cold comfort, hearing a speech like that right before I got kicked out the door. But I did appreciate that he wasn't yelling at me.

"As you probably know, I've built a rather successful business organization. But its future health depends on my ability to find the right sort of men to help me run it. I know you're quite young, but I see great promise in you. So if I can't have you as a son . . . I'd like very much to recruit you as an apprentice."

My jaw started to drop, and a mouthful of half-chewed food nearly dribbled out onto my lap before I had the presence of mind to clamp my teeth down. Which somehow caused me to start choking, and before I knew it a butler was hovering over me with a glass of water and a towel.

Pembroke smiled indulgently at me as I tried to recover.

"Is that a yes?"

"I . . . did Mrs. Pembroke . . . say . . . ?"

Pembroke chuckled and rolled his eyes ever so slightly. "Mrs. Pembroke's a bit emotional. Because, to be totally frank, she's long harbored the ambition of marrying her only daughter to a Rovian nobleman. And given the obvious mutual affection between you and Millicent"—I got a little dizzy when he said that—"she's rather concerned about the implications of your staying in our lives.

"Now—again, I'm speaking plainly, and apologies for that— I'll admit that at first blush, I shared her concern. But the more that I've thought about it . . . there's something special about you, son. You're a rare talent. I'd be a fool to let you leave us."

As my head spun, he took a sip of coffee. "What do you say? Will you come and work for me?"

"I'd love to, sir." All the gloom of the past day vanished, and I almost laughed out loud from happiness.

Pembroke and Birch traded looks of satisfaction. "Excellent. I'd like to begin straightaway. Birch here will take care of you— starting with a tour of some of our local interests."

Birch winked at me. "Eat your fill. You'll need it."

TWO HOURS LATER, Birch and I were on horseback, climbing one of the winding trails that led up the forested hills toward the timberline of Mount Majestic. We were farther up the slope than I'd ever been with Millicent—since our rides usually started in the afternoon, we couldn't get this far and still be back by nightfall— and as the trail switched back on itself, I got an occasional peek through the trees at the towering pile of rock looming ahead.

Birch had barely spoken during the ride. Early on, when I realized we were headed up the mountain, I asked if we'd be seeing the silver mine.

"Eventually," he said. "Few other stops first."

"Is it all right if I ask where?"

"You'll see."

I got the point and kept my mouth shut after that, my head

swimming with fantasies that now seemed entirely realistic. There didn't seem anything too far-fetched about Millicent marrying a young businessman with bright prospects, especially one who was a trusted associate of her father's.

I decided that as soon as I got back to Cloud Manor, I would give up novels—silly entertainment, suitable for women and children, but of no use to a young empire builder—for the self-improvement books I'd seen in Pembroke's library, like *Letters to a Young Tradesman* and *Rules of Gentlemanly Conduct*. I'd memorize these, following them to the letter until I became a man—not a boy, a man—of such impressive character that people who met me would be shocked to learn I was raised not on the vast estate of some Rovian duke, but as a lowly planter's son.

I was designing the mansion Millicent and I would raise our six children in when Birch stopped at a sharp bend in the trail, where it turned away from a steep cliff on the edge of the ridge we had been following.

We were close to the timberline, and the trees were scarcer here, hard-pressed to thrive in the rocky soil. Birch dismounted, motioning for me to do the same. Then he tied both horses' reins to a gnarled branch and stepped off the trail toward the cliff.

I followed him the thirty feet to the cliff's edge. Above and to our left was the craggy face of Mount Majestic. From a distance, it had always looked serene and peaceful—but from this close, it looked much darker, rough and threatening. It had an almost vertical face that plummeted for a mile or more, straight down from the summit into the gorge below us.

"Take a good look. Down there." Birch pointed past his boots, hundreds of feet down to the bottom of the gorge.

There was a tree next to me, so close to the edge I could see a cluster of stray roots sticking out into the air from the side of the cliff. I put my hand on a branch to steady myself and peered out over the side.

The bottom of the gorge was nothing but rock, a few giant boulders on a bed of shale. At the dead end where it terminated, there was a dark hole—tiny from this distance, but maybe five feet high and equally wide. Near the mouth of the hole were a wagon drawn by mules and three men—two soldiers with rifles and a man in work clothes. They were watching the entrance of the hole.

"What is it?" I asked.

"Exploring party. Looking for silver," Birch said. "Keep watching."

I did as I was told. In a moment, a Native came out of the hole—wearing only a ragged cloth over his midsection and carrying a bucket of earth. He dumped the bucket into a trough and disappeared again inside the hole. The man in work clothes stooped to examine the contents of the trough.

As I watched him, from the corner of my eye I saw Birch step backward. He moved casually enough, but in the last half second before he disappeared from my field of vision, he started to shift his weight lower, bending his knees slightly.

I knew that motion. It was the beginning of the crouch Adonis used to go into before he attacked.

Without thinking, I dropped to my knees, grabbing at the tree trunk for support as the full weight of Birch's body hit me from behind. I didn't have time to get my arms solidly around the tree, but going to my knees left me low enough that he couldn't push me clean out into the air, which would have meant certain death.

He had to hit me two more times to knock me over the edge, and by the time I went over, I'd managed to claw my fingers into the tree roots sticking out of the cliff. I almost lost my grip when the weight of my body swung down under me, but the momentum of his last blow had almost taken Birch over the side himself, and I had a moment to firm up my hold while he recovered his balance.

I kicked my legs in front of me, searching for a toehold, but found only air—we seemed to be on a thin overhang that jutted out some distance from the body of the cliff.

As the toes of Birch's boots appeared in front of my eyes, I flailed my legs desperately, bringing my knees up until I hit something—not wide and flat like the lip of the cliff, but tangled and uneven.

It was the tree's roots. From what I could feel with my legs, there was a thick mass of them under there—the lip of the cliff must have been so skinny that they grew out from the soil into thin air. As I started to probe them with my feet, looking for support, I saw Birch's foot draw back to kick me in the face.

"NO, MR. BIRCH, PLEASE!" I didn't expect mercy. I just needed an extra second. And begging had always bought me time with Adonis, because he loved hearing it so much. It might work with Birch, too, if he liked his cruelty the way my brother did.

Birch's foot stopped moving, the toes settling back onto the ground. I couldn't see his face, but I was sure he was smiling. He was the type who liked it.

I lowered my voice to a whimper. "Please, sir, please . . . oh, please, don't . . ."

My left leg was in the guts of the root system now, pushing

through clods of dirt as it worked its way into the stiff, thick roots. Almost up to the knee.

"Sorry, son. Boss's orders."

Birch's foot rose again, first drawing back, then moving in a swift arc toward my head. I let go, pushing off with both hands, and blue sky swooped into view, then a blur of forest and rock, and then the horizon was upside down and I felt blood rushing into my head.

I was hanging from the underside of the cliff by one leg, tangled in a knot of roots. Somewhere above me, Birch was cursing.

I managed to pull myself up far enough to grab a fistful of roots with my left hand. I was bringing my right arm up when I felt something brush against it. I should have drawn it back, into my body, but at first I was confused, thinking I'd hit part of the root.

It was Birch's hand. He got me by the wrist and began to pull me away from the tree roots.

For a long, panicky second, I fought a losing battle to keep my grip. I could feel my leg beginning to slip back through the tangle of roots when everything—me, Birch, the tree roots, the cliff—suddenly lurched downward.

Birch let go, his arm disappearing, and I felt him fall backward, away from the edge, cursing again as we both realized what was happening. The cliff was threatening to give way under our weight.

It was quiet for a moment. As I carefully readjusted my hold, digging in tightly with my arms and working my second leg into the roots, I felt the shudder of Birch's feet, walking back from the cliff toward the horses.

I was searching the underside of the cliff for some way to

escape that wasn't directly overhead when I felt him return. There were a few little tremors as he adjusted his position.

His hand reappeared with a knife. He slashed at me, blind but vicious, drawing a thin cut across one forearm and missing my head by an inch as I flattened myself against the roots.

He withdrew his hand. As I watched the blood run in little crooked lines down my arm to drip from my elbow into the empty sky, I felt him readjust, moving carefully so as not to bring the whole cliff down with him.

He'd be farther out now—close enough this time for the knife to do its job. I knew if I didn't do something fast, I was going to die.

I shifted my weight as far to one side as I could, tensing my body backward into a crouch. The knife reappeared, slashing out, missing me by a hair with the first strike. As Birch drew it back, I let go of the roots and grabbed his forearm with both hands, yanking it straight down as hard as I could. I hung on until I felt his body tumble past me, threatening to take me with him.

His boot hit me on the ear on its way down.

I swung from my knees in the air, feeling the cliff top shudder above me. My eyes were squeezed shut, praying it would hold, when I heard the echoing boom of Birch's body hitting the rocks.

Then there were more echoes, garbled voices of shock and surprise, and I could feel the men of the exploring party staring up at me as I crawled along the roots, slowly making my way back up to the top. I didn't dare look down.

Once I reached the top, I collapsed onto my back, taking deep gulps of air as I sorted out the pain in my arms and legs. They ached everywhere, my knees especially. There was a burning tightness in my sides, and while the cut on my forearm looked shallow, it was still bloody. One ear was ringing, its upper half throbbing and hot where Birch's boot had struck me as he fell.

I lay there, unable to move—not because of the pain, but because of the thoughts running through my head.

Birch tried to kill me.

On Roger Pembroke's orders.

Roger Pembroke wants me dead.

Why?

I had no idea.

But that wasn't going to stop him from trying to kill me again.

I had to get out of Sunrise. Fast.

I got up and ran for the horses.

CHAPTER 8

RUN

I took Birch's horse because it was bigger and faster, and even though I didn't know where I was going, I figured I had to get there in a hurry.

This turned out to be a mistake. It was too big, and too fast—my feet couldn't reach the stirrups, and once the horse got going down the mountain, there wasn't any stopping it. Just to keep from falling off—or getting knocked off by a low branch, because the horse seemed to be going out of its way to pass under as many of them as it could find—I had to flatten myself against its back and dig my hands into its mane, and from that position, I had trouble pulling back on the reins.

I yelled "whoa!" and "stop!" and some words that would've gotten me smacked if I'd ever used them near Dad, but they didn't do any good. So I pretty quickly gave up and just tried to hang on, letting the horse make the decisions while I tried to get my brain to work out where I was going. And what I was going to do. And why Roger Pembroke wanted to kill me.

Thoughts buzzed around in my head, dizzy and thick, like flies on a carcass.

Exploring party saw everything. They'll tell others. They'll tell Pembroke. Got to hurry. Got to get off the island.

How? The two Healy pirates, waiting offshore. No, that was weeks ago. They're gone by now. The rowboat at the dock. Is it still there? How far can I get in a rowboat? Back to Deadweather?

There's a fork in the trail down below. Got to make the horse turn right. If it goes left, I'll be back at Cloud Manor. Where Pembroke is.

He wants me dead. Why? Wouldn't let him adopt me. Why did he want to? What did he want from me? The ugly fruit plantation? My family's dead, it's mine. He adopts me, it's his. If I'm dead . . . whose is it? His?

TREE!

That was close. Branch nearly took my head off. I'd swear the horse swerved toward it. The horse wants me dead, too. Should've taken the other horse.

Need help. Who would help me? Mung. Quint. Stumpy. Maybe some of the other field pirates. Back at home.

Have to get home.

How? Need help—here on Sunrise. From who? Millicent. No. Can't go back to Cloud Manor. Anyway she's not there. Don't know where she is. Gone with Mrs. Pembroke.

Does she want me dead?

No. Doesn't matter. He does.

What's he want with an ugly fruit plantation? Not the fruit. Something Native.

That was why we came here. Dad found something Native on the plantation.

And Pembroke wants it. That king he asked me about—The Fire King. What did Millicent call him? Hut-something. Said he had a treasure.

There's a treasure. Somewhere on the plantation. It's—

TREE!

Rotten horse . . . The horse wants me dead. Its owner is dead.

I killed its owner.

No. I could never kill a man.

Did I?

He tried to kill me. For the treasure. What is it? The books could tell me. Back in Pembroke's library. The ones I couldn't get because the ladder was gone.

He took the ladder. Didn't want me to know what was in the books. Millicent knows. Wanted to talk about it.

He shut her down. Told her it didn't exist. He lied.

About everything . . .

Need help. From who? Percy. Where is Percy? Cloud Manor? Can't go there. Percy never liked me anyway.

There's a treasure. On our land. Big enough to kill for. Dad knew. Dad found it. Did he? He found something. But he didn't understand it—that's why he brought us here. To Sunrise.

Who can help me here? The harbormaster? Soldiers? No. They all work for Pembroke. He pays them. Millicent said so.

I'm all alone.

Don't think about that.

Dad took us to Sunrise because he needed to find a Native. To translate that parchment. What was on it? Native gibberish, Pembroke said. Pembroke lied. Not gibberish. What?

Why did Dad show it to Pembroke? Dad doesn't trust anybody. Why did he trust Pembroke?

Fork's coming up soon. How do I get the horse to go right? If he goes left, how do I get off?

Where am I going? Need help. Who else? Dad's lawyer. Archibald. No. He works for Pembroke, too. Dad showed him the parchment.

I saw him run. From his office back to the Peacock. Where Pembroke was.

Dad didn't tell Pembroke. The lawyer did. And Pembroke was nice to us because he knew there was a treasure on the plantation.

TREE!

The horse probably works for Pembroke. Everybody does on this island.

Pembroke is evil.

And was nice to us. No one on Sunrise is ever nice to us. Pembroke was. Invited us to stay with him. Gave us a balloon ride . . .

He wanted me on that balloon. He was angry when I jumped off. It wasn't an accident. He planned it.

He killed my family.

He killed them for the treasure.

He'll kill me for it, too. And I don't even know what it is.

The fork is coming.

The horse is going left.

I've got to get off this horse.

I grabbed everything I could—the reins, the horse's mane—and pulled back hard. The horse must have thrown me, because suddenly I was on the ground with my head ringing and one shoulder throbbing in pain.

The horse stopped about fifty feet down the hill, half hidden by the trees. I got up, rubbing my sore shoulder, and tripped on a rock, nearly falling over again.

The horse turned its head back toward the noise. Stared at me for a moment. Then turned away and started to saunter down the trail, disappearing into the trees in the direction of Cloud Manor.

I ran down the right fork, taking the steep trail as fast as I could without falling. I knew from my rides with Millicent that it emptied out onto the shore road above South Point. From there, it'd be a couple of miles downhill to Blisstown, and I needed to get to the port as fast as possible. Once the horse made it back to Cloud Manor, Pembroke would start looking for me, and if I wasn't gone by then, I might never make it off the island.

By the time I reached the shore road, I was pouring sweat. Fortunately, the road was empty. I didn't see a soul for the first mile or so, all the way down past South Point, until I neared the sentry post at the foot of the road up to Cloud Manor.

I'd forgotten about the two soldiers posted there until I turned a corner and they came into view. I must have been making a lot of noise, because they were already out in the middle of the road, watching me approach.

One of them held up his hand for me to stop. As he did, the second one unslung his rifle with the kind of motion that suggested he wouldn't mind using it on me.

I knew I couldn't stop—these were Pembroke's men, as sure as the butlers in Cloud Manor were—but they were telling me to, and had guns, and were in the middle of the road.

So I yelled, "HELP! NATIVES ARE COMING!"

It worked. The one with the gun immediately aimed it past me, up the hill.

"Where?" yelled the other one.

"BEHIND ME! THEY'VE GOT KNIVES!" I cried as I ran right between them.

I didn't look back, but I could hear them shouting to each other as they ran up the hill. This seemed helpful, because hunting Natives would occupy them for a while, but also a problem, because once they figured out there weren't any Natives, they'd probably come after me.

I tried to run faster and wound up tripping over myself, kicking up dust as I tumbled down the steep road. When I got up again, my knee didn't work quite right—every time I landed on it, I felt a warning pain like it was going to crumple. So I had to slow down and favor it, limping like a hunchback as I ran.

Half a mile later, I passed a delivery wagon coming from the other direction, and the look of alarm on the driver's face as he watched me run past made my chest thump with fear—I couldn't go into Blisstown looking like I did. If I'd been back on Deadweather, I could've walked through Port Scratch at midday and not gotten a second glance, but a dirty, bleeding, exhausted teenage boy with a gimpy leg wasn't exactly going to melt into the crowd on Heavenly Road. And how much time did I have before Pembroke knew to search for me? Between Birch's riderless horse and the men at the bottom of the gorge who'd seen him fall, probably not much.

I had to find cover. To my right, the cliff would begin tapering off toward the beach soon, but not before I had to pass the southernmost of Sunrise's two fortresses. Fortunately, the left side of the road was thick forest, so I ducked in and tried to follow the road from inside the brush. It kept me concealed, but it was rough going. The ground was covered with low, prickly shrubs that tore at my pant legs and were so thick I couldn't move at much more than a walk. I struggled through the underbrush for a few hundred yards, until I was well past the fortress and the cliffs on the other side were giving way to beach. Then I returned to the road.

I was less than a quarter mile from Blisstown now. I could see the docks up ahead, still dominated by the massive hulk of the *Earthly Pleasure* tourist ship, and the usual heavy traffic of people in and around Heavenly Road.

I ran across the road and onto the beach, taking off my shirt and shoes, rolling up my pant legs, and trotting along the waterline, hoping to look like a carefree beachgoer. I don't know how convincing it was, but the beach was mostly empty, and from there at least I could keep my distance from anyone on the shore road.

I also had a better view of the dock, and as I approached, I scanned it for the rowboat we'd tied up when we arrived. I could see a small craft in about the same spot we'd left it, and for a moment I thought I was in luck . . . until I saw a fisherman climb in and cast off.

The rowboat was long gone. If I wanted to get out by boat, I'd have to steal one.

Fear was setting in again, and I had to force myself to keep walking. I was just a hundred yards from the dock now, and I had no idea what I was going to do when I got there.

There were three little kids up ahead, all barefoot, laughing and chasing each other in the surf while their stern-looking parents watched from up the beach, holding three little pairs of shoes. The children all wore velvet short pants and silk shirts. The shirts were soaking wet, clinging to them like second skins.

"That's enough, children! Time to board!" called their mother.

They ignored her. After a moment, her husband bellowed out, "The ship's sailing! Want to be left behind? Want us to go back to Rovia without you?"

As the kids reluctantly dragged themselves from the water, I looked up at the dock. Two gangways were open on the *Earthly Pleasure,* admitting a steady stream of rich, suntanned Rovians, many of them carrying shopping bags from the stores on Heavenly Road.

I didn't want to go to Rovia. But I couldn't stay on Sunrise, and I didn't seem to have any better options.

I looked a mess, and I needed to do something about that. I put down my shoes, waded into the water with my shirt in my hand, and dunked my body in the surf.

I came out dripping wet but feeling, and hopefully looking, a bit less filthy. There was still a long cut down my forearm, stinging now from the salt water, but without all the dried blood, it looked a lot less gruesome. My shirt was too badly stained to wear, so I left it off, hoping I could pass as an avid swimmer with poor manners.

The family of five were fussing over their children's shoes at the foot of the stairs leading up to the dock. I skirted around them, up the stairs, and joined the line of people heading into the gigantic ship.

The closer I came to the foot of the first gangway, the more nervous I got. There was a uniformed porter standing in front of it, smiling and greeting the tourists as they boarded. His eyes passed over mine, ten people back, and I saw his lip curl with distaste.

This wasn't going to work. I couldn't board the ship, half-dressed and dripping wet, without getting a lot of questions.

I turned away, losing my nerve—but then I saw, up the shore road to the south, a pair of soldiers headed for town on horseback. Were they the same ones I'd sent to chase imaginary Natives? Or the ones from the exploring party that saw Birch die? Or neither? From that distance, I couldn't tell. But just seeing them made me turn back to the ship. I wasn't going to get a better chance than this.

The purser at the far gangway looked older and sleepier than the first one, so I slipped over to that line. I was getting odd looks from the other passengers, but I hoped the fact that my pants and shoes were from the Pembrokes—and as expensive as anything the others were wearing—would help convince them I belonged on board.

As the line floated forward, I folded my shirt carefully over my forearm to hide both the cut and the worst of the shirt's stains while I practiced smiling for the purser.

"Last-minute swim! Hope Mum's not cross!" I called out cheerfully as I passed him.

"Mmph," he grunted, barely looking at me.

A few moments later, I was inside the ship. The gangway led to an entry door in the second deck, where passengers were crowding down narrow, lamplit corridors into a warren of cabins. A stairway heading down into the lower decks was clogged with people, but the one going up was nearly deserted.

I climbed one flight to the gun deck, which was wide and empty except for the rows of cannons and a cluster of younger kids playing some sort of game in the middle of the deck. Strange patterns of triangles and squares with numbers inscribed in them had been painted onto the floor, and the kids were sliding large, flat stones over them using long sticks with padded bumpers on one end.

As I strode past them, trying to look like I knew where I was going, one of them yelled at me for stepping onto what must have been a particularly important triangle. He looked about ten years old, had a cruel face, and cursed me with words I thought only sailors used.

"Watch your mouth! I'll call for your father!" I told him, not because I had any intention of doing it, but because I thought I'd look even more suspicious if I let his insults pass.

"My father will sue you!" the kid shot back.

I didn't even know what that meant, so I just kept going.

When I reached the aft end, I found a row of doors, but they were all locked. There was another set of stairs, but I didn't want to take them, because the lower decks were full of passengers, and I figured if I went up to the top deck, I'd run into the crew.

I looked around. In the corner, a large canvas tarp was thrown over something wide, square, and waist-high. I gathered up an edge of the tarp—there was an excess of it, bunched around the sides—and peeked underneath.

There were four large crates of cannonballs. Not the sort of thing anyone should be needing any time soon. And there was a couple feet of space between the boxes and the bulkhead, enough to lie down in.

I looked down the deck at the children. Their backs were to me, engrossed in their game. I quickly put my wet shirt back on and crawled under the tarp, burrowing all the way to the back corner and bunching the stiff tarp up over me, keeping it propped between the box and the wall like a tent so I could lie on my back and breathe without rustling the tarp.

It was cramped but not too uncomfortable. I lay still, listening to the kids play their game. From the sound of it, they were horrible brats, arguing with each other over every move and tossing ugly threats back and forth about all the terrible things their rich and powerful fathers would do if they didn't get their way. Mostly it was torture and imprisonment, but whatever "sue" meant, there was a lot of that going around, too.

My clothes started to dry out, making me itch in all sorts of places I couldn't scratch for fear I'd jostle the tarp and reveal myself.

After a while, the noise of footsteps going up the nearby stairs began to increase, and the kids abandoned their game and went up themselves. The muffled sound of feet on the deck above grew until it seemed like the entire boat was walking around over my head.

Then there were heavy thuds of what I guessed were ropes hitting the deck, and a great cheer went up from the crowd. We were under way.

I could feel the boat moving now, lumbering out to sea. The feet slowly filtered back down to the lower decks. A bit later, the sun must have gone down, and what little light had been peeking into my hiding place died completely.

Time passed. The smell of cooked food reached me from a distant deck. I was starving by now, and as I lay there in the darkness, I wondered what the passengers were having for dinner and whether I could steal some of it later.

Somewhere below, a band began to play.

It had been silent on the gun deck now for a long time. The fear of being discovered that had kept me frozen in place for the past few hours slowly faded, and I let myself readjust my position and scratch my various itches. But I wasn't going to let myself get up and look for food until I was sure the passengers and crew were asleep, which meant hours more of lying in the quiet.

I tried to nap, but I had too much to think about. My brain was calmer now, though—the shock of everything that had happened was wearing off, and I gradually managed to wrestle my thoughts into straight lines.

We were sailing east, out of the Blue Sea and across the Great Maw to Rovia. Once we got there, I'd be safe from Roger Pembroke. Evil as he was, he only wanted to kill me for the treasure back on Deadweather. If I disappeared and never came back, he wasn't going to hunt me down across an ocean.

I could start my life over in Rovia. I'd never been there, but most of the books I'd read were Rovian, and I sort of figured I knew what I was in for. There were cities and rich people and poor people, and it was hard for the poor people to become rich, but it happened sometimes, at least in the books.

I'd be starting out poor, that was obvious, but if I worked hard, and was clever about it, things might turn out okay for me. I'd find a tradesman—a printer, maybe—apprentice myself to him, and slowly work my way up to respectability and a decent life.

I'd never have to come back. Pembroke could have the treasure. The field pirates could have the ugly fruit plantation. All I wanted from the Blue Sea was Millicent.

And someday, she'd come to Rovia. She'd talked about it with me—how much she wanted to see the cities, and the rest of the Continent. She'd show up one day, our paths would cross, and she'd be torn at first, not wanting to give up the chance to rule her father's empire. But eventually she'd realize she loved me, and she'd stay. We'd be together forever, thousands of miles from her father.

But it didn't feel right. Even with Millicent in it, there was something uncomfortable about the fantasy of escaping to Rovia. Something that made me uneasy. And more than that, ashamed.

I lay there for a long time, pressing at the feeling like a rotten tooth, before it broke loose and I saw what was under it.

It was my family. I was never much for them, Adonis especially, and I'd spent I don't know how many nights lying in my straw bed back on Deadweather, wishing I could escape from them.

But they were the only family I had. More important, I was the only family THEY had, and Roger Pembroke had killed them, and if I didn't do something about it—I didn't know what, but something—no one would ever know, or care.

And he'd take what he wanted from our land, just like it was his, and no one would try to stop him.

I didn't want any part of it. I wanted to run away, forget it had ever happened, and not think about any of them ever again, except Millicent.

But I knew I couldn't. I could run, I could cross the ocean, but someday I'd have to come back.

Because I couldn't let him get away with what he did to my family.

And I couldn't let him have that treasure.

CHAPTER 9

UNINVITED GUESTS

By the time I finally crawled out from under the tarp, I was a wreck. Everything hurt. My knee was swollen and didn't want to bend, my shoulder complained when I tried to raise my arm, muscles I didn't even know I had ached in my legs and below my ribs, and my back was so stiff from lying in wet clothes on the wooden deck for all those hours that I could barely stand up.

I was also shaky from hunger, because after three weeks at the Pembrokes', my body had gotten so used to big, regular meals that it didn't want to work without them. And the hunger wasn't half as bad as the thirst, which must have been why I was so dizzy.

Fortunately, the gun deck had been deserted for hours—if there was a watchman making rounds, I hadn't heard him pass. So I took my time getting started, holding the cannons for support as I slowly felt my way around in the gently rolling darkness.

Other than a dim glow coming from the stairwells, it was almost as black as it had been under the tarp. This seemed odd—the cannon portals were all open, and there should have been plenty of moonlight—until I looked out a portal and realized we were sailing through a fog so thick I could practically hold it in my hands.

Once my muscles loosened and I got used to both the dizziness and the pitch of the boat on the sea, I headed for the aft stairs. Oil lamps hung from the ceiling beams in the middle of every flight, and since I felt safer under the cover of darkness, I moved quickly, down through two levels of cabins to the dining room.

It was as wide and open as the gun deck, and even in the shadowy light of a few lamps hung along the walls, I could see it was spectacular. Dozens of big, round tables filled the floor, surrounded by hundreds of delicate carved-wood chairs with velvet cushions. The walls were plastered over and painted with elaborate murals of sea battles, fought between everything from ancient water gods and sea monsters to pirates and naval officers. In the middle of the room was a raised platform jutting out from the wall that I guessed was a stage for entertainment.

Unfortunately for me, the room was spotlessly clean—whatever feast had been served here that night, there wasn't a crumb left.

But there had to be a galley somewhere. At the fore end of the room, I found a wide door, secured with a latch. I quietly flipped it open and peeked inside.

It was pitch-black. I shut the door quickly—if any of the crew were asleep in there, waking them would be disastrous. But my thirst and hunger convinced me to risk it. I took an oil lamp from the wall and reopened the door.

It was the galley—and it was massive, stuffed floor to ceiling with barrels, tins, containers, and cabinets. Along one wall was a giant stove, its thick metal flue disappearing into the ceiling, and in the center of the room, a long, sturdy tabletop stood over an island of cabinets.

I started with the barrels. The first one I opened held a thick liquid that must have been cooking oil. But the second one was water, and I bent over it and drank with my hands until I could feel my belly begin to swell against my belt.

Then I moved on to the food. In a big metal tin, I found a store of salted fish and must have put away a pound of it within a few minutes, hardly bothering to chew.

The food and water made me feel so much better that I temporarily forgot to be scared—and living with the Pembrokes must have spoiled me into thinking I deserved all the comforts I figured those brats from the gun deck were enjoying every night.

So instead of doing the sensible thing and sneaking back upstairs, I started looking for dessert.

I figured there probably wouldn't be jelly bread, but there must be sweets. And there were—on a high shelf was a large, square box marked CHOCOLATE in big block letters. None of the other food containers were labeled that way, which should have alerted me that something wasn't right.

I reached up, fully extended, and tugged the box from the shelf.

A dozen empty tin cans came down with it, tied to the back of the box in a booby trap. The room filled with a deafening clatter. I could've dropped a box of cannonballs on the floor, and they would have been quieter.

The brats from the gun deck must have been here before me, on the trip out, and the cook was ready for them this time.

But I wasn't thinking that, or anything, just then. I was in a blind panic, running for cover. I was almost out of the room when I heard a door open somewhere behind me and a voice yell for me to stop, but I didn't look back.

In the dining room, I took the closest set of stairs, vaulting the steps two at a time. But whoever was chasing me was a lot faster than I was—by the time I passed the upper level of cabins, he was nearly on my heels.

I tried to speed up by leaping three steps at a time, but on the second leap, my busted knee crumpled and I fell.

Then he was on me, a big man with meaty fists that grabbed me tightly.

"What's your name?"

"James Basingstroke." I hoped he didn't read novels.

He squinted at me, taking in not just my face but my clothes, especially the bloodstains and dirt smears on my shirt.

"What cabin?"

I didn't answer. He shook me with his thick arms.

"Give me the number!"

"Six."

He didn't look convinced, so I added, "-teen."

"Sixteen? That right?"

"Yes. And my father will sue you if you don't let me go!" I narrowed my eyes, trying my best to look like an arrogant rich boy. Might as well go all in.

He laughed. My heart sank.

"So your father . . . is Lady Cromby of Esqueth?"

He started up the stairs, dragging me behind him. "Let's you and me go see the director."

TEN MINUTES LATER, I was sitting in a luxuriously outfitted cabin on the quarterdeck, my hands tied behind me with a ribbon, being stared at by a man the cook addressed as Mr. Pilcher. He was big, and not just in size—his words and his movements were all melodramatically exaggerated, like he was acting in a play and needed to make sure the people in the back of the audience didn't miss anything.

He hadn't liked being woken up—when he first opened his cabin door to find us standing there in the damp fog, he gave the cook a lecture about his need for sleep that was so emotional I thought it might end in violence.

But once the cook explained things, he seemed to warm up to the situation. It was his idea to tie my hands, and he gave the cook both the ribbon and some very specific instructions about how to use it.

Now he loomed over me, eyes bugging out under his thick eyebrows, wearing a sleeping gown of creamy silk that fit him like a tent.

"Tell me, my filthy little thief—what are you doing on my excursion without a ticket?"

I didn't know how to answer that. I wasn't about to tell him the truth—I knew Roger Pembroke was one of the *Earthly Pleasure*'s owners, which made this man another Pembroke employee. But it was obvious I'd come from Sunrise, so I needed to account for that somehow.

"Hellooooo? Anybody home?" He rapped me lightly on the head with his knuckles. As I looked up at him, he wiggled his bushy eyebrows, which made him look so comically strange it was hard to concentrate on my answer. I lowered my head and stared at the floor.

"I was . . . cabin boy. On a ship. Docked at Sunrise. The captain was cruel and vicious . . . and—"

"What sort of a ship?" He put his hand under my chin, lifting it up so I was forced to look into his buggy, dancing eyes. "Hmm? Was it a merchant? Or perhaps—"

Then he suddenly reared back with a gasp, putting his hand to his mouth.

"Oh, my . . ." He turned to the cook, a smile spreading across his face. "I've just had a brilliant idea! Keep an eye on him. Back in a jiff."

He threw on a long, fur-lined coat and dashed from the cabin. A few minutes later, he returned with another man—tall, stooped, and grizzled, with a gray-streaked beard. He wore a simple wool greatcoat and was still buttoning his pants.

Pilcher sent the cook away with a curt order to get breakfast going. Then he introduced me to the grizzled man with a grand wave of his hand.

"Captain Lanks, meet our pirate."

"I'm not a pirate," I said.

"You are now," said Pilcher.

The captain looked from me to Pilcher, still blinking sleep from his eyes. "That's no pirate. He's too well-fed. And not enough scars."

Pilcher rolled his eyes. "Captain, use your imagination! With a bit of makeup . . . possibly some wardrobe . . . I can turn this boy into a sharp-eyed devil sent to prepare an ambush by the most ruthless pirate on the Blue Sea! The advance party of Burn Healy himself! What do you think? Stroke of genius?"

He waited for the captain's response, eyes shining with excitement.

The captain just looked tired. "Not sure I'm following you."

Pilcher sighed impatiently. "It's my job to provide our guests with a thrilling journey to an exotic but dangerous land. And they've had exotic coming out their ears. But the dangerous part's been a real bust. There weren't even any snakes on Sunrise. That Native in chains we paraded around just looked depressed. And there's been grumbling. Because these people want some danger for their money—"

"And it's my job to make sure they don't get it."

"Not the real thing! Just some vicarious experience of it! A frisson of danger! The suggestion of peril. And when it comes to the Blue Sea, nothing says peril like pirates."

"Fine. Say he's a pirate—"

"I'm not—" I started to protest.

"Shut up, boy. Say he is . . . what do you want to do? Flog him?"

"Obviously that. The boy stole food, it goes without saying. But more. And bigger." Pilcher's eyes danced with intrigue. "I want to maroon him."

My chest started to thump. Marooning meant slow death by starvation. Or madness.

The captain winced. "Once we're on the Maw, there's no island within a thousand miles of latitude. And the prevailing winds will make it next to impossible to double back—"

"We're not on the Maw yet, are we? We're still in the islands! Surely there's a deserted one nearby."

The captain was silent. Pilcher pressed him.

"There is! Isn't there? Captain, don't make me assert my—"

"There's a handful. To the north, above Pig Island. But we'd have to change course immediately. And it's dark, and we're in heavy fog—"

"What's that got to do with anything?"

"If we change course now, we'll lose our escort."

"Pffft." Pilcher made a funny gesture with his hands, like he was shaking water from them. "Morning will come, the fog will lift. He'll see we're not on course. And he'll wait. We'll catch up in no time. Snip, snap."

The captain sighed. "Mr. Pilcher. Your job is entertainment. Mine's getting us back to Rovia safely. And the Blue Sea, I'd remind you, is full of ACTUAL pirates. Some of whom are actually dangerous."

"And the worst of them's protecting us! What do we have to fear?"

"Losing him! Without his escort—"

"We're not going to lose him! How long could it take?"

"Half a day, at least."

"That's nothing! This marooning's going to be priceless! I'm already imagining the ceremony in my head! Now, turn us around, man! We won't lose him in half a day."

Lose who? I vaguely remembered Pembroke boasting to my father about the precautions he'd taken to ensure the *Earthly Pleasure*'s safety . . . and Millicent telling me her father controlled the pirates. I hadn't really believed her. But apparently it was true, of at least one pirate, anyway.

The captain was shaking his head. "I'm not in favor of this."

"I don't need your approval. I just need you to turn the ship. And quickly—if we don't get the marooning done by midafternoon, I'll have to reschedule the shovelpuck tournament."

"For Savior's sake . . . Can't we just make him walk a plank?"

"There's no mystery in that! Plop, thrash, and he's dead."

"He'll die if you maroon him."

"But not while we're watching. There's a fine line between entertainment and barbarism. Now, get it done! I've got LOADS of planning to do." Pilcher opened his cabin door and motioned for the captain to exit.

"For the record, you've ordered this action against my judgment."

"Yes, yes, yes. That's fine. Cover your backside. Just do it! Shoo!" He waved his hands, and the captain trudged out, still shaking his head.

Pilcher shut the door. Then turned and leaned back against it, smiling at me like a cat with a mouse under its paw.

"My, my, my . . . I'm going to make you SUCH a nasty little pirate."

IT WAS JUST AFTER BREAKFAST, and four hundred pairs of eyes were glued to Pilcher—pink-faced and sweaty, his voice booming from the dining room stage as he narrated the breathtaking, although completely untrue, tale of my discovery and capture.

"Seaman Grimsby lay crumpled on the deck, bleeding and

unconscious, clinging to life, as the bloodthirsty cur secured the knife in his teeth and leapt to the rigging . . ."

I was the bloodthirsty cur. I stood next to Pilcher, legs in chains, my head and arms locked into a makeshift stock the ship's carpenter had built on such short notice that fresh splinters dug into my neck every time I tried to shift my position.

"The pirate climbed, catlike, up forty feet of ratline to an errant rope, from whence he swung, like some terrible ape of the darkest jungle, over the heads of Leeds and Austin and onto the poop deck.

"Austin's blood ran cold as he realized the object of the pirate's design—the swivel gun! If he reached it before them, their death was assured—the bowels of our intrepid young seamen would be splattered about the deck like a drunkard's vomit . . ."

Next to me were the heroes of the story, the three handsomest crew members Pilcher could find. Grimsby's head was heavily bandaged, Leeds had his arm in a sling, and Austin had a bright red cut down three inches of his cheek that had taken Pilcher an hour of careful work with a theater makeup kit to make convincing.

"There wasn't a moment to spare! Austin searched out Leeds, locking eyes with his compatriot across the fog-shrouded deck. Leeds's arm, broken and useless, hung by his side like a salami. But one arm—and the brave heart of a hero—was all he needed. He drew his sword . . ."

I had to admit, Pilcher told a good story. Everyone was entranced. A few of the ladies in the crowd were swooning. The men and boys glared at me with hate.

I would have tried to speak up in my own defense, but Pilcher had warned me that every time I opened my mouth during the performance, he'd add another ten lashes to the twenty he'd already promised to lay across my back before the marooning. I'd read about the lash in a history of the Rovian Navy—in experienced hands, thirty lashes could drain enough blood to kill a man.

So I kept my mouth shut. Pilcher built the story to a brilliant climax—apparently, I would have come out on top if Grimsby hadn't woken up and distracted me at a critical moment in the final sword fight—and finished up with my confessing to him my fiendish plan to slit the throats of the captain and crew and send up a signal flare to trigger the final, fatal ambush by my dark master.

"And who was this evil puppet master, his greedy eyes coveting our fair prize from across the Blue Sea? Why, it was none other than—"

Pilcher stepped over to me, grabbed my hair in his fist, and pulled my head up violently, exposing the flame tattoo he'd inked onto my neck an hour ago.

"BURN HEALY!"

There was a collective gasp. Toward the back, a woman gave a terrified shriek and fainted into her pastry.

Pilcher nodded grimly. "Cast your eyes upon him, ladies and gentlemen—this emissary of the devil."

One of the brats from the gun deck, the ten-year-old with the cruel face, rushed the stage, yelled "EVIL!" at me, and spit in my eye.

There was a tense pause as the audience looked to Pilcher for his reaction. None of them had captured a pirate before, and they didn't seem to know if spitting was appropriate behavior.

Unfortunately for me, Pilcher smiled approvingly at the brat. "Right you are, son! He's the devil himself!"

This unleashed a wave of hate, all of it directed at me. A crowd of people rushed the stage, and in the several minutes before Pilcher had enough and called out for order to be restored, I was slapped, punched, kicked, pelted with food and hot coffee, and spit on by at least a dozen people, young and old, men and women alike.

"Fear not, my good people!" he called out as they returned to their seats. "This incorrigible fiend will have his reward! We've set sail for the nearest uninhabited island! Upon sight of it—in accordance with the laws of the sea—he shall be tied to the mast, given twenty lashes, and marooned with no possessions but the mercy of Our Savior!"

A cheer went up from the crowd. Pilcher beamed with pleasure.

"The shovelpuck tournament will begin immediately afterward. Thank you! Enjoy your morning!"

ONCE THE DINING ROOM had emptied, two crew members pulled me out of the stocks, chained my wrists together, and took me down to the hold, where they tossed me inside a tiny storeroom with no light. I heard the clank of a lock being put on the door, followed by their footsteps fading away up the stairs.

I wiped the spit and the blood off as best I could in the dark. Then I cried. Not from the pain, although there was plenty of that, but the humiliation. The way I'd been treated made me feel sick and dirty inside, and the fact that it had been done by some of the finest members of Rovian society was almost impossible to believe. Even Adonis, vicious as he was, rarely spat on me.

And while I could imagine things like that happening in Port Scratch—in fact, I'd SEEN things like that happen—I'd always consoled myself, when I dreamed about life outside of Deadweather, with the thought that somewhere there were better, more civilized people, who wouldn't turn into a pack of snarling dogs because a man who was good with words had whipped them into a frenzy.

In its way, this was worse, and more demoralizing, than learning Roger Pembroke was evil and wanted to kill me. Because he was just one man. This was a whole boat full of the best sort of people, and when I was chained and helpless, they'd treated me like an animal.

And there was worse to come. I was going to be flogged, probably halfway to death, and then left alone on a deserted island with no food or water.

They might not even bother to unchain me first.

I tried not to think about it. Instead, I thought about Millicent's smile. And playing catch with Mung when I was little. And jelly bread. And Millicent again, not just her smile, but her laugh, and her walk, and the way the sunlight got caught in her hair . . .

I drifted into sleep. I'm not sure how long.

I woke up to a distant booming that I thought was thunder. I hoped the rain wouldn't delay my marooning, because I wanted to get it over with.

But it wasn't rain—I never heard the thunder again. Instead, I heard stranger things. The heavy footfalls of people running on the deck above. Distant shouting. More footfalls—dozens of them. A pounding so fierce I could feel it through the floorboards.

Then there were screams.

Then the rising thrum of feet, spreading down through the boat like a flood, bringing with it the crash and thud of objects breaking by the hundreds, accompanied by loud, rough voices sprinkled with rum-soaked laughter.

The mayhem went on for an hour or more. Finally, I heard footsteps clomping down the stairs to the hold.

An ax head struck the door, making me jump back in terror and opening a thin crack of light near an upper hinge. The ax struck twice more at the hinges, and the door fell away.

I was looking up at a scarred, ugly, heavily bearded man. He wore a bright blue velvet topcoat that he must have acquired recently, because it didn't match up at all with the filthy breeches and soiled shirt underneath.

Seeing me on the floor in chains, he burst into laughter. Then he called out to someone over his shoulder:

"Sully! Come look! 'Ey've got some kind o' prisoner!"

A second man joined him, equally filthy and unkempt, except for the powdered wig that sat crookedly on top of his head.

He laughed, too. Then gave me a wink.

"Good news, boyo—ship's under new management."

CHAPTER 10

GUTS

I stared up at the two pirates, wondering what their smiles meant. Were they friendly? Or just happy to find someone already in chains, making me that much easier to torture and kill? If they tortured me, would they use that ax?

As I sat there worrying, the one with the ax got impatient and kicked me on the underside of my foot.

"Get up! Liberation Day! Need an invitation?"

He staggered off, and a second later I heard the *chunk!* of his ax taking down another storeroom door. The other pirate, the tall one called Sully, held out his hand and helped me up.

"Come on, boyo. Get ye a drink."

I followed him up to the dining room. It had been ransacked. The furniture was broken and overturned, and big chunks of the wall plaster lay in crumbled piles on the floor. Half a dozen rough-looking pirates, all in rich men's clothes they must have taken from the passengers, clustered around the open galley door, its contents spilling out over the floor like a cornucopia.

They were mostly ignoring the food in favor of a barrel of wine they dipped into with pewter mugs. Judging by the way they swayed on their feet, they'd been at it awhile.

Sully picked up two mugs from the floor on his way to the barrel. "Look what Barney found in the hold!"

The pirates turned as one and broke into laughter at the sight of me standing there in chains.

"Wot? This a slave ship?"

"Nah. 'At's what 'appens round 'ere when ye use the wrong fork at dinner!"

"Probably didn't wipe 'is nose with a kerchief. Mummy put paid to you, eh?"

They laughed some more as Sully handed me a mug full of wine. "Drink up. Look like ye need it."

I took a polite drink, holding the mug with both hands because the chain between my wrists was only a few inches long. Almost immediately, I felt the warmth spread through my empty stomach.

Then I sort of stood there feeling awkward. The pirates had gone back to their drinking, ignoring me. They didn't seem to care one way or another what I did.

I looked at the food strewn over the floor in front of the galley. "Mind if I eat?"

"'Ave at it. World's yer oyster." The pirate nearest the galley door stepped aside to let me in.

I entered. The galley had been ransacked even more thoroughly than the dining room, but I found some bread and dried beef and had my fill.

When I rejoined the pirates, they were arguing amongst themselves.

"Shouldn't 'ave put 'em off. Valuable 'ostages is what they are."

"More trouble than it's worth. Where d'ye ransom 'em? Sunrise? And sail in range of them shore cannons?"

"Yeh! And be 'angin' around when His Majesty's frigates show up."

"Stuff it! Rovian Navy ain't put an oar in the Blue Sea since the war ended."

Sully noticed me standing there. "Want to get them chains off? Find Big Jim. Got a ring o' keys might fit. Think 'e's up on deck."

"Thanks," I said, and started to shuffle off, my leg chains clanking.

"Wait!"

I turned around. Sully was looking at me funny. He stepped over to me, staring closely at my neck.

"That a Healy mark?"

Hearing this, the other pirates immediately grew interested. And a lot less friendly.

"Are ye one of 'em?"

"No! I'm not—"

"Is 'e tattooin' young boys now? Run out o' real men?"

"Might 'ave to slit that throat of yours."

"I'm not one of them! It's drawn on! Really!" I stammered, rubbing at the spot where Pilcher had drawn the tattoo. "It's not real! The ship's director drew it on me so the passengers would think I was a pirate. But I'm not! It was like a play. I was the villain."

They were staring at me, confused and suspicious. This explanation wasn't going over well.

"Is it coming off?" I licked my fingers and rubbed the spit furiously into my neck, but I couldn't see the tattoo, so I didn't know if it was having any effect.

"Not much."

"Can you put some wine on it or something? My hands are, you know . . ."

Sully reluctantly dribbled wine onto my neck. I rubbed it into my skin, the chains on my wrists knocking painfully against my collarbone.

"Is it fading? It's only ink! Really."

Sully shrugged. I could see from his face he wasn't sure whether to believe me. "I'd stay away from the Ripper if I was you."

I CLANKED UP the stairs in my chains, my chin tucked into my chest, trying to keep my shirt collar hiked up to cover the mark as I passed various marauding, drunken pirates.

"The Ripper" almost certainly meant Ripper Jones, and I dreaded what might happen if he saw the mark. He was legendary for his viciousness—like most Blue Sea pirates, he was in and out of Deadweather, and when he left, there were usually bodies in his wake. Two years ago, we came down the mountain to buy supplies and found three burnt, headless corpses swinging in the air over the main street. One of them had played dice with the Ripper and made the mistake of winning. The second had argued for the first one's life. And the third was a tavern keeper who'd asked the Ripper if he'd mind not stringing up the corpses quite so directly in front of his tavern entrance.

And everyone knew Ripper Jones hated Burn Healy. I didn't know why—professional jealousy, maybe. But while most of the pirate captains and their crews mingled freely in Port Scratch, as friendly as pirates can be, the Healy and Jones crews kept well apart, drinking in different taverns and only crossing paths to murder each other.

If Ripper Jones was in charge, I decided it'd be best to try and get off the ship as soon as possible. But first I had to get the chains off my arms and legs, which meant I had to find Big Jim, whoever he was.

I passed the cabin decks, which were getting loudly ransacked, and the gun deck, where two pirates had found the shovelpuck sticks and were using them to pummel each other. Finally, I stepped out into the sunlight of the main deck. The fog had long since lifted, and although the sun was well on its way to setting, it still felt hot on my face.

The first thing I noticed was the massive pile of clothes in the middle of the deck, easily five feet high and three times as wide. A few pirates milled around it, trying on outfits.

One was wearing a ball gown. That seemed odd.

But less odd, I guess, than a boy in chains. As I approached the pile and started to search it—I'd had an idea, and I wanted to get on with it before someone stopped me—the men gradually noticed me and began to stare with their mouths open.

"'Oo are you?" asked the one in the ball gown.

"I was a stowaway." As I searched the pile, I kept my chin tucked down into my neck, which probably looked strange, too. "They chained me up to put on a show for the passengers."

"Then don't mind thankin' us. And wave bye-bye to the fancy folk."

He pointed across the deck to the sea. I looked over the railing.

Starting about a hundred yards from the ship, I saw a string of eight longboats—the *Earthly Pleasure*'s entire set of launches, each one stuffed full of passengers.

They were all stripped down to their underwear.

The ones in the nearest boat were just close enough to make out their faces. I might have been imagining it, but I could swear I saw the bony-shouldered captain glaring daggers at the pale-skinned blob of a sobbing Pilcher.

My mind flashed back to those few terrible minutes in the stocks. And for a moment, I found myself thinking maybe the pirates weren't all bad.

"Thank you," I said to the one in the gown.

They all grinned. One of them clapped me on the back. "Pleasure's ours, mate."

I went back to searching the pile. After a few minutes, I found what I was looking for—a long, red ascot, unknotted and badly wrinkled. Trying not to clonk myself with the chains on my wrists, I managed to get it around my neck and tie it off, covering the Healy mark.

When I finished, I looked up to see the pirate in the ball gown watching me with amusement.

I shrugged. "Always wanted an ascot."

"It's yer lucky day, innit?"

"Do you know where Big Jim is? Someone said he might have a key to these."

"Try the poop."

He jerked his head toward the elevated deck at the aft of the ship, over the cabins on the quarterdeck. I headed for the ladder up to the poop deck, passing the door to Pilcher's cabin.

From inside it, I heard a scream.

It was a horrible sound, so anguished and pitiful it made my stomach sick. I wanted to open the door and try to stop whatever was happening in there, but I knew I'd only get killed for my trouble. So I hurried up the ladder, having to make awkward frog leaps from one rung to the next because my chains were too short to climb it properly. Even so, I got up it awfully fast, because I was desperate to get away from that sound and stop feeling ashamed that I'd ignored it.

And I knew I'd been wrong about the pirates. Friendly as they might have been to me, they were all bad. And the sooner I could get clear of them, the better.

There were a handful of men on the poop, smoking cigars and passing bottles of what looked like whiskey back and forth. A little pile of clothing lay on the deck behind the ship's wheel, which was tied off and unmanned.

Seeing me, the men made a fresh round of jokes about my chains. I told them I'd been a stowaway, was looking for keys, and had heard Big Jim might have some.

"Jim!" one of them barked, kicking the little pile of clothes, which turned out to be the tiniest man I'd ever seen. He was the size of a small boy, but his limbs were thick and muscular, his face was as grizzled as any of the others', and when he staggered to his feet, it was clear he was more than typically drunk.

There was a big ring of keys hanging from his neck, but he was so brain-fogged it took several requests before he began to understand why we'd woken him up.

Finally, he tottered over to me and peered at the lock on my wrist chains. Then he made a woozy, confused effort to sort through the ring before giving up in frustration and handing me the whole set.

"Meggh! Fin' i' yerself." He curled up behind the wheel and went back to sleep, and I sat down on the deck and began trying to find a key that would fit the locks.

I was almost to the end of the ring and starting to worry when I finally found one that fit both sets of chains. I quickly freed myself, got the ring back around Big Jim's neck without interrupting his snoring, and headed for the ladder to the lower deck.

"Wot, leavin' yer chains behind? Don't ye want 'em?" called out one of the pirates.

"That's all right," I said, trying to sound polite as I hurried down the ladder.

Back on the main deck, I tried to keep to myself as I scanned the surrounding ocean. Judging by the position of the sun, we were pointed north. Off starboard was a second vessel—a sleek, heavily armed frigate that must have been Ripper Jones's ship. A pair of rowboats were ferrying back and forth between it and the *Pleasure,* carrying plundered cargo to the frigate.

Aft on the port side, the longboats carrying the *Pleasure*'s passengers were rapidly shrinking into the horizon to the southwest. They were rowing hard, but if they had some goal other than escaping the pirates, I couldn't see it.

Looking north, I saw a good-sized island a mile or two ahead. I couldn't tell if it was inhabited, but it was lush and green, so I guessed there'd be fresh water and probably fruit to eat. I didn't think I could make it swimming, but if we were floating in that direction—the sails of both ships were struck, leaving us adrift—I thought we might get close enough at some point to make a try for it.

I was wondering whether marooning myself was better than staying in the company of a pack of murderous thugs when I heard a voice boom behind me.

"S'is the boy?"

I turned around. A beast of a man was approaching me, with three of the men from the dining hall trailing behind him. He was well over six feet, shoulders wide as a horse, with a machete in his belt and a pair of pistols tied to a sash slung across one shoulder. There was something peculiar about the shape of his head, but it was hard to say what.

I tried not to look terrified, but I couldn't help shrinking back as Ripper Jones loomed over me, gnawing the meat from a bone that I hoped wasn't human. It looked like pork, but I wouldn't have put it past him.

He reached out with a hairy finger and yanked down the ascot. "Healy fire, neh?"

"N-no, sir. Not a real one. Th-they drew it on me. For sport." As I gestured toward the boats fleeing in the distance, my hand trembled. In that situation, I think anyone's would have.

He tossed the bone away. As he inspected his greasy fingers, I realized why his head looked so strange. He had the smallest ears I'd ever seen, so small they made his whole face look narrow and weasel-like.

As I wondered how many men he'd killed for making fun of his ears, he licked the grease from one finger. Then he wiped the others down the front of my shirt.

"Man pu' a Healy fire on me . . . be righ' angry."

I nodded vigorously. "I was."

The more he talked, the more I realized there was something odd about the way he spoke—something slithery, like all the hard edges had been sanded off the words. In its way, it was as unusual as the size of his ears.

He pursed his lips in a thoughtful sort of way. "Say I help ye . . . say I cu' 'er off?"

He drew his machete, raising it to my neck. The men behind him sniggered.

"All righ' wi' you?"

My whole body was trembling now. I could feel the razor edge of the blade tickle my neck.

"Rather you didn't," I managed to whisper.

Seconds passed. Finally, he laughed, clapping me on the arm as he lowered the knife. "Goo' answer."

Then he turned to the other men. "No' bad, 'is one. Figger 'e go' some fight in 'im?"

"Dunno. Should we give 'im a workout?"

The Ripper grinned. His front teeth had been filed down to sharp points, and when he showed them, he suddenly looked less like a weasel than a shark. "Neh. E'en better—le's pu' 'im an' Gu's inna ring. See 'oo's tougher."

"Right on, Cap! Should we make a show of it?"

"Yeh! 'Ave Mink se' a line."

One of the men turned and ran toward the other end of the deck, where a net full of plundered cargo was being lowered down to one of the rowboats.

"OY! BRING GUTS OVER! WE'RE FIGHTIN' 'IM!"

The Ripper winked at me. "Goo' luck. Ye nee' it."

IN THE HALF HOUR or so it took for them to ferry over Guts, whoever he was, the pirates showed a knack for organizing I wouldn't have guessed they had. The deck was cleared and sprinkled with a thin layer of sand. A large square area in front of the mainmast was marked off with chalk, and the crowd assembled on its edges in impressively straight order, considering how drunk most of them were. A complicated betting system was established by the quartermaster—bets were made and secured against odds that constantly shifted, although I was never given a better than five-to-one chance of winning.

They sat me on a stool and left me to sit alone in a corner of the fighting square. No one spoke to me, but from the conversations swirling around the deck, I got a sense of where things stood. This Guts was a cabin boy. He wasn't big, but he was tough, mean, and thought to be insane. There was something wrong with him— the pirates called it his "crip"—but the general opinion was that it wouldn't hurt his chances, and a few men even argued that he could use it as a weapon.

The fight would be to the death. No one really expected me to win, even the ones who bet on me.

The longer the wait went on, the more sick to my stomach I got. I'd already been the entertainment on the *Earthly Pleasure* once that day. This time promised to be much worse. I would have jumped overboard if I thought I could make it to the railing without getting tackled.

So I tried to distract myself by studying the crowd. At the far corner stood a handful of pirates who kept to themselves, apart from the others. They were swarthier than their mates, with the same tiny ears as Ripper Jones, and at one point I caught a snatch of their conversation, which sounded like mushy gibberish until I realized they were speaking a foreign language. It occurred to me that they must be Cartagers, which came as a surprise. I'd never seen one in person before, and I never would've guessed that Ripper Jones not only had them on his crew, but was one himself—which explained not only his ears, but his slithery accent.

Toward the end of my wait, when the boat carrying Guts had arrived and the net had been lowered to haul him up, one of the less drunk pirates, who'd been standing in the front row to my right and staring at me curiously for a while, finally opened his mouth.

"Yer from Deadweather, aren't ye?"

I nodded. He grinned, nodding in recognition. "Yeh! Yer that fruit picker's son! I seen ye in the Scratch. Where's yer Dad?"

"He's dead," I said.

The man shrugged. "Don't worry. Probably see him in a few."

A cheer went up from the crowd. The net had cleared the deck rail, its human cargo wriggling inside. Someone unhooked the net, and Guts tumbled out.

He sprang up fast, short and skinny, eyes darting under a mop of tangled hair that fell below his shoulders and was so blond it almost looked white. His head and limbs moved in unpredictable, spastic twitches, like a trapped and desperate animal.

He might have been nine or sixteen or anything in between. It was hard to tell. I'd never seen a human move like that. If someone had told me his father was a wolf, I would have believed it.

He was in such constant motion that it wasn't until he'd been herded into the far corner of the ring that I realized his left hand was missing. At the end of his forearm, right where the left wrist should have been, his arm suddenly ended in a rounded-off stump.

Someone whispered in his ear, and his eyes landed on me, burning fierce. If one of the pirates hadn't been holding him back by the arms, he would have rushed me right then. They pulled him down onto a stool, holding him in place.

I felt hands press down on my shoulders from behind. They didn't want me starting early, either.

Ripper Jones made his way toward a plush, high-backed chair that had been set up for him on one side of the square.

"Las' bets, gen'lemen!" he called out. "Show's abou' start."

"Final line is eight to one!" announced the quartermaster.

"'Ow d'ye figure?" yelled someone else.

"Gutsy's hungry! Forgot to feed him today."

There was laughter and catcalling. I tried to block it out. I needed to think, to loosen the grip of fear tightening around my brain and come up with some kind of plan for staying alive. I didn't think I could kill this boy, or whatever he was. But I didn't want to die, either.

I looked around for a third option. The crowd of pirates had closed around us—there wasn't an inch of open space around the square. I looked up and saw a dozen men in the rigging above us, peering down like spiders in a web.

There was no getting out of here without giving them what they wanted. Which was blood.

The Ripper settled into his chair.

"You know rules, boys. Las' one breathin' wins."

"On my count!" yelled the quartermaster. "Three . . . two . . . one . . . 'Ave at it!"

The kid sprang at me, closing the open space like a bird in flight. I ducked him, diving under and to his left, where he didn't have a hand that could grab at me.

I hit the gritty deck hard, rolled, and was halfway to my feet when he charged again.

I tried to duck him a second time, but he got me by the hair and we went down together. There was a tangle of limbs, and I was thrashing frantically, swinging and kicking with no aim at all. I got hit a few times and tried to twist away, and for a second I didn't know which way was up and then there was a searing pain at the base of my shoulder, and I somehow thrashed away and as I pushed backward with my feet I got a look at him and there was blood in his mouth and I think it was mine.

I was on my back, still scrabbling backward with my feet, when he jumped at me again. But he was too far away and I had just enough time to kick him hard in the middle of the face and he flopped to one side and then I had time to stand up.

I backpedaled in a crouch as I watched him get to his feet. His nose was crooked and streaming blood.

We circled, keeping our distance, catching our breath. My shoulder burned where he'd bitten me. He wiped the blood from his face with his good arm, but more kept coming out his nose.

"'Ey, Gussie!" yelled the Ripper. "Bonus if you chew that mark off 'is neck!"

He snarled and jumped me again. I tried to get low on him, and we knocked heads so hard I saw colors. Then his mouth was going for my neck, but I got my hand up under his chin and tried to rip his jaw away from his skull. He gurgled and tried to punch me in the ribs, but it was his bad arm and the stump didn't do much. I got a good grip on the fingers of his hand and wrenched them around, so he had to roll off me or they'd break.

Then I got him by the wrist and twisted his arm behind him as I sat on his back, and he was flailing, all wild fury, but he was flat on his stomach and couldn't get any leverage with his legs.

A roar of surprise went up from the crowd. He struggled some more, but I had him good and stuck.

"Kill him!"

"End it, boyo!"

He was mine to finish. I thought about sinking my teeth in his neck, or bashing his head against the deck, or choking him out.

But I couldn't make myself do any of those things. I don't know why. Maybe it was the memory of that scream coming from Pilcher's cabin. The one from the poor soul I hadn't tried to help.

I lowered my head toward his ear. "I don't want to kill you," I said.

He flailed again, like a fish in a bucket.

"If we stop, they can't make us fight. We don't have to finish. Do you understand?"

He didn't say anything, but I felt his body go slack. I kept my grip, just in case.

"I'll stop if you stop. Both of us together. Will you?"

He didn't answer. The pirates were getting angry.

"Finish him!"

There was a thud that I felt through the planking of the deck, followed by a low, gritty rumble. I turned my head. Rolling toward me, on a straight line from the Ripper's chair to my hand, was a five-pound cannonball.

I looked up and caught the Ripper's eye. His mouth was split in a grin, the sharpened teeth glistening.

"Do it!"

"Kill him!"

"Bash his head in!"

The cannonball rolled to a stop against Guts's bad arm. His stump bumped uselessly against it.

"I don't want to kill you!" I said again. "Promise you'll stop and I won't."

His cheek was pressed against the deck, his eye dancing as he tried to look back at me. Under his nose, blood was dripping into a little pool on the deck.

I moved my head so it was in his field of vision. His eye stopped moving and settled on mine.

"Just promise!" I was practically begging him.

He jerked his head a little, up and down.

"Say it."

"Promise." His voice was weak and gurgly.

"The fight's over?"

"Fight's over."

The crowd was yelling louder. They could see what was happening, and they didn't like it.

"No more," he said, louder this time. "Promise." His eye was still watching me. The fierceness was gone from it.

I kept my grip. I wasn't sure of him yet.

"Friend?" he asked, his voice breaking.

I nodded. "Friend."

I rolled off him onto the deck to the sound of fury erupting all around us. The pirates were shaking their fists with rage.

I didn't care. I was done with it. They could do what they wanted, but I wasn't going to be like them. They weren't going to make me kill some poor half-animal crippled kid.

I looked around the square, watching them yell themselves hoarse. I should have been terrified, but I wasn't. They might kill me for this. But I felt like I'd won.

I was starting to smile when I saw their faces change, the eyes all darting to my left in surprise.

Then Guts hit me in the side of the head with the cannonball.

Everything went screwy for a moment. By the time my eyes refocused, he was straddling my chest, all the fierceness back in his eyes as he swung the cannonball toward my head again.

I had just enough time to curse myself for being an idiot before it all went black.

What a stupid way to die.

CHAPTER 11

PIGS

My first impression of being dead was that it was awfully loud. There were screams and shrieks and great blasts of noise and chaos, and when I opened my eyes, I was still sprawled flat on the deck, but there was fire and blood everywhere and something was hurtling down through the sky at me. I rolled out of the way in a hurry, and it thudded to the deck right where I'd been lying, making the planks shudder.

It was a body. Actually, part of one—when I looked up into the mast, the rest of it was still hanging there, tangled in the ropes.

Then I heard a cracking sound and looked to the forward mast in time to see the upper third of it splinter and tumble halfway to the sea before it snagged on its own ropes.

I sat up. Dead pirates lay all around, the deck red and slick with their guts. The ones who weren't dead were either scrambling to raise what was left of the sails or running belowdecks to man the cannons. I couldn't see Ripper Jones, but I heard him somewhere behind me, bellowing orders.

I got to my feet and swooned, almost falling back over. Something was making it next to impossible for me to stand up straight. I put a hand to the side of my head and found an angry lump the size of a fist where Guts had hit me with the cannonball.

I looked around for Guts and saw him standing at the deck rail, struggling to heave a barrel almost as big as he was over the side of the ship. As I watched, he managed to get it over, and the barrel plummeted out of sight.

He turned, scanning the deck with his fierce eyes, and saw me. We stared at each other for a long second.

Then he went over the side.

It took me a few seconds of wondering why he'd jumped in the ocean before I realized that whoever had just unleashed the volley of cannon fire on us was probably reloading, and this was a stupid place to be standing once they finished.

I ran to the spot where Guts had been and looked over the side. The barrel was bobbing in a field of debris—everything from clothing to bodies to big hunks of wood from the ship—and Guts was frog-swimming through the junk to get to it.

I looked out across the sea. It was almost sunset, and the island in the distance looked even farther away than it had been the first time I'd seen it.

But it beat waiting for the next round of cannon fire.

I took a deep breath and jumped overboard.

It was a long way down. I felt like I was in the air forever, and most of the way I regretted jumping. Then I was plunging down through the cold water, and I wasn't coming back up fast enough, and I realized my shoes were pulling me down.

I broke the surface and was gasping for air when a wave hit me and I got a lungful of water instead. Then I was choking it back out, but the shoes were still sucking water and pulling me down and I couldn't kick them off.

Then there was another wave, pushing me back toward the ship, and I was thinking the sea hadn't looked nearly this choppy when I was fifty feet above it and this was definitely a mistake because I was going to drown. I tried to pull a shoe off with my hand, but I couldn't keep my head above the waves that way, and I was starting to get panicky when I heard a distant cluster of booms, like a string of firecrackers going off.

Almost instantly, there was an avalanche of noise behind and around me as the round of cannonballs hit—splintering and tearing and splashing and screams—and pieces of wood and metal and people and who knew what else were hitting the water all around me, and I don't know what kind of luck kept anything from conking me on the head because that would have been the end of it.

Another wave came, and as I wriggled to keep my head above the crest, I caught sight of something floating in the trough. It passed out of view, but I struck out toward it, and after the next wave crested, I got a hand on it.

It was a section of deck rail, two big lengths of wood maybe four feet long joined by half a dozen crosspieces, splintered on either end but otherwise intact. I hung on to it with one hand while I used the other hand to finally pull off my shoes.

It would have been a good idea to hang on to the shoes, but it wasn't like I was planning ahead right then, so I let them sink.

I firmed up my grip, turning the rail sideways and holding it by the top crosspiece with my arms in front of me so half of it was under my chest and supporting my body. Then I started kicking furiously, straight into the current, because I wanted to put as much distance as I could between myself and the *Earthly Pleasure* before the next round hit.

When it came a minute later, raining more debris down around me, I realized I was swimming straight for the ship that was firing on us. I was changing course to the right when the first of the *Earthly Pleasure*'s cannons discharged practically over my head, so loud my ears rang.

Underneath the roar of the cannon came a second sound, more delicate but similarly destructive. It took me a moment to realize it was the sound of glass breaking on the ship's portal windows. A second cannon went off, the noise and the recoil shattering the few remaining panes. I guess whoever designed those glass windows hadn't counted on the ship's cannons actually getting fired.

I was swimming across the current instead of against it now, and a couple of cannon rounds later, I'd cleared the prow of the ship. I wasn't completely out of danger—at one point, a stray cannonball hit the water close enough to capsize me—but eventually I got far enough away to catch my breath and get my bearings.

I was moving north, toward the island. It was going to be a long slog to get there, and the current wasn't completely with me. If I didn't swim at an angle against it, I knew I'd end up missing the island and get carried out to sea. But I figured if I kicked hard enough, I'd be okay.

I was wrong. By the time the sun went down ten minutes later, it was obvious the kicking wasn't doing much and I was going to miss the island by a good quarter mile unless I could figure out how to use my arms to paddle against the current. After a lot of trial and error, I worked out the best way to hold the deck rail with one hand while I paddled with the other.

That got me back on course, but it hurt like anything. One shoulder was still busted up from when the horse had thrown me, and the other was burning where Guts had bitten into it. So I could only paddle for a minute or two on either side until the pain got to be too much and I had to rest, lying across the deck rail while I stared at the island up ahead in the moonlight, always pulling off to the left, never seeming to get any closer.

And it wasn't just my arms, or my busted knee, giving me trouble. The twin lumps on the side of my head from where I'd been hit with the cannonball—at first, I thought there was just one big lump, but as I probed it more carefully, I realized there were two of them, bunched together like the summits of a little mountain range—were so swollen that every heartbeat sent a little pulse of pain through them, and the longer I swam, the more dizzy and sick I got.

At one point, I quit. I stopped paddling and kicking and just let the current carry me as I floated on my back, holding the rail across my stomach and watching the battle rage in the distance behind me. The *Earthly Pleasure* was burning now, the light from her fires dancing over the water. But the other two ships—Ripper Jones's frigate and whatever had attacked us—were still trading cannon fire, although they were both under sail and moving out to sea, away from the burning hull of the tourist ship.

I watched them for a while, thinking about how pointless it all was, how stupid and cruel men were, how they made life just one kick in the teeth after another, and what a relief it would be to give up and let the waves pull me under.

Then I turned over and kept going.

I don't know how long it took. I don't even remember feeling the sand under my feet. I just remember how good it felt to put my head on something dry and fall asleep.

I WOKE UP with the sun burning my face, glad to be alive.

Then I tried to move, and I was a little less glad. So many parts of me hurt I couldn't even count them all.

And there was a bug biting my arm.

I started to laugh. I don't know why the bug struck me so funny. I think partly I was a little delirious from getting conked on the head. But after everything I'd been through, two days of getting pushed off cliffs, thrown from horses, locked in chains, punched, kicked, drowned, stabbed, and spit on . . . what did this bug think it was going to do to me?

"Bring a gun next time," I told the bug.

Then it flew off before I could get around to squashing it, which struck me even funnier. I was practically shaking with laughter, which made everything hurt more but feel better, when I heard him.

"SHUT UP!"

I looked down the beach. A hundred yards away was a barrel, exactly like the one Guts had tossed over the side of the ship. Next to it were a pair of bare feet and some scrawny legs, their owner's head obscured in the shade cast by the barrel.

As I got up and started over to him, I noticed the smell for the first time—a low, outhouse stink carried on the breeze. I looked around for the source of it, but there was nothing on the beach except sand, trees, me, the barrel, and Guts.

I was close enough to see the ragged tears in his breeches when he sat up with his usual quick, jerky motion and snarled at me.

"Sod off!"

I stopped. "Or what? You'll hit me with another cannonball?" The swelling had gone down some by now, but I was still bitter.

"Worse'n 'at." He held up a knife.

"Where'd you get that?" I was glad he hadn't had it during our fight.

"Sod off!" he yelled again, swiping the knife through the air.

"Don't be stupid. I'm done fighting you."

"No'f ye get any closer."

I sighed and held out my hand. "Let's call a truce—"

"Nuts to that! Jus' want the water!"

So that was why he'd taken the barrel. I had to admire his survival instincts. He'd washed up on the beach with fresh water and a knife. All I'd done was lose my shoes.

He was barefoot, too, but I was pretty sure he'd started out that way.

"I don't want your water. Maybe we can—"

"SOD OFF!"

Now I was getting annoyed. "I could've killed you, you know. Back on the ship. But I didn't."

"'At's yer problem."

It was pointless. I gave up.

"Fine. Have it your way." Remembering what happened the last time I turned my back on him, I walked backward so I could keep him in view until I was inside the tree line.

Then I went looking for water of my own. The forest was hilly and strewn with rocks, some of them as big as buildings. The awful stink I'd first smelled on the beach was still there, but it wasn't as heavy higher up the hill. I walked for a while, my ears straining over the buzz of insects and the occasional rustle of an animal in the brush, until I heard what I was listening for—running water.

I followed the sound until I found a stream that emerged from an underground spring. I drank from it with my hands for a long time, pausing now and then to lie across the mossy ground and stare up at the trees. It felt good to rest.

It's funny how you don't appreciate things until you lose them for a while. Like being able to just lie quietly without somebody trying to kill you.

As nice as it was to lie there, I was famished, so I forced myself to get up and start looking for something to eat. Up the hill, I found a cluster of bushes with fat, dark berries hanging from them. The lower branches had all been picked clean by animals, and I didn't see any corpses lying around, so I figured they weren't poisonous.

I ate until I'd gone through all the ones within easy reach. Then I figured I'd look for something else, but my stomach was full enough by then that I got sleepy, so I went back to the mossy ground by the stream and lay down for a nap.

I woke up to an odd grunting noise that made me startle for fear something was about to eat me.

A little downstream, maybe ten feet from the end of my foot, was a wild boar—four feet long, bristly and black, two tusks curling up from under a long piggy snout—plopped on its belly in midstream. My sudden movement must have startled it, because before I could even think to get up and run, it was off like a shot, crashing through the underbrush.

Once my heart rate got back to normal, I realized this was a good sign. Not only did the boar seem as scared of me as I was of it, but its being there meant there was enough food on the island to grow wild boar to a few hundred pounds.

I spent the next couple hours foraging up and down the hillside, trying to think like a wild boar. What did they eat? Whatever it was, I didn't find much other than more berries and more wild boar. They were all over the place, big and scary-looking but mostly skittish.

Toward the top of the ridge, I came upon a field of loose rocks and pocketed a couple of small, flinty ones that looked like they might be good for sparking tinder into a fire, which I figured I'd have to do sooner or later. I'd never started a fire myself, but that was how the tribe of cavemen in *The Savages of Urluk* did it, and I hoped the author knew what he was talking about even though it was a lousy book.

Around midafternoon, it occurred to me that I should probably try to build a shelter. I was making my way down the hill and mulling over where to build it when I heard the scream—not human, but animal, somewhere up the ridge above and behind me, and close enough that I could hear it thrashing in the underbrush.

Something—probably a boar, but I couldn't be sure—was fighting for its life.

I looked around for anything I could use as a weapon, because I knew wounded animals were dangerous, and whatever was trying to kill it might be even worse. I'd just picked up a coconut-sized rock from the ground when I realized the thrashing was getting closer.

Whatever it was, it was headed in my direction.

There was a big rock outcropping jutting up out of the ground nearby, six feet high and maybe twice as long, with what looked like a wide, flat top. I figured I'd have an easier time defending myself from up there, so I hoisted the rock I was holding onto the top and then climbed up myself.

I'd just swung my legs up over the side when the wounded boar burst into view. As I turned to watch, it passed below me, almost close enough to touch, streaming red blood from a fat gash on the side of its back. As it disappeared again into the trees, I caught a glimpse of something sticking out of the wound.

Then came the thing that was hunting it—Guts, stumbling barefoot through the brush, carrying a rock in his hand and looking as fierce as ever. He plunged into the woods, following the trail of blood left by the boar.

I stared after him, dumbfounded. The kid sure was fearless. That boar was easily five times his size, and he must have gotten right on top of it to bury his knife in its back like that. I thought for a moment about climbing down and following him, because if I could help him kill it, he might share the meat with me. But I figured he was less likely to appreciate the help than he was to knife me for trying to horn in on his food, so I stayed put.

The sound of the chase had died away, and I was about to climb down off the rock when I heard a cry of surprise from Guts, followed by more crashing through the brush. They were headed back my way.

I flattened myself against the rock, lying on my stomach, and waited.

A moment later, Guts reappeared, running for his life. He tripped on a root and fell heavily to the ground. As he got up, his eyes wild with terror, I yelled to him.

"UP HERE!"

He only hesitated for an instant. Then he ran to the outcropping and tried to climb it. I held my hand out to help him up, but he shook it off. Which was stupid, because he quickly got stuck—he managed to get his good hand up over the top of the rock, but he couldn't find a hold wide enough to support the stump of his forearm, and with just the one hand, he didn't have enough leverage to pull up his legs.

The boar came roaring back at full speed, crazed and murderous. Some instinct must have clicked on in its head, like it realized it was going to die and decided to quit running and take its killer down with it, so when it saw Guts pinned down on the rock, it charged him.

Guts heard it coming and started to scrabble desperately against the rock with his legs, but he couldn't find a toehold. I reached over the side of the rock and grabbed his bad arm just below the stump, lifting him up several inches as the boar's jaws snapped in the air where his foot had been an instant before.

The boar hit the rock hard and fell backward, landing on the side of its back where Guts's knife was still sticking out of it. It let out a shriek, but quickly staggered to its feet, lurching and bloody.

Guts was halfway up the outcropping now, and I was trying to pull him along, my arm hooked under his armpit, when the boar reared up on its hind legs and lunged.

It grazed him on the lower leg with its tusks. Guts grunted in pain and lost his handhold, but I managed to keep my grip on him and he stayed up, just barely.

The boar lunged again. It missed his flesh this time but hooked its tusks on the seat of his breeches, and it started to shake its head violently, trying to dislodge him from the rock. I was hoping the breeches would tear away, but the fabric held, and his body was getting wrenched from side to side, and I was pulling and he was hanging on with all he had but I could feel him starting to slip.

I looked to one side and saw the rock I'd brought up with me, less than an arm's length away. With my free hand, I grabbed it and hurled it straight down past Guts, right at the boar's head.

It caught him on the snout. The boar tumbled back to the ground, and by the time it regained its feet, Guts was wriggling onto the rock next to me. He panted, catching his breath, as we watched the boar screech with fury below us—it lunged a couple more times, getting its front legs up on the side of the rock, only to slide off helplessly.

Finally, it gave up and sank to the ground. We watched in silence as the life twitched out of it.

Guts checked out the bite on his leg, which didn't look that bad. Then he turned his head to me.

The fierceness was mostly gone from his eyes. I couldn't help smiling as I waited for him to thank me for saving his life.

But he didn't. Instead, he looked down, motioning with a nod of his head at the dead boar below us.

"We can eat 'im," he said.

PARTNERS

My plan for starting a fire didn't work. Once Guts and I had piled tinder and kindling into a little pyramid around a circle of stones just off the beach, I spent a good half hour knocking the flinty rocks together. But they never made a spark. Maybe the rocks I'd found were no good, or maybe the author of *The Savages of Urluk* didn't know how to start a fire any better than he knew how to tell a story.

Either way, after a while Guts—who couldn't seem to stop moving, and whose eyes and shoulders twitched even when he tried to sit still and watch me bang the rocks together, his blue eyes blinking impatiently under that long, shaggy mop of blond hair—got sick of waiting and took over.

"I'll do it," he said. "Get more wood."

I went off to gather more kindling, and when I got back, he'd split a thick branch in half and was carving a groove down the middle of it, using his knees to hold it in place while he worked the knife with his good hand. He sent me off again for bigger pieces of wood, and by the time I returned from that, he'd finished the groove and was crouched over the branch, trying to work a sharp stick back and forth in the groove. It was tough work for somebody with one hand, and I was about to offer my help when he spared me the trouble of asking.

"'Ere," he said. "Do like this."

On his direction, I rubbed the stick over the groove until a little heap of wood dust built up. After that, he had me tilt the branch up on my knee so the dust collected in a little pile on the bottom, then start working the stick back and forth in the groove as hard as I could.

Ten minutes in, my shoulder hurt, my hand was cramping, and I was starting to wonder what the point of it was when a thin wisp of smoke curled up from the dust. Guts lowered his face to it and blew soft, rapid puffs of air over the pile until it suddenly ignited. He grabbed the branch fast and got it over to the tinder. Within a few minutes, we had a good-sized fire going.

I stayed to watch over it while Guts took his knife back up the hill to butcher the boar. He came back at sunset, so covered in blood and guts he looked like he'd crawled inside the carcass. But he'd managed to carve some good pieces of meat, and I cooked them while he washed off in the ocean.

It was dark when he returned. We ate sitting on a log in the hot, smoky light of the fire, taking our time to savor the meat.

Guts ate hunched over his food, like he thought somebody might come along and take it away. Every couple of minutes, he'd jerk his head around and look over his shoulder to make sure nothing was sneaking up on him. And his face never really stopped twitching, even when his big, prominent teeth were tearing into a hunk of meat.

For a long time, neither one of us talked.

"What's your name?" I finally asked.

"Guts is fine." He turned his head to look at me. "Wot're you?"

"Egg," I said, because I liked it better than Egbert. And because it reminded me of Millicent.

"How long you been a pirate?" I asked.

"I'm not."

"Did they capture you?"

"Nah. Bought me."

"From who?"

He was silent, head down, bangs hiding his eyes, nose pointing past his bony knees to the ground. I asked him again.

"Who sold you to them?"

"Shut up."

He said it quietly, not so much angry as sad. I felt bad for asking twice.

"Want more food? There's plenty left."

"Nah. Wrap it in some leaves. Have it in the mornin'."

I did as he suggested, carefully putting the leftovers on top of the water barrel we'd dragged over from the beach. Then I added a few more branches to the fire and sat down again.

"Got family on that ship?" he asked.

"No," I said, shaking my head. "I was a stowaway."

"Was it fancy? Looked fancy."

"Yeah," I said. "But not for me."

We were both quiet for a while, staring at the fire.

"You know what I think?"

"Wot?"

"I think rich men are just as bad as pirates," I said.

"Dunno 'bout that." He looked at his stump as he said it.

"Not in some ways. But . . . what I mean is, they both think they can take whatever they want. And people like you and me are just . . . meat. What they don't chew up, they throw out."

I poked at the edge of the fire with a stick, knocking the gray ash off a branch that still glowed red underneath. As I stared at it, I thought about everything that had happened to me over the past few days. Pembroke. Birch. The passengers who'd spit on me. The pirates who'd gambled with our lives.

"No more," I said, shaking my head.

"No more o' wot?"

"No more taking it from them." I sat up straight, raising my chin and squaring my shoulders. Everything still hurt, but I had a belly full of food, and I could feel myself getting stronger.

And I was going to fight back. It was the same feeling I used to get with Adonis. I could only take his abuse for so long before I had to give him some in return. It didn't matter how much bigger and stronger he was, or how much worse he'd wallop me for fighting back. Enough was enough.

"There's a man who lives on Sunrise Island," I told Guts. "A rich man. They say he's more powerful than any pirate. He's after a treasure. It's buried on my family's land somewhere. He killed them for it. Then he tried to kill me."

The fire was hot on my face. I turned to Guts, staring him in the eye.

"But it's on my land. That makes it mine. So I'm going to find it before he does. Then I'm going to kill him. And then, someday . . . I'm going to marry his daughter."

I don't know if I really believed all of that, or any of it. For all I knew, Pembroke had already found the treasure and made off with it. And I wasn't sure I could kill anybody, even him.

But it sure felt good to say those words out loud.

"Need a hand?" Guts asked.

I looked at him closely. He didn't seem like he was joking.

I thought about it for a moment. Anybody with that much fight in him could be a real help. But he was crippled, and he'd nearly killed me once, and I still wasn't sure if he was crazy or not.

"What's in it for you?"

"Share o' that treasure."

"I wouldn't give you half. It's too much."

"A third, then."

"Dunno. You've only got one hand."

"Yeah, so—one, two, three." He nodded at my hands, then his own. "Three hands, three shares. Two fer you, one fer me."

"How do I know you won't crack my head open and take it all?"

"Wouldn't."

"You already did!"

"Now's different."

"How's it different?"

"'Cause."

"What?"

His face twitched as he scowled. "Gonna make me say it?"

"Say what?"

"I owe you one, you——." He finished the sentence with one of the foulest oaths in the language.

"Just one?"

He twitched again, shaking his head in exasperation.

"Two. All right?——!"

He'd definitely spent a lot of time around pirates. There were curses in there I'd never even heard before. But coming from him, they were weirdly comforting. He was crippled, and he might be crazy, but I was pretty sure I could trust him.

"All right, then," I said, sticking out my hand. "Partners?"

He shook it with a grip as firm as a man twice his size.

"Partners."

He added more wood to the fire, then yawned and stretched himself out on the grass, folding his arms over his chest.

"Where's this treasure?"

"Deadweather Island. You heard of it?"

"Course. Close by. Day or two, as the crow flies." He stared up at the shadowy silhouettes of the trees overhead. "Too bad. Woulda liked to stay a bit."

"Probably have to. Take us time to build a raft."

He snorted. "Not buildin' nothin'."

"How else are we going to get off?"

"Same's the pigs."

"What do you mean?" He wasn't making any sense.

Guts lifted his head, sniffing the air. "Smell that?"

I nodded. Even with the smoke from the fire, the undercurrent of stink was still noticeable.

"What is it?"

"Dung. This 'ere's Pig Island."

"What's Pig Island?"

"Wot it sounds like."

He lowered his head and closed his eyes, and in less than a minute, he was snoring.

BY EARLY THE NEXT AFTERNOON, we were standing on the ridge that split the island into its two sides—the wild, uninhabited one where we'd come ashore, and the side we were looking down on now, that stank to high heaven and, according to Guts, was the main source of meat for the islands around the Blue Sea. On the nearly treeless hillside below us, hundreds of head of cattle and sheep grazed in fenced-off meadows. At the foot of the hill, closer to the sea, were half a dozen giant pens holding thousands of pigs, all wallowing in muck.

Even from that distance, the smell was fierce.

A short way from the pigpens was a cluster of buildings, connected by a stretch of dirt road to a dock that jutted out into a horseshoe-shaped bay.

There was a cargo ship half a mile offshore, sitting high in the water. Guts pointed to it.

"She'll come in on the tide," he said. "Load up, go out on it in the morning. Just gotta get aboard."

I wasn't too thrilled about stowing away on another ship, but I had to admit it made more sense than trying to build a seaworthy raft.

"How do we know she's not headed to the Continent?" I asked him.

"Don't ship pigs 'cross no ocean. Next port she makes, we'll jump ship to Deadweather."

He gave a twitchy shrug, then stepped back off the top of the ridge. "Jus' need to wait fer dark."

We found a good shady spot just inside the forest and lay down on the grass to wait out the sun. Even though I'd slept plenty the night before, I dozed off pretty fast. When I woke up a while later, Guts was standing nearby, bare-chested. He was so skinny the sun practically shone through him, and I could see every one of his ribs. He was holding up his stump, squinting at it as he turned it at various angles. Then he feinted with it few times, like it was a knife he was using to attack someone.

He smiled, pleased with his fantasy. Then he noticed me watching him and grimaced, dropping his arm quickly to his side as he looked away.

"What's that about?" I asked.

"Shut up."

"What were you doing?"

"Nothin'!"

"Aren't we partners?"

"So?"

"So you can tell me."

"Not 'ardly."

"I'd tell you."

He snorted. Then he sat down on the grass.

After a few moments of quiet, he said, "Want to get a hook."

"For the end of your hand?"

He nodded.

"So why don't you?"

"Need a blacksmith. Money to pay 'im."

"A third of a treasure would probably take care of that."

"'Pends on the treasure."

He reached over to where his shirt lay on the grass. He must have taken it off to use as a pouch, because there was a large pile of berries on top, picked from a nearby bramble. He scooped up a handful and then motioned for me to take what I wanted.

"Wot is it?" he asked through a mouthful of berries.

"What?"

"The treasure."

"Oh . . . I don't know, exactly."

"Gotta know somethin'."

"It's Native. There was a ruler, a hundred years ago. I forget the name. They called him the Fire King—"

Guts made a strange choking noise that I gradually realized was a laugh.

"What?"

"The Fire King? Tell another!"

"What?"

"It's bunk! Don't exist!"

"How do you figure?"

"Wot, never heard the jokes?"

"No. What are they?"

"Like . . . if a pirate's spoutin' off, like, 'I can whip this whole crew at leg wrestlin',' another'll say, 'That an' a map get ye the Fire King's treasure.' Or he says, 'Ten more cannons, we could out-gun Burn Healy,' an' the other one says, 'Yeh—an' if I 'ad the Fire King's treasure, I could retire.' It's a joke!"

"That's not a joke. Just says it's valuable. Doesn't mean there isn't one."

"Yeh, it does."

"If it's all a joke, then why's my family dead?"

"Dunno. 'Ow'd they die?"

I told him the whole story from the beginning, starting with Dad coming down the hillside acting funny and ending with Birch trying to throw me off the cliff. By the end, he wasn't laughing anymore.

"Gotta be somethin' on that land," he said. "Don't make sense otherwise."

"So what do they say about the Fire King's treasure?"

"Who?"

"Everyone. The men who joke about it. What do they say is in it?"

"Dunno. Just . . . big."

Then he scrunched his eyes until they were nearly shut, like he was thinking hard about something.

"And more'n that . . . Magic, too."

"What kind of magic?"

He thought some more.

"Killin' magic . . . Power o' the Gods."

"How?"

"Dunno."

One thing that hadn't really made sense to me—if Pembroke was already rich, why go to so much trouble just to get richer?— suddenly got a lot clearer.

It wasn't just treasure he wanted. It was power.

But Guts was shaking his head. "Bunk."

"Why's that?"

"If the Fire King 'ad magic power . . . wouldn't'a lost."

"Who says he lost?"

"Ever see a Native?"

"Not up close. Just in the distance. Working the silver mines on Sunrise."

"Yeh. Bunch of slaves." Guts shook his head, twitching with distaste.

"I'm not sure they're slaves," I said, remembering what Pembroke had once said about slavery being illegal.

"Close enough." He gave a twitchy shrug. "So much for magic."

FROM A CONCEALED SPOT on the top of the ridge, we watched the ship dock—two of the men from the island, no bigger than ants in the distance, met the boat and tied up the lines thrown onto the dock by the ship's small crew. Then the crew disembarked, and they all disappeared into one of the outbuildings.

A few men reappeared an hour before sunset and made their way to the pens as the pigs crowded in a throbbing pink swarm around what must have been their feed troughs. Then the men went back inside. Smoke began to curl up from a chimney in the main building.

Once it was good and dark, I nudged Guts.

"Should we go now?"

He shook his head. "Just 'ave to wait in the ship longer."

So we stayed there, drifting in and out of sleep, until Guts shook me awake in the middle of the night and we made our way down the hillside to the dock. We skirted as wide of both the humans and animals as we could, taking a roundabout route along the shoreline.

The closer we got, the worse the smell was. I nearly gagged on the approach to the dock, but I told myself (why, I don't know, because it was particularly stupid thinking) that it would get better once we were on board.

The crew were all bunked on land, and we crossed a gangplank onto the deck with no trouble. Guts searched until he found a hatch in the flooring with a big iron ring, which he managed to lift with his good hand.

Even worse smells wafted out of the opening as he beckoned me in. It was pitch-black down there and impossible to tell how far down the floor was. I started in feet first, my upper arms braced against the deck, and slowly lowered myself, hoping to find the floor with my feet before I had to let go.

I got as low as I could manage, but my legs were still dangling in air.

"Drop!" Guts muttered.

"It stinks in there!"

"Come on, fancy," he growled as he shoved me off.

It wasn't a long drop—the hold was maybe six feet high—but I landed in a squish of straw and manure that made my feet slip out from under me, and I fell backward onto my rear with another heavy squish.

I was gagging from the stench and the general disgust when I heard Guts whisper, "Heads up!"

His feet slipped as he landed, and he fell just like I did—only I was already there, so he plopped right on top of me. There was more squishing, and I suddenly wished we'd built a raft instead. If this was better than drowning, it wasn't by much.

"Disgusting!"

"Wait till the pigs come in."

I tried to get used to the light, only there wasn't any.

"I can't see a thing."

"Find a wall. Feel along that."

"This is stupid! When somebody comes in, they'll see us."

"Not if we're in the straw."

"You can't be serious!"

"Who'd go lookin' for us?"

"What a stupid idea!"

"Too late now."

It took some doing, but we managed to feel our way to a corner and pile up straw on top of ourselves. After a while, a few cracks of bluish light started to appear overhead as the sun came up and the light began to filter through the seams in the ceiling planks.

And so began the longest day of my life. I never got used to the smell—or, for that matter, the sensation of lying in a bed of manure—and Guts turned out to be right: when the pigs showed up, it got worse.

They came in squealing an hour after dawn, through a door in the side that flooded the room with light when it opened—and revealed that we'd done a lousy job of hiding ourselves under the straw. Fortunately, none of the men herding the pigs had any more interest in looking inside than I had in being there, so we went unnoticed.

The pigs ignored us, and we did our best to ignore them. But once the door closed and everything went dark, they started to squeal in fright, and as the ship got under way and began to lurch with the waves, they got even more scared, which made them squeal all the more. Finally, someone opened the overhead hatch, giving the pigs (and us) enough light to see by, and the noise died down a bit.

Sometime around late afternoon, we docked. Guts and I had burrowed in pretty good by now, but even so there were some tense moments when a herder came in to hustle the less cooperative pigs out the door. After they were gone, I looked to Guts, my eyes begging him to let us stand up.

He shook his head.

"Wait till dark," he whispered.

We lay motionless until the daylight faded away. Then we lay there some more. Finally, Guts nudged me. We got up and felt our way along the wall to a ladder on the opposite side of the hold, then climbed up to the deck.

The ship was moored at a dock on the edge of a good-sized port—a forest of masts and rigging surrounded us. At the rear of the ship, the crew were playing cards and drinking around a barrelhead. We moved away from them, monkey-climbing a mooring line to the dock. I was taking my first step toward the port when Guts suddenly pulled me back behind a pile of crates.

I peered around the crates and realized what had concerned him. Standing at the end of the dock was a pair of armed soldiers. They were facing away from us, but there was no way to get off the dock without going right past them.

We had a brief, mostly silent argument, making our points with hand gestures. I wanted to jump in the water and swim for the shore, but Guts was worried the splash would attract the attention of the soldiers.

Guts eventually gave in, and we jumped. But he was right—the first thing I heard when my head broke the water was the sound of feet running on the wooden planks overhead. I took cover behind the closest piling under the dock, out of view of anyone peering over the side, and tried to stay as still as possible.

Guts was doing the same at the next piling. We listened as the soldiers debated what they'd heard and whether it was important enough for them to look closer. Eventually, they shrugged it off and returned to their position at the head of the dock.

We waited awhile and then began to swim the length of the dock toward the sea, working our way slowly down a line of moored ships until we figured we were far enough from the soldiers to move out across the adjacent docks and into the bay of open water between the last dock and the shore.

I was so preoccupied with being quiet, and so glad to be out of the filth, that at first I didn't pay attention to the outline of the island ahead in the moonlight, with its long stretches of beach that ended in a pair of cliffs slowly rising along the shore to either side of the port.

Then I noticed the silhouette of a fortress sitting atop the nearer cliff, and I felt a pang of recognition in my gut. I turned in the water to look back at the town, which was slowly coming into view as we cleared the line of ships along the dock.

There was no mistaking the familiar spread of the buildings.

As the pang turned to fear and spread through my body, I uttered one of Guts's pirate curses.

"What?" he whispered.

"We're on Sunrise," I said.

CHAPTER 13

NIGHT PROWLERS

Dunno why yer all in a twist."

"Because there are people on this island who want to kill me!"

"Yeh, but *yer* gonna kill *them.*"

"I can't kill anybody like this! I'm half naked!"

We were huddled in our underpants behind a large rock on the dark, empty beach north of Blisstown. The rest of our soggy clothes lay in a pile nearby. We'd stripped them off when we reached land, and once I realized how disgusting they still looked and smelled, I knew that was it for them.

Guts was harder to convince. "Put this lot back on."

"It's all covered in pig dung!"

"I've worn worse." He shrugged, or maybe just twitched. It was hard to tell with him.

"It's no good. We've got to find new ones."

"Ye can take '*is* clothes. Soon's ye kill 'im."

Once I'd told him where we were, Guts had gotten it into his head that this was a perfect opportunity to kill Roger Pembroke. Just the thought of it filled me with dread, but I couldn't exactly tell Guts that, because it had been my idea in the first place. So I had to make do with more limited objections.

"I'd never fit in his clothes! He's very tall. Anyway, I can't kill someone in my underwear."

"Course ye can. 'Appens all the time."

"Really?"

He nodded. "I seen it. More'n once. Get to it! Which way's his house?"

"This is crazy. Look, I don't even have anything to kill him with."

Guts handed me his knife, which he'd been holding because he couldn't exactly stick it in his underpants.

"Now ye do. 'Ave at it."

The knife felt heavy and strange in my hand. I tried to imagine using it on Pembroke, and I shivered. Partly because I was standing in wet underwear on a cool and windy beach. But only partly.

"I'm not going anywhere without clothes," I said firmly.

"Where we gonna get 'em?"

I looked down the beach, toward Blisstown.

"We'll have to steal them."

WE LEFT OUR ruined clothes behind the rock and moved quickly up the beach, pausing in the weeds by the side of the shore road to let a lone rider on horseback pass before we crossed into the forest. The trees were so thick there was barely any moonlight to see by, but we didn't have to travel far before we reached the first row of houses on the edge of Blisstown.

We crept from house to house, sticking close to the buildings and sprinting across the roads. Fortunately, it was late enough that most of the town had gone to sleep. Just a few windows showed a hint of candlelight, and the only people we saw were a pair of half-drunk men on their way home. They were easy to avoid, and I was glad for the sight of them, because to anyone looking out a window, they offered a reasonable explanation for the handful of dogs we set to barking when we passed.

I figured the big clothing shop on Heavenly Road was our best target, although I kept hoping we'd come across a line of laundry left out to dry so we could avoid breaking into the store. But I guess people don't dry laundry overnight, because we didn't cross paths with so much as a flapping sheet before we wound up crouched by the side of the street meat shack, staring across the street at the shop.

It was a squat, two-story building, its lower windows shuttered and latched. The second floor windows were wide open, but I guessed that was where the owner lived, so there was no point in trying to get in that way. The front door didn't look too sturdy, but from across the street I couldn't tell what kind of lock was on it.

Not that I knew anything about locks. I was hoping Guts did.

"Dunno," he said when I asked him. "Let's 'ave a look."

At the top of Heavenly Road, there were a handful of men talking on the porch of the Peacock Inn, but they were too far away and too involved in their own conversation to notice us as we slipped across the street.

Guts was just ahead of me, and his first step up the short stairs to the shop's porch produced a noisy creak. The sound froze us in place for a moment, but it didn't seem to alert anyone, so after a nervous second, we continued, taking care to step on the far edge of the stairs where the creaking wouldn't be as bad.

At the top of the steps on either side was a column supporting the porch roof. As I passed the one on the right, I noticed a foot-long sheet of thick paper tacked to it. In the moonlight, it was hard to make out what it said, and I would have kept going without a glance if a word in the three-inch headline hadn't caught my eye.

Guts was already at the door, inspecting the lock. I paused for a closer look at the poster.

WANTED FOR MURDER.

That was the headline. Below it, in slightly smaller type, were the words $5,000 REWARD FOR CAPTURE—DEAD OR ALIVE.

Below that was a picture of me.

It was drawn in ink, and accurate enough that I recognized myself immediately. When I did, I felt the bottom of my stomach drop to somewhere around my knees.

"Guts," I managed to croak, "look at this."

Guts turned away from the lock, which he'd been trying to jimmy with his knife, and joined me on the edge of the step. He squinted at the poster.

"Wot's it say?"

"Wanted for murder."

He leaned in closer, studying the picture. "That you?"

"Yeah."

"Five thousan' silver?" He nodded approvingly. "Good price."

I wanted to smack him for that, and I might have done it if a voice from behind us hadn't suddenly made me jump out of my skin.

174

"You boys from the boat?"

I spun around. Two feet past the bottom step was a stout, balding man wearing the expensive linen coat of a well-to-do Sunriser. He was squinting up at us in the moonlight, looking confused.

I would've run for it right away, but I couldn't get down the stairs without coming less than an arm's length from him. As my eyes darted around the porch, looking for the best way to flee, he kept talking, in a friendly and soothing voice.

"Don't be scared, son. You're safe now. No pirates here. Just come ashore, did you?"

He took a step toward the stairs, a little wobbly on his feet, and as I watched him, several things occurred to me at once—that he was a bit drunk, that he didn't mean any harm and in fact clearly wanted to be helpful, and that he must have mistaken us for passengers from the *Earthly Pleasure*.

"Expect you're hungry. Need clothes, too. Whyn't you come with me? I'll get you set—"

Just then, something hurtled through the air, sailing from the corner of my eye straight into his skull just above the eyebrows, where it made a heavy *THUNK* sound, which was followed by a much heavier *THUD* as the man's pear-shaped body toppled backward onto the street.

As the heavy brass porch spittoon rolled back and forth on its lip a few feet from the man's motionless body, Guts stepped forward with a satisfied grin.

"Ace shot, wannit?"

"What'd you do that for?!" I hissed.

"Savin' us!"

"From what? Getting fed and clothed?"

"Nuts! Woulda strung us up." He bent over and picked up his knife, which he'd had to put down in order to hurl the spittoon. "Quick, check 'is pockets."

I was just putting the words together to express my disgust at the idea of robbing the poor man when a shout from up the street turned both our heads. The men at the Peacock Inn, attracted by the commotion, were all starting toward us—two of them at a run—and the cold-cocked body at our feet meant we didn't have much in the way of options.

We both leapt from the steps and took the shortest route out of sight, pivoting sharply down the alley between the clothing shop and the building next to it. We ran flat-out, too panicked to worry about the noise we were making, and by the time we'd raced across the first street behind Heavenly Road, it sounded like every dog in town was barking.

I didn't slow down to look back until we reached the edge of the forest a few blocks away on the far side of town. There weren't any pursuers in sight by then, but we kept moving until the barking died away and it felt safe to stop and take stock of the situation.

"Why'd you hit him? He could've helped us!" I was still angry.

Guts shook his head, long tangles of hair swishing across the scowl on his face. "No man like 'im 'elps the like o' us."

"He would've! He thought we were rich folk! From the boat."

"Yeh? 'Ow long till 'e made ye fer the murderer?"

It was a fair point. But I didn't care for that word.

"I'm not a murderer," I said quietly.

His face twitched. "Course ye are."

"It's not murder if someone tries to kill you first."

"Yeh, it is."

"No, it isn't!"

"What d'ye call it, then?"

I thought about it for a moment. "It's a gray area."

"Wha's a gray area?"

"It's not black and white. It's both. Like how people aren't all good or all bad. They're a little of each."

"Not true."

"What, everyone on earth is either completely good or completely bad? No in between?"

"Yeh." He nodded.

"What are we, then?"

He was quiet for a while, and I thought I'd won the argument. But then he answered.

"We're bad."

I snorted. He wasn't just being stupid. He was making me angry.

"If we're bad, who's good?"

He was quiet again for a moment.

"Nobody."

"I don't believe that," I said.

"Find somebody good, gimme a poke. Like t' see it."

"You're an idiot."

"Must be. Look who I'm followin'. Wot we do now?"

I chewed over the situation for a while. We didn't just need clothes. We needed food and water, none of which I knew how to find in Blisstown with no money, in the middle of the night, when I was wanted for murder. And that wasn't even taking into account all the barking dogs and newly alert men on the lookout for a pair of attempted burglars.

But there was one place on Sunrise where I *did* know how to find all of those things, even in the dark—a place where no one locked the doors at night, and where the dogs were kept in a kennel away from the main house because they made Mrs. Pembroke sneeze.

And breaking into Cloud Manor was the last thing Roger Pembroke would expect me to do. At least, that's what I hoped.

I told Guts my idea. He gave a little snort of disgust.

"What?"

"Whyn't we do it in the first place? Back when I said it?"

"It doesn't matter," I said, starting off in the direction of Cloud Manor.

Guts crossed his arms and stayed put. "Does to me," he said.

"What do you want me to do?"

"Say it was my idea."

"It was your idea! Satisfied?"

He started to follow me. "Gonna kill 'im while we're there?"

My stomach flopped a little at the thought of it. "We'll see."

WE FOLLOWED THE SLOPE of the hill to the shore road. It was slow and painful. The prickly shrubs that grew thick near the bottom of the hill left our arms and legs scribbled with small scratches and cuts. But once we got to the road, we made good time even though it was all uphill. We took to the trees again a little below the sentry post where the road branched off from the shore, but the forest was thinner there, and it wasn't long before we crossed back onto the branch road to Cloud Manor.

The whole way there, I thought about Millicent. She'd almost definitely be home and just as definitely asleep. What did she think of me now? That I was a murderer? Would she be afraid of me? Or would being a wanted man make me seem dangerous and alluring, like the outlaws in books who made women swoon?

Should I wake her up?

No. It'd be too big a risk. And anyway, I was in my underwear, which made looking dangerous and alluring pretty much impossible.

But I thought maybe, while I was still up on the second floor, after I'd gotten the clothes that I hoped were still in my old bedroom, I could slip into her room and just look at her for a moment . . .

Or write her a note and leave it beside her pillow . . .

No. I'd need parchment and ink for that, which I'd have to get from Pembroke's study, and that would take too long. But maybe I could leave her something, a sign of some sort, to let her know I'd been there and was thinking of her. Like a copy of *Basingstroke,* our favorite book, which I could probably find in the library downstairs . . .

It was all completely stupid, but fantasizing about it kept my mind off of wondering what would happen if I ran into her father—and I knew if I stopped to think about that, I was going to lose my nerve completely.

I was still thinking about Millicent when we reached the edge of the great lawn, and Guts got his first look at Cloud Manor, silhouetted against the moonlit sky.

It took a while for him to get over the idea that a family of just three people lived in that massive castle of a home.

"Got 'orses in there? Stables and such?"

"Nope. It's just them."

"Not cows, neither? Jus' them? In all that space?"

"That's how rich folk live. You ready?"

"In a minute." As I watched him gaze up at it, slack-jawed, it occurred to me just how small and awful his life must have been. A month earlier, I'd never seen a place like Cloud Manor, either, but at least I'd read enough books to know they existed. Guts was staring at the place like it had fallen out of the sky from a whole other world.

Finally, I gave him a shake on the arm and started for the mansion. "Remember, food and water. Then clothes. Then we get out."

"And if ye get the chance—"

"I won't—"

"But if ye do—"

"Yes! I'll kill him. All right?" By now, I was deeply regretting ever having said that back on Pig Island.

"Want the knife?" He held it out for me to take.

"You keep it."

Around the side of the mansion, a single door led from the herb garden to the kitchen. As we got closer to it, I felt the fear start to rise in me. What if it was locked? What if everything had changed since I ran away, and Cloud Manor had become an armed camp? What if there were guards watching us even now, waiting for us to close the distance before they opened fire? What if Pembroke was awake and waiting inside?

The door was open. There were no guards. Whatever threat he thought I posed, Roger Pembroke clearly didn't find it serious enough to lock his doors or post a watch.

Nothing had changed inside, either—even the leftover jelly bread was right where the pantry maid usually kept it.

We ate and drank quickly and silently. Then came the hard part. We had to get upstairs to my old bedroom and hope my clothes were still there, either the ones I'd been wearing when I arrived or the several outfits the Pembrokes had given me.

I motioned for Guts to follow me. We left the kitchen through the dining room, where moonlight from the tall windows shone off the brightly polished table. At the entrance to the main hall, I paused and looked back to see Guts gaping at the opulence of the room.

"Ever eat in 'ere?" he whispered.

"Three times a day," I told him. "The butlers served us."

He answered with one of his foulest curses, packed full of amazement.

We had to step carefully in the main hall not to create an echo, and for the first time since I lost my shoes, I was glad to be barefoot. Up ahead, the door to the study was shut.

But the library door was open, and there was light coming from inside.

My heart thumped a little, remembering how Pembroke used to stay up late at night reading. I tiptoed up to the door and peeked my head around the side.

There was a small fire burning in the fireplace, and a candle flickered on a side table next to one of the big, high-backed chairs facing the fire. I couldn't see him from where I stood, but I knew he was in that chair.

Guts nudged me from behind. I turned, and he mouthed the word *what?*

It's him, I mouthed back.

His eyes lit up. He held out the knife.

My heart raced. I wasn't ready for this.

He urged the knife on me, practically forcing it into my hand. After I took it, he leaned in, his lips practically touching my ear.

"Killed yer family," he whispered.

My stomach went all knotty, and I wanted to throw up the food I'd just eaten. But I knew he was right.

I had to do it. And I'd never get a chance as good as this.

I took a few deep breaths, trying to slow down my thumping heart. Then I slowly crept into the library.

The firelight cast long, trembling shadows around the room. It was so quiet I could hear the flames lick at the logs.

Ten feet away . . . From the other side of the chair, I heard the sound of a page turning. He was awake.

But he'd be unarmed. And unsuspecting.

Was it fair, sneaking up on him like this? Should I make a noise, give him a chance to defend himself?

Did he give my family a chance?

Five feet away . . .

I paused to look back. Guts was halfway between me and the door, all skinny limbs and bony ribs. His eyes glowed, and he nodded gravely at me.

I turned back to the chair and stepped forward, raising the knife in my hand.

There's no honor in this. Heroes in books don't kill men this way.

But was there honor in the way Birch tried to kill me?

And who said I have to be a hero?

It's got to be done. He'd do it to me if he could.

No. He'd have someone else do it. That's the rich man's way.

No honor in that, either.

Two feet away . . . The knife was over my head. One step to the side, one step forward, and I could plunge it into his chest.

Maybe it'll be easy.

Maybe I'll even like it.

Fat chance. I was shaking so badly I had to hold the knife with both hands.

What if the first thrust doesn't kill him? What if I have to pull it out and do it again?

Got to get it right the first time. Left side of the chest. Straight through the heart.

One step to the side. One step forward.

Just do it.

I forced myself to move.

As my body crossed the plane of the chair and I made the turn toward him, starting the knife on its downward arc, I saw the glint of honey-gold hair.

And I froze.

"AAAAAAAAAIIIIEEEEEEEE!!!"

You could have heard Millicent's scream all the way to Blisstown.

I stumbled backward, trying to hide the knife behind me as she leapt to her feet, her heavy book thudding to the floor.

"Egg! What are you doing?"

"Nothing! I was—"

"Are you trying to murder me?"

"Course not!"

"Then what were you doing with that knife? Combing your hair with it? And why aren't you wearing any clothes? Have you gone mad? And who on earth are YOU?"

Guts's good hand was cocked back, ready to take a swing at Millicent. I shook my head vigorously, waving him off as a door slammed somewhere in the recesses of the manor.

"*Millicent . . . !*"

Mrs. Pembroke's voice rattled through the great hall from an upstairs corridor, sending a bolt of panic through me.

Millicent ignored the voice, spinning back to face me. "What are you doing here? And where have you been? Were you on the boat? How'd you get past the soldiers?"

"What soldiers?"

"The ones who searched the rescue boats when they came in—"

"MILLICENT!" She was on the stairs now.

"Blast! She'll wake the houseguests."

"What houseguests?"

"From the boat. Hide yourselves! I'll deal with her." She ran from the room, calling to Mrs. Pembroke as she went. "It's nothing, Mother. Just reading a ghost story—"

She slammed the heavy door behind her on the way out, reducing the rest of their exchange to a series of muffled grumblings.

I took cover behind a couch along a side wall. Guts stared at me like I was crazy.

"What ye doin'?"

"What's it look like I'm doing?"

"Cowerin'! We're dead men stayin' 'ere!"

"We're not—"

"You heard 'er! Gonna bring soldiers back to kill us!"

I shook my head. I hadn't completely understood what Millicent was talking about, but I felt safer trusting her than not.

"She wouldn't do that."

"Wot if she does?"

"She wouldn't. You've got to trust her."

"Nuts to that! Gimme my knife back."

"Promise you won't use it?"

"Wot's the point o' havin' it?"

"Only in self-defense, then."

"Whatever. Give it."

I handed it back to him. He glowered for a moment, looking around.

"Goin' out the window—"

"Just give her time! Please."

"Why ye so sure ye can trust her?"

I probably should have thought it over, at least for Guts's sake. But I didn't want to live in a world where Millicent would give me up to her father.

"I just am."

"She the one ye gonna marry?"

"Don't talk about that."

"Wot? Don't she know it?"

"I said don't talk about it! Just forget I ever said that."

He snorted, shaking his head. "Wot we gonna do? Sit here?"

I looked at the shelves behind us. "You could read a book."

"Shut up." He joined me behind the couch, twitching and scowling as he glared at the closed door.

A minute later, it creaked open. I kept my head above the back of the couch long enough to see that it was a maid, plodding sleepy-eyed toward the fireplace.

As I sank back down, I saw Guts was readying his knife. I grabbed his arm and shook my head no.

He brushed me off with a scowl, but let the maid live. A moment later, the shadows stopped dancing on the walls as she put the fire out. Then she was gone, and we sat in the darkness for so long I had to put down three or four mutinies from Guts.

Finally, Millicent slipped back into the room. She was carrying an armload of clothes, a rucksack, and a pair of shoes.

The shoes were mine, the ones I was wearing when I first came from Deadweather. She had the rest of my old clothes with her, too, and I was surprised at how glad I felt to put them on, even the itchy shirt. I left the other outfit, a much nicer one that Pembroke had given me, to Guts.

"You're lucky," Millicent said as she relit the candle and locked the door behind her. "Mother had those laid out to take to town in the morning. There's a terrible shortage of clothing ever since the tourists came back."

"From the *Earthly Pleasure*?"

She nodded. "If these hadn't been laid out to donate, I would've had to sneak past Lord and Lady Winterbottom to get them. They're staying in your old room. They snore like bears, you can practically hear it downstairs. But they're not as bad as Lady Cromby. She complains about *everything*. Yesterday at lunch—"

"How many of them are here?" I finished tying my shoes and stood up.

"Six . . . no, eight. Sorry about the shoes, by the way. There's just the one pair."

Guts gave a twitchy shrug. "Don't wear 'em."

"And there's food and water in here." Millicent handed me the rucksack.

"Why are they all staying here?"

"Daddy said it was the least he could do. They were all horribly shaken—"

"Where is he?" Guts barked at her.

"Excuse me?"

"Where's yer dad?"

"Guts—" I tried to cut him off.

"You're quite rude, aren't you?" She turned to me. "Is he one of your field hands? One of the hands with no hands? Because that's no way for a servant—"

"I'm no servant, ye———!" Guts rattled off a string of vile words, tying them up with a snarl as he tightened his grip on his knife.

I quickly moved to stand in between them, wishing I'd never given Guts the knife back, as Millicent curled her lip at him.

"What *are* you, then? Certainly not a gentleman."

"This is Guts," I said. "He's my . . . partner."

"Partner in what?"

"Just . . . things. Where *is* your father?"

"Offshore, at an emergency meeting. The pirates who attacked the *Pleasure* are going to pay for it, I'll tell you that."

I felt a wave of relief spread through me at the news that Pembroke wasn't even on the island. "When's he back?"

"In the morning." Then her voice turned quieter. "Is it true, Egg? Did you really murder Mr. Birch?"

"I didn't have a choice. He tried to kill me."

"Why on earth would he do that?"

I didn't know how to answer her. Guts broke up the silence.

"'Cause yer dad told him to."

"Guts—"

"That's ridiculous!" Her voice rose in anger. "My father loved Egg! And who are you to speak like that? In clothes my father paid for? You've got no right—"

"Let's not talk about this," I said quickly. "In fact, why don't the two of you not talk to each other at all?"

"Egg—" Millicent cupped my face in her hands, forcing me to stare into her eyes. The feel of her skin on mine sent a shiver through me. "You don't believe that rubbish, do you? Daddy loved you! He told me he wanted to make you his son."

The look in her eyes said she believed it. And the look in my eyes must have been easy to read too, because she dropped her hands to my chest and shoved me.

"Don't be stupid! Why on earth would he want to kill you?"

"Because of the treasure."

"What treasure?"

"The Fire King's. It's on our land. Back on Deadweather."

She laughed. "That's ridiculous! Even if it exists, the legend says it's on Sunrise."

"The legend's wrong. My father found it. That's why your father got rid of him."

It took her a moment to answer. Whether it was just because she was sorting out the implications of what I'd said, or because a part of her was wondering if it was true, I couldn't say.

"Ridiculous! That was an accident!"

A sudden, metallic rattle made us all turn at once toward the entryway. It was the doorknob, and it was followed by a pounding on the door itself.

"Millicent! What are you *doing* in there?"

Guts raised his knife. I put a hand on his shoulder—carefully, because I didn't want him stabbing me—and motioned for the window. Reluctantly, he headed over to it.

"Good-bye," I said. "Thanks for everything."

I shouldered the rucksack. Mrs. Pembroke was pounding and yelling on the other side of the door, and Guts was halfway out the window, the knife in his teeth, but I lingered for a second anyway, trying to memorize as much of Millicent's face as I could in the dim light.

She was scowling at me. But I thought, or maybe just hoped, there was more than anger in her look.

"You can't stay on Sunrise. They're looking for you."

"I know," I said.

"How will you get off?"

"I'll figure it out," I said.

"MILLICENT!"

I'd never heard her mother so angry. As she began to call for a servant to get out of bed and come force the door, I hurried to the window.

"Good-bye," I said again. I tried to catch her eye to say more than that, but she was already turning away.

"Be careful!" I heard her whisper as I swung my legs out the window.

GUTS WAS LOOKING highly annoyed as I dropped to the ground next to him.

"Ye stop fer tea?"

"Shut up," I said. There was a lump in my throat that made the words hard to get out.

We were halfway to the trees when I heard her voice.

"Wait!"

Millicent was bounding across the lawn toward us in her night-gown, hair streaming behind her in the moonlight like a nymph.

I was dumbfounded. "What are you doing?"

"Saving your life," she said. "Follow me."

CHAPTER 14

THE BOAT

"o's she think she is? And where's she goin'?"

Guts and I were struggling to keep up with Millicent, who was racing up a footpath that snaked through the wooded hills above Cloud Manor. It was almost too dark to see the ground, but she knew the path so well that she could hurdle the various rocks and fallen tree trunks without so much as looking at them.

Guts and I, on the other hand, kept running headlong into things and falling on our faces.

"Nuts to this!" Guts was angry. I was just confused.

"Millicent, could you stop so we can talk about this?" I pleaded.

"I don't think that's wise," she called over her shoulder. "The servants will be out looking for us in no time. Probably on horseback. And possibly with dogs."

"What?!"

"You know how Mother is. She'll probably send half the household after me."

"You're going to get us killed!" Now I was getting angry too.

"Don't be stupid! I'm saving you!"

Guts stopped running. "I've had it. Not chasin' *her* no more."

I stopped too. "Millicent . . ."

She was so far ahead I couldn't even see her in the darkness. But I heard her stop and snort with exasperation. She came back down the path, fading into view like a ghost in her billowing white nightgown.

"Egg, you've *got* to follow me. Every man on Sunrise is looking for you—"

"I know! I've seen the poster."

"Brilliant picture, wasn't it? I drew that," she said proudly.

"That's terrible!"

"What do you mean? It looked just like you."

"It's a WANTED poster! Couldn't you have made it *not* look like me?"

That caught her short. But only for a second. "Whatever. The point is, you've got to get off Sunrise. And you can't go by the port, because Daddy's got soldiers searching every ship top to bottom for you before it leaves."

"So what can *you* do?"

"I've got a boat."

"But you just said the port—"

"It's not at the port! Come on!"

She started off again. Guts and I looked at each other.

"This island's hundred-foot cliffs all round," he said. "No port but the port."

"Worth a look," I said, and ran off after Millicent.

Once he finished cursing, Guts followed us.

THE FOOTPATH ENDED half a mile later, somewhere along the upper reaches of the shore road. We crossed over to the cliff side and followed the road for a while as Millicent studied the shallow line of trees fronting the cliffs. Twice, she stopped and doubled back, which made Guts roll his eyes and snort in disgust.

I asked her if there was anything I could do to help.

"Yes," she said. "Make him shut up."

"Didn't say nothin', you——."

"Do you kiss your mother with that mouth?"

"Speak of 'er again, I'll slit yer—"

"Oh, good! Here it is."

She stepped between a pair of large pines to a barren, unremarkable spot at the top of the cliff. As Guts and I followed, she picked her way over a few big rocks to reach the edge, which seemed to plummet straight down to the sea below.

"Follow me," she said. Then she stepped out over the edge into what looked like thin air.

We watched, dumbfounded, as she slowly disappeared, half a foot at a time.

"Come on!" she called to us as her head sank out of view.

"Yer first," said Guts.

I gulped and followed Millicent's path to the edge. On the seaward side of the rock, invisible to the eye until you were almost on top of it, was a narrow row of a dozen steps cut into the side of the cliff. Millicent was at the bottom of them, leaning lightly against the side of the cliff and smiling up at me.

As I started toward her, she took a few more steps and disappeared from view beneath an overhang. By the time I reached the end of the first section, the next one had come into view, leading down the cliff's face. Millicent had paused again to look back at me.

"Is he coming?"

I looked up. Guts was on the steps behind me.

"Keep movin'! Got nowhere to go."

I started down the stairs toward Millicent.

"Whatever you do, don't look left," she said as she started moving again.

I looked left—and immediately went dizzy with terror, because there was nothing but air between the side of the step and the sharp rocks rising out of the sea a hundred feet below me.

I clutched the side of the cliff with both hands and pressed my head against the rock wall to try and make the dizziness go away. Behind me, Guts let out an annoyed grunt.

"What'd ye stop fer? Almost ran into ye!"

"Sorry!" My voice sounded like someone was strangling me.

"You looked left, didn't you?" Millicent called out brightly. "Try not to do that."

We were on the stairs for maybe two minutes, but it felt like an hour. Finally, about twenty feet above the waterline, they turned sharply inward, disappearing through a little archway that we had to crouch down to squeeze underneath.

Inside, it was pitch-black and ten degrees colder.

"Hand me that sack," I heard Millicent say from somewhere just in front of me.

I held out the rucksack of food and water she'd prepared for us, which I'd been carrying on my back since we left Cloud Manor.

She took it from me, and a few moments later, she struck a match, lighting the immediate area.

We were on a platform cut into the wall of a narrow, high-ceilinged cove. A small, single-mast boat bobbed in the water below us, tied up to iron cleats hammered into the rock.

"Give me a minute. I'll find the lantern," Millicent said. She was halfway down the steps to the boat when her match went out. I expected her to strike another right away, but she knew her surroundings well enough that the next one she lit was to fire up a lantern she'd retrieved from somewhere on the boat.

She beckoned for us to get on board.

"Oars are under that bench. Keep to starboard getting out of the cove—there's some nasty rocks just under the waterline to port, but it's a deep channel otherwise. There's a jib and a main in the cabin, but the jib might be more trouble than it's worth. Wait till you're out to raise the main. All right?"

She had her foot on the deck rail, ready to step off the boat.

"I'm not sure I got that," I said.

"Which part?"

"The jib and the . . . raising the . . ."

"Don't you know how to sail?"

"Not really, no."

"For Savior's sake, Egg! You grew up on an island!"

"I grew up on a mountain! That happened to be on an island. We didn't exactly leave very often."

She turned to Guts. "What about you?"

He shrugged. "Know from a jib an' a main. Don't mean I can sail."

195

I stared at him in disbelief. "Didn't you live on a ship?"

"Yeh, moppin' decks. Loadin' cannons. Weren't the pilot."

Millicent was shaking her head in amazement. "I can't believe it. Neither of you knows how to sail?"

"We've got oars. Can't we just paddle?"

"Not if you actually want to get anywhere! How far are you going?"

"Deadweather."

She sighed. "I'll just have to take you myself. Ridiculous! And dressed like this!"

"It favors you."

"Don't make me blush. Now get those oars out."

"Hang on." Guts was staring suspiciously at Millicent. As he spoke, he gestured at her with his knife. "Just 'cause yer comin' don' mean yer sharin' the treasure."

"Don't be stupid. I don't need any treasure. Besides, you're barking mad if you think you're going to find it on Deadweather."

"Good enough for me," I said, handing Guts one of the oars. The thought of Millicent coming with us was making me a little light-headed.

Reluctantly, he put down the knife to take the oar. Then he leaned in, muttering in my ear. "Don't trust her. She's witchy."

"She's not," I said. "Believe me."

"I'm not what?" asked Millicent.

"Nothing," I said.

"Witchy," said Guts.

"Oh, terribly! In fact, I'm planning to kill you both at sea," said Millicent. "Now, give me that oar," she said, holding her hand out to Guts.

"Why?"

"Because they work much better when you've got two hands."

His face twitched with anger, and he drew back the oar like he was going to swing it at her. I quickly got a hand on it.

"Don't. Please. She's only teasing."

He made an odd, angry gurgling noise. But he let me take the oar. As I turned to give it to Millicent, he snarled at her. "Watch yerself!"

"I'd suggest you do the same, but I don't know how you could watch anything with all that hair in your eyes. Next time you're play-acting with that knife, why not use it on your bangs?"

There was another angry gurgle, and he went for his knife. So did I. He got there first. But at least I managed to put myself in between him and Millicent.

"She's only kidding. Really. Even though she's being an idiot."

"Excuse me?"

"You are. Seriously." I took my eyes from Guts just long enough to glare at her.

Guts growled again. "Don't have to take this."

"You're welcome to step off. Wait for another girl to come by with a boat."

"MILLICENT!"

"No? Right, then. Why don't you make yourself useful and fetch the main? It's in the sack down in the cabin."

"Not yer—— servin' boy!" Guts took a step toward her, and I had to put my hands out to make sure he couldn't stab her without hitting me first.

"Of course you're not, and she's being a complete idiot—"

"Who's the only one among us who knows how to sail. And happens to own the boat."

"And there's that. So please, please, don't stab her."

"And do fetch the main. It's rather critical to the entire under-taking," she said with a smile.

Guts twitched like he was halfway to a seizure, and made some more growling noises, but he let me steer him toward the cabin.

"She actually does mean well," I told him quietly.

"Keep her out my way." He stomped down the cabin steps, twitching and muttering.

When he was gone, I lit into Millicent. "For Savior's sake, would you stop winding him up? Do you *want* to get stabbed?"

"He'd never use that knife."

"He would, actually. He's quite violent. And not well in the head."

"What kind of 'not well'?"

"The kind that stabs people! Look at this." I opened two but-tons on my shirt and pulled it far enough off my shoulder to give her a good look at the blood-crusted bite mark on my shoulder.

"Oh, that's awful! Does he have a dog?"

"No, that was *him.*"

Millicent's eyebrows jumped. "Right, then. Good to know. Thanks for the tip."

Millicent laid off Guts after that, settling for bossing me around instead. She tried to give me orders like I was an ordinary seaman, but she quickly realized that words like *clew* and *halyard* were going straight past me, so she had to settle for pointing and using simpler instructions, like "pull down on that rope" and "let Guts do it."

And "watch out for the boom." Which I wish she'd said a little faster, because then I might have ducked in time and not gotten clouted across the back when the arm of the sail swung over the cockpit. But at least it didn't hit me in the head.

Eventually, we got under way. Millicent set a course to the west and settled back in the cockpit with her hand on the tiller.

"It's chilly," she said, hugging her arms to her chest. "Can you fetch me a blanket from the cabin?"

I went inside and found Guts already fast asleep, curled up in one of the cabin's small but cozy beds. I took a wool blanket from the other one and brought it back to Millicent. She wrapped it around herself like a shawl as I took the seat beside her on the other side of the tiller.

It was still an hour or so before dawn, and the sea was calm under the moonlight. I watched Millicent for a while, studying the curve of her cheekbone and the long wisps of hair that the wind blew across her face, until she caught me at it and I had to stop.

"What are you looking at?"

"Nothing." I turned away and studied the water instead.

"Tell me what happened," she said. "With Birch."

I told her the whole story, careful not to look at her when I got to the part where Birch said "boss's orders." I knew she wouldn't like hearing it, but I wasn't going to leave it out.

"That's not how they told it at all," she said when I was finished. "Who's 'they'?"

"The men in the gorge. The ones who saw it happen."

"What did they say?"

"That Birch was waving to them from the top of the cliff, and they were waving back when they saw you step out from behind and push him over the edge."

"They told you that?"

"No. They told Daddy. He was very upset."

"Millicent . . . I'm telling you the truth." I could feel my jaw tighten as I spoke.

"Sometimes when things happen very fast, especially if they're scary—"

"It's got nothing to do with scary! He tried to kill me! You think I'm lying?"

"No, I just—"

"Why on earth would I push him off? I didn't even know him!"

"Don't get angry—"

"And he didn't know me! Why would *he* try to kill *me*, if someone hadn't told him—"

"STOP!" It was a sharp, sudden burst of temper, a kind I'd never seen from her. And one that reminded me of her father.

Just like him, she quickly reeled it back in. When she spoke again, it was practically in a whisper.

"Let's not talk about it. We're not going to convince each other of anything. And I believe you. I'm sure Birch attacked you first. But I also know, in a million years, Daddy wouldn't have ordered him to do that. Somehow there's been a terrible misunderstanding. And I'll get it worked out. I'll fix it, I promise. I'll make it right between you and Daddy."

There was no point in arguing. Like she'd said, we weren't going to convince each other of anything. So I changed the subject.

"Why don't you think there's any treasure on Deadweather?"

"Because Daddy would have told me. And it's not part of the legend."

"What *is* the legend?"

"Of the Okalu?"

"What's the Okalu?"

"Seriously? You don't know any of it? With all the books you've read?"

"I never read one about that."

She sighed. "Right. Where to begin . . . ? A hundred years ago, when the Cartagers first came to the New Lands, there was a Native tribe that ruled the whole area. They called themselves Okalu. The People of the Sun.

"And they were quite advanced for savages. They had cities and writing, and supposedly they could do things we can't even imagine. Like setting things on fire just by looking at them. Some people think there was a trick to it, like a technology or something we don't know about.

"But others think, and the Okalu themselves said, that they had magic powers. Which they got from the sun—they said it was a living thing, a god in the sky that they called Ka. Every morning, the whole tribe would bow down to worship the sunrise and give it thanks. And every night, they'd do the same to the sunset, and ask it to come back again and renew their powers for another day.

"They had two main temples. One back on the mainland, that they used all year round, and one on Sunrise, on top of Mount Majestic, that they only went to once a year. I've been there. It's mostly ruins now, but looking at it you can imagine, back then, it must have been magnificent.

"No one lived on Sunrise. It was sacred ground, just used for the temple. And once a year, at the summer solstice, the whole tribe would cross the Blue Sea from the mainland and come there, and they'd have a huge ceremony, called the Marriage of the Sun.

"They'd take one girl from the tribe—the Princess of the

Dawn—and they'd cover her in gold and jewels and offer her up to the sunrise to be Ka's wife. And supposedly, she'd rise into the heavens, draped in her jewels. And never return."

Millicent smiled. "When I was little, I used to pretend I was Princess of the Dawn. And I lived in the sky, and ruled over everyone."

That wasn't hard to imagine.

"In exchange for his bride, Ka would grant his powers for one more year to the head of the tribe, the Fire King, who he blessed with a sacred object, the Fist of Ka, this sort of"—she gestured toward the knuckles of her hand—"giant ring or glove, or something. It's unclear exactly what it was. But when the Fire King wielded it, he had all the powers of Ka: to burn, to kill, even to heal.

"And then the Cartagers came. Just a few explorers at first, but eventually they sent a whole fleet of soldiers to conquer the mainland. And they had guns and horses, neither of which the Natives had ever seen, and the Okalu thought they were Thunder Gods, come to destroy the People of the Sun.

"At first, the Cartagers won every battle, and they got all the way to the gates of the main Okalu city, where the Temple of the Sunset was. But then the Fire King, Hutmatozal, raised the Fist of Ka against them, and supposedly, most of the Cartagers were struck dead in an instant. The only ones who survived were those who'd agreed to worship Ka themselves.

"What was left of the Cartagers retreated to their ships and were about to set sail when another tribe—the Moku, who'd been ruled by the Okalu forever and hated them—came to the Cartagers and offered to help. They told the Cartagers about the yearly pilgrimage for the Marriage of the Sun, which was just about to happen.

"So the Cartagers set a trap on Sunrise. They took the cannons from their ships and set them up on the harbor cliffs, where the fortresses are now. The Okalu arrived. And supposedly, because they thought the reason they'd nearly been wiped out by these Thunder Gods was because they hadn't been generous enough to Ka, they brought with them their entire treasury as the princess's dowry—every bit of gold and jewels the tribe had. The moment they landed, the Cartagers opened fire and slaughtered them all. And that was the end of the Okalu.

"But the Cartagers never found the dowry. It disappeared, along with the princess and the Fire King himself and the Fist of Ka that supposedly gave him his power. The legend is that they disappeared inside Mount Majestic. And someday, the Fire King will reappear, along with a new princess, and offer the treasure again as her dowry. And Ka will give his blessing, and the Okalu will rise again.

"That's the legend. And that's why, if the Fire King's treasure really exists, it must be on Sunrise somewhere."

It was a lot to absorb. And I didn't know what was real and what was just legend. Nobody did, from the sound of it.

"All I know," I said, "is there's something on Deadweather. And it's Native. And it was important enough to make my dad come to Sunrise and look for someone to help him understand it."

"That could be anything," she said. "But I wouldn't go thinking it's some huge treasure. Let alone the Fire King's."

I didn't know what to think. "Guess we'll find out."

"Guess we will." She stretched her legs out across the deck and leaned her head back against the seat, cocking it toward me. I wished the tiller weren't between us, because if it hadn't been, she might have rested her head on my shoulder.

"I missed you, Egg," she said.

She missed me. My heart soared.

"I missed you, too." I turned toward her, opening my mouth to spill out my guts, to tell her how much I loved her. But before I could form the words, she caught my eye and grinned, scrunching up her nose.

"It's no fun with just Daddy and Mother."

No fun?

I came back down to earth, slumping back in my seat. I'd read enough books about star-crossed lovers and doomed romances to know that when the person you love gets accused of murder and has to run away, there's a lot of ways you can react. Inconsolable weeping, suicidal hysteria, violent rage—even silent brooding's okay, as long as you're plotting something underneath the silence.

But saying it's "no fun"?

She might as well not have missed me at all.

I crossed my arms and went into a heavy sulk. But she didn't even notice. She was staring up at the dimming stars.

"Mother wants to send me away. Off to some boarding school on the Continent. Thinks I'll never be a proper lady if I stay on the island."

Fine. Go. See if I care.

"Daddy will never let her, though. He needs me too much. Hasn't got nearly enough levelheaded advisers. This whole *Earthly Pleasure* fiasco made that perfectly clear—"

Given everything that had happened, it was also perfectly clear that Millicent wasn't half the confidant of Roger Pembroke she thought she was. But the words were tumbling out of her so quickly that all I could do was shake my head and roll my eyes.

"—although Daddy seems strangely thrilled about it, like there's some kind of opportunity to be had. Which I can't fathom in the slightest—I mean, Rovia's finest families, robbed blind, stripped to their underwear, scared to death, and abandoned at sea? How on earth could that be a good thing? But Daddy thinks there's some angle to be played involving Cartage and the New Lands . . . It's a terrible waste, you know, the Cartagers control this whole continent full of resources, and they never *do* anything with it. Still, I can't for the life of me understand what that's got to do with a pirate attack. But that's the thing about Daddy—he's brilliant, always three steps ahead of everybody else, and he plays his cards *very* close to his chest—"

"Millicent."

"What?"

I was staring at the horizon. Straight ahead of us, the skyline was turning pink.

"Are you sure we're headed west?"

"Of course."

"Then why's the sun rising in front of us?"

She sat up straight, staring at the bleeding edge of dawn.

"That's the strangest thing . . . It's rising in the wrong place."

My jaw dropped. "Is *that* what you think?"

"What else could it be?"

"We're going the wrong way!"

"Impossible. I had us going west."

"What's more likely—the earth started turning in the other direction, or you went the wrong way?"

She let out a little huff of annoyance. "Whatever. We'll change course and it'll be fine."

BUT IT WASN'T FINE. We'd been under way well over an hour by then—long enough for Deadweather to be on the horizon if we'd been headed the right way. Instead, there was nothing but ocean in all directions.

We sailed west, the direction we should have gone in the first place, until Guts woke up and started an argument about whether it was the right way to fix the problem. All three of us had a different opinion, but no one knew for sure, and the maps we found in the cabin were useless because we didn't know where to locate ourselves on them. West of Sunrise? East? South? How far?

The sun climbed higher, searing our faces and making everyone sweat up a thirst. But we only had a skin of water, and it was two-thirds gone before we realized we'd need to make it last.

We took to the cabin to escape the sun, tying off the tiller and sitting in a tense silence while taking turns poking our heads out to see if anything—a spit of land, another ship—had appeared on the horizon.

Nothing did. Hours passed. We were well and truly lost, trying to make our way west, because at least that way we'd eventually run into the New Lands. And while they were mostly trackless jungle, sailing in any other direction could guarantee us a slow death on a thousand miles of open sea.

But the sun was high, and the wind kept shifting, and soon we weren't even sure which way was west.

Millicent and Guts picked at each other until a screaming fight broke out. After the yelling burned itself out, both of them refused to speak. Not that there was much to say. Just bitterness and fear. Fear that we wouldn't sight land or another ship, and fear that we would, only to find ourselves at the mercy of pirates—or, in my case, anyone who knew five thousand pieces of silver were theirs for delivering me to Roger Pembroke.

The sun started to drop, and the wind died down, leaving us nearly becalmed. My head hurt from lack of water, and I realized it had been almost two days since I'd slept.

So I wedged myself into the corner of one of the beds and fell into a heavy sleep, full of strange nightmares—of gods dressed as pirates, and savage battles, and pigs feasting on jewels that spilled from the guts of slaughtered Native children.

I woke up to the sound of Millicent's voice.

"We're saved!"

Guts had been asleep as well, and we both tumbled out of our beds and scrambled up to the cockpit.

It was well past dark, our sails were struck, and Millicent was waving the lantern over her head in the direction of a three-masted galleon, closing fast on us from less than a hundred yards ahead.

"She would have gone right past, but I signaled her, and she turned!" she said excitedly.

I stared at the ship, close enough now that I could make out the carved wooden figurehead on its bowsprit. On the Blue Sea, nearly every ship's figurehead is the same—a winged Goddess of the Sea, who's supposed to guarantee the crew divine protection. It's such a common superstition, and sailors take it so seriously, that I've heard of crews who refused to sail without one, or returned to port just to fix a broken goddess figurehead.

This figurehead wasn't a goddess. It was a skeleton, grotesque and distorted, the jaw of its skull wrenched open in a terrible shriek.

There was only one ship on the Blue Sea with a figurehead like that, and a captain and crew cocky enough to defy the superstition and sail behind it.

I opened my mouth to speak, but Guts beat me to it.

"Fool!" he yelled at Millicent. "It's Burn Healy!"

ON THE GRIFT

There was no mistaking the *Grift,* Burn Healy's flagship. And not just because of the skeleton figurehead, but because no one else on the Blue Sea commanded that kind of sleek, saddlebacked galleon. Only the Cartager Navy had the skills and the money to build such a ship, and only Burn Healy had the guts and the muscle to take it from them.

There was no point in trying to escape—not only was the ship almost on top of us, but I knew the only victims who survived an encounter with Healy were the ones who surrendered instantly and offered up everything they had as plunder.

What scared me most right then was that the only thing we had worth taking was Millicent.

I turned toward her, my brain churning to think of where on the little sailboat we might hide her away from a crew of rough men all but certain to treat her with unspeakable horror—and I couldn't believe my eyes. She was smiling.

More than smiling. She looked thrilled.

"Burn Healy? That's brilliant! He works for my father!"

Like it usually does when it gets a piece of news it can't handle, my brain shut down completely.

Guts was quicker to react. "Nuts to that! Healy don't work fer nobody!"

"My father's hardly nobody. And Healy owes him. He was supposed to guarantee the *Earthly Pleasure* safe passage, and he completely botched it! Daddy was only just meeting with him last night, and he was *very* cross before he left, so I'm sure Healy's gotten an earful, and he'll be desperate to get back in Daddy's good graces. All I've got to do is tell him who I am, and he'll fall all over himself—"

"MILLICENT!" I screamed. There were so many things wrong with what she was saying that little explosions kept going off in my head with every sentence, and I had to make her stop long enough to let the smoke clear.

"Savior's sake, Egg, there's no need to yell. I'm right here."

"Yer out of yer tiny little mind! They'll tear ye apart!" barked Guts, pointing his finger at the ship looming over us.

Millicent sighed and rolled her eyes. "I don't think you understand how the world works."

"I know 'ow it works with a crew o' pirates an' a pretty girl."

Millicent's jaw dropped. She looked genuinely shocked.

"Pardon me!? *No one* is going to lay a hand—"

CHUUUNK! A grappling hook landed on the foredeck,

sending up splinters of wood as it dug its teeth into our boat. A rope ladder snaked from the hook up onto the deck of the *Grift*.

"Evenin' to ye," called a mocking voice from somewhere above us. "Whyn't ye climb on up and say 'ello?"

Millicent took a step toward the rope ladder. "Just you watch—"

I grabbed her by the arm, stopping her in her tracks. My brain had settled enough by now to sort out exactly what I needed to warn her about.

"These are bad men," I said urgently. "They do awful things. And if they really do work for your father, they'll kill me."

"Not if I tell them—"

"You're not your father! You can't control them! They'll do what they want!"

She stared at me, her eyes slowly widening. For maybe the first time in her life, she looked unsure of herself.

"Come on, up the ladder with ye." The voice above us was getting impatient.

"They wouldn't dare," she whispered.

"They would," I assured her. "And worse."

"Wot's this?" called out the voice. "'Ave we got us a gimp?"

Guts was working his way up the ladder, and they'd noticed his missing hand. I saw him twitch at the insult, but he kept his mouth shut.

I looked back at Millicent. "Let me do the talking for us. Please. I've got an idea."

She nodded. I went up the ladder behind Guts. Waiting on deck for us was a pair of scruffy-looking men. The larger one was built like a brick. His companion had the narrow face and beady eyes of a weasel. Neither one had the flame tattoo of a Healy pirate on his neck, which made me wonder if I could have been wrong about the ship.

They smirked with amusement at Guts and me, but when Millicent came over the side in her nightgown, the smirks disappeared as their eyes locked onto her.

"'Ello, love. Wot a pleasure," croaked the brick.

I stepped in front of her, but he shoved me out of the way. "Mind yourself, boy."

"Sorry, it's just, my sister's very sick, and I wouldn't want it to spread."

"Sick 'ow?"

"She's got the jack." I didn't know what the jack was, but I'd heard pirates on Deadweather complain bitterly about getting it.

It worked, for a moment, anyway. The men drew back, and the weasel wrinkled his nose.

But then the brick grinned. "See about that." He was raising his hand to shove me out of the way again when a voice from behind stopped him.

"Who's this?"

A third pirate was approaching. This one had a flame tattoo, and it was clear from the way the others stepped aside at the sight of him that he was in charge.

"Dunno. Only just hauled 'em in," said the brick.

The new man stared at us with cold, unblinking eyes like a hawk's. Unlike his mates, he didn't look twice at Millicent.

"What d'you carry, and where you bound?"

Guts and Millicent both looked at me for an answer.

"Just ourselves," I said. "Bound for Deadweather, but we're lost." My throat was so dry that my voice cracked.

"What business have three whelps got on Deadweather?"

"Our father lives there," I said.

"Wot, in the Scratch? Ye sure 'e wants to be found?" asked the weasel, who'd been silent until now. The others laughed.

"Brothers and sister, are you?" the hawk asked.

We nodded, a little too eagerly.

"Don't look like it."

"Mummy had lots of friends, I'd say." The weasel cackled at his own joke.

"We don't want any trouble," I said. "There's not much on board, but it's yours."

"That goes without saying," said the hawk matter-of-factly. "Got any provisions?"

"Bit of food," I said. "Been out of water awhile now."

"Search the boat," the hawk told the weasel. Then he turned to the brick. "Give 'em water if they need it. Then watch 'em till the captain wakes."

The brick nodded. "Why don't I take 'em back down to—"

"Stay on the deck," said the hawk firmly. "Plain sight."

"C'mon, Spiggs—"

"Mind the Code."

The hawk turned and strode off. The brick and the weasel scowled at his back. Then the weasel went over the side, disappearing down the rope ladder to our boat.

The brick jerked his head toward the foredeck.

"This way, kiddies."

There was a barrel of water near the foremast, and the brick gave us a wooden cup to share. While we drank our thirst away, he disappeared for a few minutes, returning with three biscuits. They were hard as rocks, but they weren't mold-crusted or wormy, and even Millicent ate hers gratefully.

"Be mornin' soon," he said when we were finished. "Lie down. Get some sleep."

"That's all right," I said.

"I said lie down, boy." It wasn't a suggestion.

The three of us curled up on the deck, huddling together against the chill. No one slept, or even tried to. The brick kept his eyes fixed on Millicent, and I kept my eyes on him.

The weasel returned and lit a pipe. They passed it back and forth while they kept up a hushed conversation. When the pipe was finished, the weasel went to the deck rail and knocked out the ashes while the brick raised his head and addressed the rigging over our heads.

"Hssst! Hssst!"

A moment later, a man dropped down in front of us—he must have been on watch in a crow's nest somewhere above. He was long and skinny, with an odd wattle under his chin that made him look like a pelican. His eyebrows rose at the sight of Millicent.

The brick put a hand on the pelican's back and whispered in his ear. The pelican nodded and smiled.

My stomach started to churn. They were planning something.

The brick squatted in front of us and addressed Millicent.

"Got the jack, eh?" he asked her.

"Yes," she said in a halting voice.

"See 'bout that," he snorted.

He reached out to grab her hands. I moved to get between them, but someone pulled me back and shoved me down onto the deck from behind, trapping me on my side with my left arm pinned under my body and the full weight of my attacker on top of me.

I tried to squirm free, but there was a cold tickle at my throat, and I heard the raspy voice of the weasel in my ear.

"Feel the knife? Make a noise, and I'll kill you." I couldn't see him, but I could feel his breath on my face, rotten with the stink of decay.

The brick had both Millicent's wrists clamped together with a single massive hand. With his other hand, he pulled a rag from his pocket.

"Stop! My father's Roger Pembroke! He'll have you killed!"

The brick stuffed a rag into her mouth. She tried to scream, but it came out muffled and tiny.

"I'm yer father now, dearie," he said with an evil grin as he pulled a length of rope from his pocket.

As Millicent struggled, I caught a glimpse of Guts lying helplessly beyond them, wrapped up by the pelican with a knife to his own throat.

Millicent was desperate to get free, but the brick easily held her as he tied her hands together.

"'Urry up, Mike," growled the weasel. "Don't take all day."

I had to stop them. And I couldn't do it by myself. They had knives, I wasn't strong enough, it was impossible.

But they had to be keeping quiet for a reason. The hawk, or

someone, would step in if he knew what was happening. I just had to figure out how to raise an alarm.

I let my body go slack. "I've got gold," I whispered to the weasel. "I'll pay you if you make it stop."

He snorted. "Where is it?"

"In my pocket."

"Pull it out, then."

"I can't get it. My arm's pinned."

"Which pocket?"

"The left."

He must have brought his leg up, because I felt the iron hardness of his shin bone press down on my side. Then I heard a low, hollow *thock* near my ear—the sound of him setting his knife down on the deck.

As he started to roll me forward onto my stomach, I screamed at the top of my lungs and lashed out with every muscle in my body, twisting away from the weasel and heaving myself toward Millicent.

I got a hand on the brick's arm and tried to pull him off, but the weasel grabbed me and yanked me backward, driving me to the deck and landing hard on top of my back.

That knocked the wind out of me, and I couldn't scream anymore. The weasel flipped me over and pinned my arms with his knees, searching the deck for his knife as he snarled "I'll kill you, you——!"

There were feet pounding on the deck, coming toward us.

The weasel found his knife and drew himself up over me, raising the blade over his head to plunge it into my chest.

Then a boot kicked him in the side of the head, knocking him cold. His upper body fell away from me, and I squirmed out from under his legs. I was about to scramble to my feet when I felt another body on me.

It was Millicent, burrowing into my chest like a frightened child. As I put my arms around her, I saw Guts. His neck and collar were red with blood, and I realized he must have had his own struggle with the pelican.

The weasel was still unconscious a couple of feet from us, but the brick and the pelican were standing now, faced off against two other men: the hawk who'd quizzed us earlier and a big bear of a man with a Healy mark on his neck. They were shouting at each other, filling the air with an angry swirl of accusations, and the pelican was gesturing with his knife in a way that said he might use it.

Then there was a gunshot, and they all went quiet.

Everyone turned to see a man striding slowly toward us out of the predawn gloom. He was wide-shouldered and handsome, with a tangled thatch of curly hair. Even dressed as he was, in a heavy black greatcoat hanging open over a knee-length white nightshirt, bare calves rising out of a pair of weathered boots, he gave off an aura of commanding self-confidence. He could have walked up to us naked, holding a baby's rattle, and there would have been no question he was in charge.

Just now, though, he was holding a smoking pistol.

Burn Healy—I'd seen him before, back in Port Scratch, but never up close—came to a stop in front of us. As he looked over the group, he raised the barrel of the gun to his face, using it to give a thoughtful scratch to a spot on his stubbled cheek.

"So I've just been woken up," he said. "And I'm wondering why."

No one answered.

He looked down at us—Millicent, Guts, and me, all sitting on the deck. A few feet away from us, the weasel was moaning softly and clutching his head.

"Spiggs, who are these children?"

"They were adrift in a small boat," said the hawk-eyed man. "It's under tow off port. Told Mike to keep an eye on them till morning."

"Seems simple enough." Healy looked at the brick, who was hanging his head like an angry schoolboy.

"Nothin' 'appened, Cap," he muttered.

Healy pocketed his pistol and crouched down in front of me and Millicent, who was still trembling in my arms.

"Are you all right, young lady?" She raised her head from my chest to meet his eyes, staring at her with concern.

"I am now, sir," said Millicent in a shaky voice.

"What happened?"

"He attacked me." She nodded her head in the direction of the brick.

Healy straightened up. "What do you say to that, Mike?"

"Weren't going to hurt her none, Cap." The brick managed to smile, but it wasn't a laughing smile. It was a nervous one.

Healy took a few steps toward him. The brick stepped backward, trying to keep his distance.

"How long you been with us? Three weeks? A month?"

"'Bout that." Healy kept backing him up until the brick ran into the deck rail and had to stop.

"Long enough to know the Code. What's it say?" Healy closed

the distance, leaving their faces just half a foot apart. The brick had two inches of height and at least fifty pounds on Healy, but he seemed to be shrinking under the captain's steady stare.

"Every man his master." The brick's voice was so quiet I could barely hear him.

"Not the relevant part, unfortunately."

Without taking his eyes off the brick, Healy called over his shoulder. "Spiggs! What's the Code say about children?"

"Treated with mercy in every respect," Spiggs answered.

"In every respect," Healy echoed.

"Hardly kids, these—look at 'em! The whelps may be 'alf grown, but the girl's nearly—"

"Spiggs?" Healy called out again, interrupting the brick. "Are these children?"

"Certainly seem to be, sir."

"I'm forced to agree." Healy's voice was mild, and I couldn't see his face from where I was sitting. But there must have been something terrifying in his look, because the brick was turning pale, and his voice was pleading.

"Just a bit o' fun, Cap'n. That's all."

Healy nodded. "I'm certainly sympathetic to that. I mean, the days are long, the work is hard. And fun *is* fun . . ."

"Yeh!" The brick was nodding, too, a little hope creeping into his fearful look.

"But rules are rules."

In one quick, violent motion, Healy lifted the larger man off his feet and threw him over the side of the ship.

Then he turned on his heel, so quickly he was two steps back to us by the time we heard the splash.

The weasel had staggered to his feet by now, and he and the pelican were both white with fear. Healy barely glanced at them.

"Go below and mop the decks until you're told to stop."

They were off and running before he'd even finished the sentence.

Then he turned to us. "Please, children, stand up."

We stood. He looked at each of us in turn, his eyes grim with concern.

"I apologize for your treatment. It won't happen again."

His eyes met mine last, started to move on, then went back to me, his eyebrows bunching together slightly, as if he'd just recognized my face.

"What's your destination?"

Fear started to creep through me, and for a moment I wondered if I should lie to him.

"Deadweather Island," I said.

He turned to Spiggs.

"Chart a course for Deadweather. Need to replace those three, anyway. Fire the other two without share. If they complain, shoot them in the head."

"Yes, sir."

"And make these children comfortable. See about cleaning that boy's wound," he said, motioning in the direction of the cut on Guts's neck. "And for Savior's sake, dress her in something that's not a nightgown."

"Right away."

I was beginning to think his second look at me hadn't meant anything after all when Healy turned back to me.

"You're Hoke Masterson's boy, aren't you?"

Hearing my father's name was such a surprise that it took a moment before I understood the question. Finally, I nodded.

"Come with me."

He turned and strode off toward the quarterdeck. I looked at Millicent and Guts. They looked as bewildered as I was.

I followed Healy. It wasn't like I had a choice.

HIS CABIN WAS CLEAN and comfortable, but with none of the rich furnishings and velvet cushions I'd seen in the cabin on the *Earthly Pleasure*.

He lit a pair of lanterns and motioned for me to sit in a straight-backed wooden chair at a square table in the middle of the room. I did as I was told, staring across the table at a writing desk against the far wall while Healy disappeared over my shoulder, where the bed was. When he came back around, he was fully dressed. He took a seat at the table across from me.

"I heard about your father. Sorry for your loss."

"Thank you," I said, not sure if it was the right thing to say, and wondering how he could have known about my father.

"Now, then . . ." He sat back, stretching out in his chair and yawning. Then he settled his gaze on me. His eyes were a bright blue flecked with gray, and even with the whites veiny and the lids swollen from sleep, they drilled right through me.

I could understand why the brick had seemed to shrink under his stare.

"By strange coincidence, I've just come from a meeting with a very powerful man. And your name came up."

As my heart began to race with fear, he reached back behind him and plucked a piece of stiff paper from his desk. He studied it with a frown.

"Do you know what this man asked me to do if I saw you?"

He slid the paper across the table to me. I didn't have to look at it to know what it was.

"He asked me to kill you."

I didn't know where to put my eyes—on the wanted poster with my face looking up at me, or on the pirate captain staring at me from the other side of the table.

I settled for looking at my hands. I wondered if I could ask him to shoot me instead of throwing me overboard. It'd be over faster that way.

"Don't worry. I'm not going to."

I looked up. There was a hint of a smile at the corners of his mouth.

"I do a volume business. Five thousand silver's not enough to get me out of bed. Can't say the same for most men, though. And hats off to you." He tapped the wanted poster with his finger. "Murderer or not, that's quite a price for a fruit picker's boy. Why is that? Is it the company you keep? Or is it something else?"

I stared at my hands again. I didn't want to lie to him, but if I told him about the treasure, I was sure he'd try to take it, and that was the last thing I needed.

"Come now, son. What is it that makes you so important to Roger Pembroke?"

The silence was unbearable. I had to fill it with something.

"It's . . . complicated."

He laughed out loud. "Funny, that's exactly what he said." Healy stood up. "Leave it be, then. If I didn't make him explain, why should you have to?"

He made a casual nod toward the door. The conversation was over. I stood up and gave him an awkward sort of bow.

"Thank you, sir."

"Nothing to it."

I had my hand on the door when he called to me.

"A bit of advice—"

"Yes?"

"Roger Pembroke's not a man who gives up easily. If I were you, and he was that bent on killing me . . . I'd think seriously about killing him first."

My face must have given away my reaction, because he gave me a grim smile.

"Might be unpleasant, but it beats the alternative. Safe travels."

CHAPTER 16

HOME

I found Guts and Millicent back on the foredeck, trying to stay out of the way of the crewmen who were darting about the rigging, groggy and surly after being woken up to change course for Deadweather. Guts had a fresh white bandage over the cut on his throat, and Millicent was dressed as a boy, in long pants and a striped shirt that were both much too big. Her thick mane of hair had disappeared inside a shapeless cap.

"Wot happened?" Guts wanted to know.

"Your father told him to kill me," I said, looking at Millicent. She looked away.

"Why didn't he?" Guts asked.

"I don't know."

"Don't make sense. He's Burn — Healy!" Guts exclaimed, giving Healy a shockingly foul middle name. "Why's he bein' so . . ."

"Friendly?"

"Yeah! Don't figure."

I shrugged. It was hard to make sense of it, but there wasn't much point in wondering.

Guts looked around at the murderous-looking crew, all hard at work, and shook his head admiringly. "Say this, his lot's got discipline. Ripper Jones don't get this kind o' hop from his men 'less there's a prize on the horizon."

I watched the crew for a moment. Guts was right. Even half awake and grumpy, they all moved with a remarkable smoothness and efficiency. There was hardly a wasted motion among them, especially compared to the drunken chaos around Ripper Jones, and seeing them in action made me realize why Dad had always hired Healy men when he had a choice.

That got me thinking about Dad, and I was starting to get a heavy, sick feeling in the pit of my stomach when Millicent's arm brushed against mine. She'd been standing right next to me, but she was so quiet I'd almost forgotten she was there.

"Are you all right?" I asked.

"These clothes smell horrid," she said sullenly. "And I look dreadful, don't I?"

"No," I said, shaking my head. And I meant it. Gathering up her hair had uncovered her slender, delicate neck, and it was impossible to hide the sharp curve of her cheekbones, or the sleek line of her jaw, or—

"Come on! I look like some putrid cabin boy."

"'At's the point, stupid!" said Guts.

"Don't yell at me," she said quietly. It was a very not-Millicent reaction, small and defensive instead of strong and confident.

She was like that for the rest of our time on the *Grift*—drawn in, timid, constantly on my arm and never letting me get too far away from her.

And this was the strange thing: after all my fantasies about being a hero to her—about saving her from pirates, or burning buildings, or her evil father—I finally *had* saved her, and from actual pirates. Or at least helped save her, even if all I did was yell very loud and almost get myself killed.

And she was acting just like she had in my dreams—meek and grateful, cuddling up against me like a damsel saved from distress.

And I will say the cuddling-up part was sort of wonderful, even though she was dressed as a boy, and kind of a smelly one at that, and Guts was with us, and we were surrounded by pirates.

But mostly it was scary and unsettling.

Because Millicent had always been confident and fearless and all-knowing, and even though sometimes that could be really annoying—like when she blamed the sun for rising in the wrong place—it was also a comfort. She seemed invincible, like nothing could touch her. And being with her felt like sailing behind one of those Goddess of the Sea figureheads—stick with her, and I'd be invincible, too.

I'd spent the last I don't know how many days being scared out of my wits at every turn, and when she first climbed on the boat with me and Guts, cocky enough to set sail over a pirate-infested sea in her nightgown, a part of me thought, *Thank the Savior. Now we'll be okay.* For a while at least, she'd taken my fear away.

Now it was obvious, to both of us, that she wasn't invincible. We might still be okay, but we might not.

Which meant there was no getting rid of my fear. Whatever happened, I was going to have to carry it with me.

SOMETIME AROUND MIDDAY, the wind died, the *Grift*'s sails went slack, and a hot, thick blanket of muggy air fell on our heads.

"Ugh! What *is* that? The air's turned to soup!" Millicent was pulling at her clothes, which like everyone else's were starting to stick to her body with sweat.

I couldn't help smiling. It was unpleasant, but in such a familiar way that I instantly felt at home.

"Why do you think they call it Deadweather?"

"Didn't know it was so literal."

"There she is," said Guts, pointing to the horizon.

I never would have thought I'd be glad to see that sunken, rotting island emerge from the haze. But I was more than glad. I was finally going home again.

The only problem was I didn't know what, or who, I'd find there. Had Pembroke gotten there first? Had he sent others for him? Had they already found the treasure?

Was there even a treasure?

The tide was out when we reached the mouth of the harbor, and the *Grift* dropped anchor to wait until it came in again and she could dock. Rather than wait with it, the three of us got back into the little sailboat, dug the grappling hook out of the deck, and were preparing to row our way in when Burn Healy popped into view, calling down to us from the *Grift*.

"When you tie up, find a wharf rat. Tell him that's my boat and he needs to watch it for me. Otherwise, they'll steal it before you're ten yards off the dock. And don't spend long in town. They'll figure out soon enough she's not a boy."

As we rowed away toward the shore, Guts shook his head again in amazement.

"Burn — Healy. Maybe he's gone soft."

"We did watch him kill a man."

"True."

"Daddy's certainly never going to hire him again," said Millicent.

"Why not?" I asked.

"Doesn't do his job! He couldn't keep the *Earthly Pleasure* safe. And he didn't kill you like he was supposed to."

She grinned at me. I smiled back, not because I liked it, but because it was the kind of wicked joke only a fearless Millicent would make, and I was glad to have her back.

We tied up on the dock between two barnacle-crusted pirate ships, *Blood Lust* and the *Sea Goblin*. Several of their crewmen leered at us with interest from the decks above. Just down the dock, a dirty man in a three-cornered hat with a scorched hole where one corner used to be lounged against a piling, a bottle of rum between his legs.

I called out to him, hoping I was loud enough to be heard on the other ships.

"Excuse me! Could you keep an eye on this boat? It's Burn Healy's," I said, jerking my thumb at the outline of the *Grift* on the horizon.

The dirty man looked amused until he saw the *Grift* in the distance. Then he looked worried. He nodded quickly.

"I'm yer man."

"Thanks much."

We left the dock and started up the main street. Millicent put her hand to her face.

"Savior's sake! What's that smell?"

"It's a combination of things," I said. "Watch where you step."

There was a baker at the edge of town, and we stopped in there because he knew my family and I figured I could get credit for a few loaves of bread.

He was missing an eye, but the other one widened in surprise at the sight of me.

"Thought ye were dead," he said. "That's what the fat man said."

"What fat man?"

"Y'know, whatsisname. Yer guv'nor."

Percy. For a moment, I hoped—unreasonably, I knew—that he'd only come back to fetch his books.

"How long has he been here?"

"Showed up 'bout a week ago. Brought thirty soldiers with 'im. Marched 'em right up the mountain behind a wagonload of shovels."

My blood went cold. "Thirty soldiers?"

The baker smiled.

"Don't worry. Most of 'em left. Ripper Jones plucked a passenger ship 'bout a day out of Sunrise. Soldiers got called back to make the richies feel safe. Word is, Healy's got himself involved, and there's war brewin' 'tween him and Jones over it. Bad for us all if it washes up on shore."

"You said most of the soldiers left?"

"Yeh. But not all."

"How many are still up there?"

"Dunno. 'Alf dozen?"

I nodded. Half a dozen was bad, but it was better than thirty. "Can I get three loaves on credit, please?"

"Depends. Those soldiers lookin' for ye?"

"Not fer long," growled Guts.

The baker laughed. "Points for spunk," he said, taking three loaves from his shelf and handing them to us.

"Yer dad back, too? Brother an' sister?"

"No," I said. "They're dead."

"Ye were, too, up till a minute ago." He patted me on the back as he walked us to the door. "Try to stay alive—ye owe me ten."

"Ten?"

"Fat man paid on credit, too."

THE BREAD WAS just half a day old and still soft inside. We ate it as we walked up the familiar rutted road through the muggy half jungle. Along the way, I kept my ears alert for the sound of anyone coming down the mountain from the other direction. I didn't know what to do about Percy and the soldiers, and I sure didn't want to run into them on the road.

Millicent's mood had improved since we'd left Port Scratch and she was able to shed her cabin boy clothes. She loped along, swinging her arms in the confident way she had, occasionally darting over to the side of the road to investigate the strange cries of one of the forest birds.

Guts carried his knife in his hand as he walked. "'Oo's this fat man?" he asked.

"My old tutor," I said.

"Any chance he's on yer side?"

"Not much," I said.

"'Ave to kill him, then. What's his weakness?"

"He's fat, lazy, and stupid."

"Then how'd he get thirty soldiers to follow him?" Millicent asked.

The answer was so obvious it made me angry. "Because he's working for your father!"

"You don't know that," she said stubbornly.

"Savior's sake, Millicent!"

"Thought we been over this," said Guts.

"Your father's trying to kill me—"

"Only because you killed Birch, and Daddy's loyal to—"

"No, because there's something up there that he wants!" I pointed up the mountain. "Why can't you see that?"

"Because he would have told me! It's too big! And that would mean that he . . ." Her voice trailed off for a moment, her eyebrows knitted together in a frown. "If what you think happened is true, everything I know about my father is wrong. And it's not."

I turned back up the road. There was no point in arguing.

"Come on. It won't be long now."

I LED THEM OFF the road just below the lower orchard, hoping to keep out of sight until I found a friendly field pirate who could tell me what was going on. I wasn't sure how many of them would be on my side—they might have worked for Dad, but they weren't exactly devoted to him, and anyway they were pirates, and in it for themselves. I figured I could count on at least a few them, though. For one thing, they couldn't be too thrilled about sharing the plantation with a bunch of Rovian soldiers.

But I couldn't find a soul. The orchard was empty and silent. Big, squat cargo crates stood unattended in the middle of the rows, half full of ugly fruit and abandoned in mid-harvest.

We slipped through the trees, stopping at every row to search for signs of life. There was no one, and the eerie emptiness of it made my stomach tighten.

I stopped at one of the crates and picked up a fruit.

"Anybody want one?"

Millicent and Guts both joined me, peeling away the loose, wrinkled skin and tearing out the thick sections of citrus.

"It's not as bad as I thought," said Millicent through a mouthful.

I ate three. The others stopped at one and waited impatiently for me. When I couldn't put it off any longer, I led them up toward the house, on a roundabout path that took us past the stable. There were four horses in the outside pen that I didn't recognize, along with a large wagon that must have been the one the baker told us about. But there were still no people.

We climbed the hill a little farther, and the main house came into view. The roof looked even more saggy than ever, but the big porch and the shark's jaws over the door were exactly the same, and my throat got lumpy to see the place again.

I led Guts and Millicent around to the side door, and we went inside. The smell was instantly familiar. Even before we'd crossed the hallway to the kitchen, I knew I'd find Quint the house pirate in there, cooking a stew over the big black stove.

He was in his usual spot, perched on top of the counter, his head not much higher than the top of the pot, stirring the stew with a long wooden spoon half as tall as he was.

"Quint?"

He nearly fell off the counter at the sight of me. Then he broke into a wide smile, dropped the spoon, and vaulted onto the floor, waddling over to me on his stumps.

"Egbert! Give us a hug, boy!"

I fell to my knees and hugged him tightly.

"Percy said ye was dead!"

"He lied."

"Shoulda known. Pink-fingered crapsack." Then he waddled backward a bit and looked up at Millicent. And smiled maybe a bit too keenly.

"Hel-lo! 'Oo are *you*?"

Millicent wrinkled her nose and crossed her arms in front of her.

"This is Millicent and Guts. They're friends of mine. And this is Quint," I told them as Quint stepped to the butcher's table, reached up with his arms, and swung himself onto the tabletop, putting himself more or less at eye level with us.

"So where ye been, boy? What 'appened?"

"You first. Where are the soldiers?"

"Diggin' up the mountain, 'long with the others. Lookin' for the Fire King's voodoo."

"Did they force the field pirates to help?"

"Didn't have to force nobody. Percy said the new owner'd share whatever we found with us."

"What new owner?"

"Man who adopted ye. It's on the papers."

"What papers?"

"Over 'ere."

Quint vaulted to the floor again, and we followed him as he

waddled into the den, where Dad kept all the plantation paper-work in big, messy piles on a long table.

He hopped onto a chair and pulled several documents from one of the piles, handing them to me one by one as he read their titles.

"'Certificates o' Death'—probably need to rewrite yers, seeing's how yer not dead—'Certificate o' Legal Adoption' . . . 'Transfer o' Title' . . ."

I'd seen the adoption one before, although now it contained a signature forged as mine, right next to Pembroke's. The death certificates were made out for each of our family members and signed by Archibald the attorney.

The transfer of title to our plantation was signed by Roger Pembroke as the recipient.

I handed them all to Millicent without a word. As she looked at them, her face grew pale.

"Think I need to sit down," she whispered.

"'Ere, luv." Quint hopped to the floor, and she sank into the chair, still staring at the documents.

"Where on the mountain are they digging?"

"Upper orchard, 'tween 'ere an' Rottin' Bluff. That's where yer dad was 'eaded when he found whatever it was set him off. Stands to reason it's the place to look. Course, nobody's had much luck."

"Do the soldiers carry their guns with them?"

"Not lately," said Quint. "They're in the next room."

I couldn't believe our luck—five rifles were lined up in a neat row against the wall by the front door. While Guts and I loaded two of them, I gave Quint a quick summary of the past month.

By the time I was halfway through, he'd started loading a rifle of his own.

We gathered up extra powder and shot, then hid the remaining two rifles behind a cabinet in the den. Millicent was still sitting there, staring into space.

"We're going up the hill. Do you want to come?" I asked.

She shook her head slowly.

"Men do awful things sometimes," I said. "All of them."

She didn't answer.

"We'll be back soon," I said, and we left her there.

WE STARTED UP the hill, through the upper orchard toward Rotting Bluff. I carried Quint's rifle for him so he could keep up with us by walking on his hands.

Within fifty feet of the house, the holes started to appear, in sizes ranging from a few spadefuls to gaping, ten-foot-wide excavations. The farther we climbed up the mountain, the more plentiful they were. Pretty soon, we began hearing scattered voices.

Then the field pirates started to appear, working alone and in small groups, digging here and there without any apparent strategy or direction. When they saw me, most of them gaped in surprise. A few smiled and waved.

All the way up the mountain, I could feel my courage growing. Holding a rifle in each hand helped, as did having Guts and Quint on either side of me. But so did the fact that these were my family's fields, and seeing them torn up so mindlessly was making me angry. I was going to find the men who had done this and throw them off my land. And it would be right and fair.

A few hundred yards below Rotting Bluff, we ran into Mung, who gurgled an incomprehensible greeting and hugged me so excitedly I almost shot him by accident.

Finally, he let me go and babbled something, a questioning look in his eye.

"I'll explain it later," I said. "Right now, we've got to get rid of Percy and those soldiers."

He nodded, then picked up his shovel and brandished it with a fierce look. I smiled and nodded back, a little lump rising in my throat. Like Quint, he was on my side, no questions asked.

By the time we got close to Rotting Bluff, a clutch of field pirates had abandoned their digging to follow us. Unlike Mung, I couldn't tell whether they were joining our march out of solidarity or because they smelled blood and wanted to watch it get spilled.

The trees were thinner at that point, and Rotting Bluff came into view when it was still forty yards away. It was unrecognizable—the rampart was still there, with its cannon pointed out over the cliff, but all the land around it had been dug out in a trench so wide that I was surprised the rampart hadn't broken off and fallen into the sea.

And they were still digging over at the base of one of the massive rocks near the cliff's edge—a cluster of pirates, five Rovian soldiers stripped down to their bare chests, and Percy, who wasn't actually digging so much as pretending to dig, leaning on his shovel as he wiped the sweat from his meaty forehead.

I gave Quint his rifle and trained mine on Percy. We were twenty yards away when the first soldier noticed us and called out to the others, who gradually turned in our direction.

Percy's jowls sagged at the sight of me.

"Egbert . . . so glad you're all right. Feared the worst—"

"Put down those shovels and get off my land," I said. We

stopped at the lip of the big trench, our guns pointed across the sunken no-man's-land at them.

"No need for that, boy—"

"Put them down and get off my land," I said again.

The soldiers looked at each other, not sure how seriously to take this.

"Put 'em down, or we'll kill ye, ye——," said Guts.

Percy was trying to smile, but it looked more like a grimace. "Let's us talk about this—"

"There's nothing to talk about. Put down the shovels and leave."

They didn't move.

"Do it!" barked Quint.

They still didn't move. The soldiers seemed to be waiting for a word from Percy, who was frozen in place.

"'Oo do I shoot first?" asked Guts loudly.

"Not yet!" I whispered to him. I was suddenly wishing I'd put a little more thought into strategizing. We had the guns, but even if you didn't count the pirates, there were twice as many of them as there were of us, and once we'd each fired, it would take more time to reload than it would for them to close the distance between us. And if it came to a fistfight, I didn't like our odds.

Then there were the pirates. I had no idea whose side they were on. From the looks on their faces, I don't think they knew, either. I could hear Mung growling supportively behind me, but he and Quint were the only ones I felt sure of one way or another.

"You," I said, pointing my gun at Percy, "and the five of you"—I waved the barrel at the soldiers—"need to get off my land. Or die."

I tried to sound calm and deadly, but I couldn't quite get the flutter out of my voice.

Percy set down his shovel and started down the far side of the trench, slowly moving toward me.

"Trouble is, boy," he said in a friendly voice—as friendly as he was capable of, anyway—"this isn't your land. It's your father's."

"My father's dead."

"Not your old father. Your new one."

"He's not my father!"

"Shoot 'im!" hissed Guts.

Percy was halfway across the no-man's-land, smiling up at me.

"Afraid he is. I've seen the papers."

"Lies on paper are still lies." My face was starting to burn hot, and the rifle was getting heavy. I was shifting its weight in my hands when I heard a *pooft* sound from off to my left.

Everyone startled, turning toward Guts, who was glaring at his smoking flintlock, which had been aimed at Percy when it misfired. Guts shook the rifle, bellowing angrily at it, and it suddenly discharged with a loud roar. The round kicked up a harmless cloud of dirt in the trench twenty feet from Percy.

As Guts cursed with frustration and dropped to his knees, frantically trying to reload, two of the soldiers took a step toward him, only to stop when Quint turned his own rifle in their direction.

With a nervous glance at Guts, Percy quickened his pace toward me, his voice growing urgent.

"Think, boy! Can't kill us all. Even if you do, more'll come. Hundreds! There's no stopping it."

He paused at the near end of the trench, just ten feet away from me. "Besides, you're too good a boy to shoot an unarmed man."

"Shoot 'im!" yelled Guts, twitching so angrily that he spilled half the black powder he was hurriedly shaking into his rifle's muzzle.

Percy started up the short slope toward me, close enough now that he'd be impossible to miss. My finger tightened on the trigger.

"Come any closer, and I'll shoot!" I yelled at him.

Percy stopped. Two more paces, and he'd be close enough to grab the barrel of the rifle.

"Would you, really? Shoot your old Percy? Unarmed, helpless as a dog? You're too good for that. You know your lessons. You know that's a sin."

"SHOOT 'IM!" screamed Guts, his rifle cradled in the crook of his elbow as he yanked out the ramrod with his good hand.

Percy looked at Guts and shook his head, his fleshy neck jiggling against his collar. "No. Egbert's a good boy. He'd never shoot an unarmed man."

He looked back at me. "Isn't that right?"

"I'll shoot you if I have to," I said. But I wasn't sure I believed it.

Percy didn't. He took another step toward me.

"DO IT!" screamed Guts. Out of the corner of my eye, I could see him drop the ramrod. Once he filled the pan with powder, he'd be ready to fire again.

My heart was pounding in my chest. I could feel my finger against the trigger, but I couldn't bring myself to pull it.

"I will!" I warned Percy through gritted teeth.

"You won't," said Percy softly, taking the final step, his hand reaching out for my rifle.

Then the gunshot was echoing off the rampart, and he was tumbling backward into the trench.

As Percy writhed in the dirt, crying out and clutching a

shoulder stained red with blood, I looked down at the gun in my hands. The flintlock was still poised over the pan. It hadn't gone off.

I looked at Guts to my left. He was still on his knees, holding the open powder flask over the pan as he stared past me, his mouth open in surprise.

I followed his gaze to my right, to the figure standing just behind Quint.

It was Millicent. She was holding a rifle.

She stepped forward and addressed the soldiers, her face cold with hate.

"Get off this land, or we'll kill you all."

CHAPTER 17

NIGHTFALL

After Millicent shot Percy, the soldiers put down their shovels and left in a hurry. We let them take their wagon and horses—Guts wanted to hang on to them, but it felt like stealing to do that, so we only kept the guns.

The sun was beginning to set as we watched them rattle down the hillside in the wagon, with Percy clutching a rag to his wounded shoulder and crying out in pain with every bump. Quint had gone back to finish his stew, and the field pirates had disappeared to their barracks for dinner, leaving Millicent, Guts, and me alone on the porch of the main house.

"Any chance that wound will kill him?" I asked.

"Not if it don't turn to cheese," said Guts.

"We can only hope," said Millicent darkly.

She was sitting on the porch steps, the rifle still in her hands. She held it by the barrel, digging the edge of its stock into the dirt as she brooded.

"Are you all right?" I asked her.

She looked up at me. Her eyes were still cold and hard. "He lied to me. About so many things."

"That's what men do."

"Not my father. Not to me."

She lifted her chin and stared at the reddening sky. "They'll be back, you know. Daddy won't wait. He'll come right away. With a hundred men, at least."

"We've got to find that treasure before they get here," I said.

"Say we do," said Guts. "They'll still come."

"But we won't have to be here," said Millicent. "We can run."

"I'm tired of running," I said.

Guts stared at me. "Gonna stay an' fight a hundred soldiers?"

"I don't know. Maybe."

"Nuts to that! Couldn't even shoot whatsisname. Standin' right in front o' ye."

I shook my head. "That's because it wasn't fair. He was unarmed."

"Won't have that problem again. Be a hundred of 'em next time. Then ye'll see what not fair is." Guts's whole face and shoulders twitched after he said it, like he was shuddering at the thought.

"You can't fight them with five guns," said Millicent.

"My father's got a hunting rifle."

"So you've got six? Oh, that changes *everything*."

"Plus a cannon," I said.

"Still not enough."

"And fifty pirates."

They were both quiet for a moment, thinking it over.

"Would they fight for you?" Millicent asked.

I stood up. "I don't know. Let's find out."

THE FIELD PIRATES had just sat down to their usual meal of slop when we entered the long, lamplit barracks. It was noisy with chatter, but as they realized we were there, the talking fell away. It was an unwritten rule that only the field pirates were allowed in the barracks—even Quint wasn't welcome in there—and a hundred unfriendly eyes glared at us.

Although it was more like eighty unfriendly eyes, because a lot of them weren't working with a full pair. And Mung actually seemed happy to see us.

"What can we do for ye?" asked Otto the foreman coldly. He'd been the foreman for years, because he was the smartest of the bunch, and because he'd beaten the last foreman to death with a brick.

"Need yer bottom wiped?" someone yelled at me from the crowd, to snorts of laughter.

"Soldiers are coming to take back this plantation," I said in as loud a voice as I could muster. "Will you help me fight them?"

There were a few more snorts of laughter. Mostly it was silent.

"Wot's in it fer us?" Otto asked.

"They're after a treasure," I said.

"That's hardly news, sonny."

"If we find it instead of them, we can all share it equally," I said.

Behind me, I heard Guts quietly curse. It must have occurred to him that he stood to keep a lot less than a third of the treasure if this deal held up.

"Same offer the soldiers made," said Otto. "Wot's the difference?"

"The difference is I'm not lying to you," I said.

"Not good enough, sonny," said Otto. "Best o' luck to ye."

He picked up his spoon and returned to his slop. The others followed, and the barracks quickly filled again with the clanking of spoons and the growling of voices.

I thought for a moment. If I didn't get them on our side, we were doomed—the best I could hope for would be to flee across the ocean and hope Roger Pembroke wouldn't send anyone to follow us. But that wasn't likely, especially if Millicent was with us.

It was going to be a long shot stopping him with this bunch, anyway. But Burn Healy's warning was fresh in my mind, and I felt sure if I ran away now, the odds of my killing Pembroke weren't going to get any better down the road.

So I had to convince them to help us, with whatever I had. And all I had, really, was one thing:

"What if I give you the plantation?"

The spoons stopped clanking.

"'Ow's that gonna work?"

"Same as the treasure," I said. "We'll all own it equally. Effective immediately."

There was a short silence, followed by a sudden burst of noise as fifty pirates all started talking to each other at once.

Otto stood up and pointed at the door. "You three wait outside. We gots to discuss this."

We didn't have to wait long in the moonlight outside the barracks—within a few minutes, the door burst open, and the whole crew ran past us for the orchard. A few held lanterns. The rest carried harvesting hooks.

Otto paused in front of me, his gray teeth glinting in the lanterns' light as he smiled.

"Got yerself a deal, sonny," he said. He held out his hand, and we shook on it.

"Where are they all going?" I asked.

He rubbed his neck, looking a little sheepish. "Bit of a crisis. Cargo ship's due into Port Scratch in three days. S'pposed to carry the early harvest to Pella Nonna. We been slacking off o' late, first 'cause yer dad was gone, then 'cause we was lookin' fer that treasure. But if we don't get the harvest in and loaded on that ship, likely as not, the plantation goes under."

"What does that mean?" I asked.

"Means the contract's busted, ship sails without us, fruit rots in the fields, an' we can't lay in stores. No food, no money . . . whole racket falls apart."

I was furious. "Why didn't you think about all that before a minute ago?!"

"Weren't our problem. Up 'til a minute ago, we just worked here."

I MANAGED TO CONVINCE Otto to let Stumpy the driver ride down to Port Scratch and let us know when Percy and the soldiers managed to set sail so we'd have some idea of how much time we had before the reinforcements returned from Sunrise.

Other than that, Otto insisted he couldn't spare any men to help look for the treasure in the morning. The pirates would only stop their frantic harvesting long enough to fight when the soldiers returned.

And that wasn't our only problem—none of them had guns (Dad had forbidden it, which if you think about it, was a pretty sensible policy), and there wasn't any money available to go to Port Scratch and buy some.

"There's got to be money somewhere," I pleaded with Quint when we got back to the house.

"Not till we sell the harvest. And most of that's pledged to provisions. Can't buy guns with it 'less yer not plannin' on eatin' again till spring. And this lot won't stand fer that."

"Didn't Dad keep any money in reserve?"

"Some, yeh."

"Where is it?"

"Sewn into his coat."

"Which coat?"

"The one he wore to Sunrise."

THERE WASN'T MUCH TO DO after that but go to bed and hope things looked a little less bleak in the morning. Millicent disappeared into Venus's bedroom upstairs, and Guts sacked out on Dad's bed, snoring almost as soon as he hit the mattress. I could have slept upstairs with them, in Adonis's room, but I wanted the comfort of being in my own bed for the first time in a month. So I retreated into my familiar little windowless box off the kitchen to lie in the darkness and worry about how I was going to come out of this mess alive.

The comfort was spoiled a bit by the fact that my bed smelled like a soldier, not to mention the fact that I'd just traded away my family's plantation for the allegiance of fifty crippled pirates who'd be useless against armed soldiers unless I could somehow find guns for them.

Then there was the treasure. Assuming it was there, I had no idea how to find it. Dad had stumbled upon it on his way up to clean the cannon, which meant it was somewhere between the house and Rotting Bluff. But Percy had known that, too. And even with upward of fifty men, all digging frantically for a week, he hadn't found a trace of it.

Although the more I thought about it, the more pointless all that digging seemed. Dad didn't have a shovel with him when he went to clean the cannon that morning. So why would anyone need to dig to uncover whatever he'd found?

It seemed utterly stupid, but then it was probably Percy's idea, and he'd never had much in the way of brains.

I could find it—I just had to be clever enough to think it through. To think like Dad.

What path did he take up the hill that morning? Straight up? Or something roundabout, like following the cliff's edge? That's a longer and harder climb, but there's a view of the ocean.

Is that thinking like Dad? Did he ever take the scenic route anywhere?

Not if he could help it. Dad didn't go places without a purpose. He'd—

I heard the creak of the wooden steps. Someone was coming downstairs. A moment later, there was a dull *thop,* followed by a barely audible *"mph!"* as whoever it was stubbed a toe on my door frame.

"Who is it?" They were only a few feet away, but without a lantern it was pitch-black, and I couldn't see a thing.

"Did I wake you?" asked Millicent.

"No."

"Can I stay down here for a bit? I can't sleep, and my bed smells like a soldier."

"Mine does too," I said.

"That's all right." I felt her bump into the side of the bed frame. "Is that you?"

"Yeah." I felt her weight push down on the thin straw mattress, and I wriggled to the far edge of the narrow bed to make room for her.

Her arm pressed down on mine, and something soft landed on my head. "I brought a pillow."

"Oh." I shifted my head over to make room for her pillow. My heart was beating fast, but my brain felt thick and slow. I wanted to say something clever, or charming, but I couldn't think of anything.

We were silent for a while. The part of her arm that was on top of mine felt warm and soft through my shirt, except for what must have been her shoulder blade, which was digging painfully into my upper arm. I wondered if I should roll onto my side, or if that would ruin everything.

"Your soldier doesn't stink as bad as mine did," she said. Then I felt her shift position, turning away from me, and I thought I'd ruined everything just by doing nothing.

"Give me your hand."

I raised my right hand, the one closest to her, and searched in the darkness until it grasped hers awkwardly.

"No, the other hand . . . now turn onto your side."

I did as I was told, turning toward her. She took my left hand

and pulled it across her like a blanket, tugging me closer until my chest was against her back and her hair tickled my nose. I could feel the gentle rise and fall of her body as she breathed.

It was wonderful. I just hoped she couldn't feel my heart thumping through my chest.

"I'm sorry for not believing you," she whispered.

"That's all right," I said.

"I can't ever go back," she said. "Not after what he did."

"You can stay here."

She sighed. "No. Neither of us can. They'll overrun this place. Even with the pirates on your side. Let's just run."

I thought about it. What I wanted, more than anything else in the world, was to stay with her like this, lying quietly, with my arm around her, forever.

But as long as he was alive, Roger Pembroke wasn't going to let that happen.

"Are you sure your father will come here with them?"

"Definitely."

"Then we've got to stay."

"Why?"

Because I have to try and kill him.

"Because I can't let him take that treasure."

"If there *is* a treasure . . . we'll find it in the morning," she said. "Together. Then we'll run away with it."

Her hand found mine again in the dark and squeezed it tightly.

"All right?"

"I'll think about it," I said.

WE SLEPT LIKE THAT all night. In the morning, we stepped into the kitchen to find Guts and Quint there. Quint was making biscuits, and Guts was watching him.

"I thought I might wash up a bit," Millicent said. "How exactly does one do that around here?"

"There's a fresh bucket of well water in the room with the tub," said Quint, gesturing down the hall with a wooden spoon.

"Thanks so much," Millicent said, and sauntered off down the hallway. As soon as she was out of earshot, Guts turned to me with a skeptical look.

"Why's she in yer room?"

"Didn't want to be alone, I guess."

He kept looking skeptical.

"What? I didn't even kiss her!"

"Why not?" asked Quint.

"I don't know," I said.

But I did know. Because even after all that, I still couldn't tell where I stood with her. And I didn't want to make a hash of things by going and making a fool of myself.

Guts narrowed his eyes. "Take care round 'er. She's witchy."

"Shut up," I said.

Millicent returned, her face bright and damp.

"Does your sister have any clothes I could wear? This nightgown's getting a bit iffy."

"Yeah. Upstairs in her room."

"Biscuits are ready," Quint said, heaving a hot iron tray onto the countertop. They were like all his biscuits—chewy for the five minutes until they cooled and hard as rocks after that.

"Oughta fetch that twelve-pounder from the cliff," Guts said through a mouthful of biscuit. "Been thinkin'—set 'er on the porch, get a clean shot down the road. Can move it quick if they flank us, too."

Millicent looked at me. "Is all that really necessary?"

"We'll do it later," I told Guts. "First let's find the treasure."

BUT WE COULDN'T FIND IT. I wandered the hillside with Guts and Millicent all morning and half the afternoon, trying every imaginable route between Rotting Bluff and the house, racking my brain for some clue to what my Dad might have been thinking or doing that morning that would have led him to a hidden treasure.

In the end, all I got for my trouble was the realization that I didn't really know much about my father.

I mean, I knew the obvious things. Like how he never smiled. And he never ate vegetables.

He liked pork better than chicken.

He smacked his kids when we broke the rules, although somehow he ended up smacking me more often than Venus or Adonis, even though I broke fewer rules than either of them.

He didn't care for talk of religion or the Savior—but sometimes when he thought no one was watching, he'd pray on his knees with his hands clasped over his bed.

When there was rum in the house, he'd drink it. And afterward, he'd sing to himself in a low, melancholy voice.

But the important stuff—what went on in his head, how he thought about his life or any of us who were in it—was all a mystery. Even the plantation—he gave his whole life to it, working his fingers to the bone every day from sunrise to sundown, but the why of it, whether he cared about it for its own sake, or whether it was just a way to put food on the table, that he would've abandoned in a heartbeat if he knew an easier way . . . I had no idea. No one did.

The one thing I thought I knew for sure was that he didn't trust anyone, ever. But then he'd gone and gotten into Roger Pembroke's balloon when he'd only just met the man. So even that was wrong, I guess.

As the hours dragged by and we trudged back and forth through the dug-up orchards, I got more and more frustrated, and then angry, and finally hollowed-out and despairing.

Maybe there wasn't any treasure after all. Maybe we were all going to get killed for a few acres of ugly fruit trees and some piles of dirt.

Maybe we should do what Millicent wanted and run.

But there was nowhere to run. If we stayed on Deadweather, they'd hunt us down. If we left in Millicent's sailboat, we'd only get lost at sea. And if we could somehow find a ship and depart before the soldiers arrived . . . they'd still hunt us down. And anyway, if we went to sea, how could I protect Millicent? What had happened on the *Grift* would happen again, only Healy wouldn't be there to stop it.

So we couldn't run.

But we couldn't stay, either, because Millicent was right—we couldn't beat them. Not with six rifles and a cannon.

We were doomed either way, but I didn't know what to do, so I just kept wandering the hillside looking for the treasure, long after I'd given up on finding it.

When Guts finally grumbled that it was getting late and we needed to bring the cannon down to the house, it was almost a relief to quit looking.

Millicent begged us not to give up, and as I followed Guts to the cliff to get the cannon, she stormed off toward the house in a sulk.

It was tough work dragging the cannon through the trench that Percy and his men had dug around Rotting Bluff, because the wooden wheels couldn't get traction in the loose earth. But once we got it up the far side, gravity took over, and pretty soon the challenge wasn't getting the cannon to roll but keeping it from barreling out of control down the hill.

By dinnertime, we'd maneuvered it into position on the front porch and were filling empty fruit bushels with dug-up dirt from the hillside for use as fortifications. Two full bushels, stacked on top of each other behind the porch rail, were the perfect size to shoot over from a crouch. I didn't know how well they'd stop a bullet, but it wasn't like we had any other options.

Millicent eventually came out of the house and helped us, scowling the whole time. We had the front of the porch pretty well socked in when we heard wagon wheels on the road.

Guts and I went for our guns, and Millicent grudgingly retreated inside. But it turned out to be Stumpy, in a small open wagon pulled by the horse he'd ridden down the hill.

He reined the horse to a stop in front of the house and grinned at me from the seat.

"Took 'em till noon to hire a boat. Then the tide was out. Didn't push off till four. Not likely 'ey'll be back before morning."

"Where'd you get the wagon?"

"Present for ye. 'Long with the cargo. Think ye'll like it."

Guts and I climbed into the wagon bed. Inside were half a dozen long crates. I opened the top one.

It was filled with rifles—at least two dozen of them, Cartager made and so new the metal plates around the flintlocks shone like mirrors. Guts made a noise that was somewhere between a laugh and a shout.

"There's pistols and grenades as well," said Stumpy. "And paper cartridges—sight faster to load'n loose powder and shot."

I couldn't believe my eyes. "Where did it all come from?"

"'Ang on—came with a note." Stumpy pulled a small card from his pocket, drew himself up to his full height of four feet, and cleared his throat with a big show of formality.

"A-ha-hem . . ." He held the card in front of his nose, with a snooty look like a royal attendant. Then he chuckled as he handed over the card with a shrug.

"Pullin' yer leg. Can't read a word."

I looked at the card in my hands. It was a heavy, fine ivory stock. Written on it, in an elegant hand, were the words:

Good luck. You'll need it.
Burn Healy

I read it out loud to Guts. He shook his head slowly. "Burn — Healy. Why?"

I was wondering the same thing. "Maybe he just doesn't like Pembroke."

"Maybe." Guts pulled a grenade from one of the crates and

held it up for me to admire. "Changes the odds, don't it? 'Ow many soldiers ye think one o' these kills?"

"A lot." I was smiling from ear to ear when I realized Millicent was glaring at us from the porch steps.

I nudged Guts to put the grenade away. "Let's get this unloaded."

We stored the crates just inside the house, where Quint cooed over them excitedly. As we emptied the wagon, Stumpy fed and watered his horse so he could make the trip back down the hill to watch for the soldiers' return.

After he left, Guts wanted to test the cannon to fix its range on the spot where the road first emerged through the trees. I was about to help him load a cannonball when Millicent pulled me aside.

"Can I speak with you privately?" she asked.

"Sure."

Guts shook his head in disapproval as I followed her into the yard, far enough that we wouldn't be heard.

Millicent fixed me with a worried stare. "This is madness! A handful of guns doesn't change anything."

"It's a lot more than a handful," I said.

"All it means is more people die! You can't win, Egg! We've got to run."

"Millicent, I have to—"

"No, you don't! You're just being stupid! There's still time to get out of here."

"What the——?!" I turned to see Guts pull his arm out of the cannon barrel with a loud curse and a twitch of distaste. He swiveled his head to yell at me. "Thought yer dad cleaned it!"

"He did."

"Nuts to that! Nest o' rats been livin' in 'ere. Look—" He stuck his knife deep into the barrel, scraped around, and pulled it out to reveal a knotted clump of filth, straw, and animal hair.

"He must have found the treasure before he got to the cannon," I said.

Guts snorted. "Look at these droppin's. Dry as dust."

"So?"

"'Asn't been cleaned in years."

"That's impossible," I said. "My father cleaned it all the time."

"Ever see 'im do it?" Guts asked.

"No. He'd go alone. Take the brush and bucket, and go up the hill . . ."

My voice trailed off. The three of us stared at each other, all coming to the same realization.

"Why ELSE would he go up that hill?"

The answer came so quickly I couldn't believe I hadn't thought of it before. I started up the hillside.

"Follow me," I said. "And hurry. There's not much daylight left, and it's all the way around the mountain."

"What is?"

"My mother's grave."

CHAPTER 18

THE GRAVE

I led Millicent and Guts up the mountain, half a mile past Rotting Bluff to where a wide stretch of mossy scrub separated the tree line from the black crumble of the lava fields. From there, we turned and skirted around the western slope of the volcano to the only field of wildflowers on the entire island.

My mother was buried in the middle of it. Dad took us there twice a year to pay our respects, but I realized now that he must have gone alone much more often, which explained why, even though the surrounding hillside buckled and cracked with every new earthquake or sputtery cough of lava, the grave always looked clean and undisturbed, its lonely wooden cross standing perfectly straight at the top of a low rectangular border of white stones.

The sun was almost touching the horizon when we got there. I stood at the foot of the grave, the sun at my back, and looked around. Stretched out above me was the long slope of the volcano, a glum expanse of rough black rock that tapered as it rose up to the rim, where a few thin curls of smoke wafted into the sky.

It looked just like it always had, a colorless wasteland . . . except for one spot, off to the right a hundred yards above the grave, where a section of rock had crumbled away to reveal a sharp seam of nearly white granite, jutting six feet straight up out of the earth like the blade of a knife. I'd never seen it before, but it must have been there all along, buried under a frozen crust of black lava, and had reemerged after some minor earthquake shook its cover loose.

I started toward it, and Millicent and Guts followed. As we approached from the side, an opening came into view. It was a two-foot-wide crack down the middle of the granite face. The sunlight was hitting it at an angle that revealed the beginnings of a cave inside.

Guts nudged me. "You first."

I squeezed sideways through the opening, stepping to one side once I'd entered so the others could come in behind me.

We were in a wide, low-ceilinged chamber, twenty feet across and half as deep, and not quite tall enough for me to stand up straight inside it.

At first, it seemed barren. But once my eyes got used to the dim light, I realized there were markings on the far wall—dozens of small, squarish figures, painted in a dark color on the smooth white surface of the granite. They were arranged in two large clusters of long, straight rows, set two feet apart with a series of random-looking squiggled lines and marks in the space between the clusters.

Each little square figure was about the size of a fist, a blotch of wavy lines inside of rectangles, forming geometric shapes . . . no, they were hieroglyphs, picture-writing—a bird, a spear, an eye . . . a face, with long hair and lines radiating out from its head . . .

Millicent shrieked, startling me so much that I recoiled and hit my head on the ceiling.

"What?"

"Look—" She was pointing down, at something lying across the floor along the wall under the markings. At first, I thought it was just one of the thin, irregular rock formations created by fast-cooling lava.

But no. It was too symmetrical, a double row of slender lines arcing up out of the ground and meeting at a long, smooth plate.

It was the rib cage of a skeleton. I followed the line of the breastbone with my eyes until I found a human skull, dimly visible in the gloom. Peeking up out of the ground in a semicircle under the skull was a broken line of small, colored stones that ended in a little lump of earth just under the jaw. One of the stones glinted brightly, its surface catching a stray ray of sun coming in through the entrance.

I was bending over them for a closer look when I heard Guts say, "More behind ye."

I turned to find two more sets of bones in jumbled piles on either side of the cave entrance. A pair of leg bones stuck straight out of each pile, parallel to the entrance.

It looked like they'd died sitting up, guarding the entrance, and the skeletons had collapsed as the bodies decayed.

Millicent knelt in front of the skull of the first skeleton, brushing the dirt from the semicircle of stones. As the earth fell away from them, it became clear that they weren't just rocks but gems: most were obscured under a layer of caked-on grime, but I saw glimpses of what looked like rubies, emeralds, and even a diamond.

"It's a necklace," she said. She worked her fingers into the dirt under one of the stones and tugged, pulling loose a limp, dirt-encrusted tendon of something that at first I couldn't place.

"What's that?"

"A feather. There was one between each stone."

"How do you know?"

"Because that's how the books describe it. Along with this—" She dug under the lump of earth at the base of the necklace until it crumbled, revealing a three-inch pendant. She scraped the dirt from the pendant to reveal an intricate, multicolored bird, wings extending up over its head, with a diamond for an eye and ruby feathers speckled with sapphires and emeralds.

Even clodded with dirt, it was magnificent. Millicent's eyes were wide with wonder as she stared at it.

"It's a firebird. That's his insignia."

"Whose?" demanded Guts.

"The Fire King's."

"Then where's the treasure?" asked Guts, looking around the chamber. Other than the skeletons, there was nothing in it but a pile of debris in the corner—a couple of small bowls, a rounded stone in the shape of a pestle, and some crumbling chunks of dry fabric that looked like they came from rotted-away containers.

"Maybe my father took it," I suggested.

Millicent was crouched in front of the painted markings on the wall. "No," she said. "There'd be too much. And I don't think it was ever here."

"'Ow d'ye know?" Guts asked.

"Because why else would they draw a map?"

We crowded around the wall, studying the drawings as Millicent tried to make sense of them.

"Look," she said. "That third hieroglyph at the top—a fire-bird, just like on the necklace, with two lines and a dot beneath it—that's the mark of Hutmatozal. And that one—" She pointed to a hieroglyph somewhere in the middle of the first cluster that looked like a lightning bolt over a fist. "That's the Fist of Ka."

"And this . . ." She made a large, sweeping circle with her finger, taking in the area between the two clusters of hieroglyphs. There was a mess of scattered markings across it—dotted lines, crooked squiggles, X's, and a few random hieroglyphs. "That's got to be a map."

"To what?"

"That must be what the rest of it tells us," she said. "How to read the map."

As the sunlight died, I studied the strange pictures and mysterious shapes. They were all gibberish to me. But the closer I looked, the more convinced I was that Millicent was right.

This was what my father had copied onto the parchment he brought with him to Sunrise. Pembroke had let that copy drown somewhere in the ocean along with my family, because he knew he could find the original back here.

This was what he'd killed my family to get his hands on. This was what he was coming for.

It was getting too dark to see. We left the cave and made our way back around the mountain and down to the house, to eat a meal of Quint's stew and try to decide what to do when the sun rose and the soldiers returned.

WE WERE FINISHING our dinner when Otto turned up at the front door.

"Harvest's comin' along," he said as I let him inside. "Keep the pace up, we'll be ready to load in when that ship docks." He looked down at the crates beside the door. "These the guns Stumpy brought up?"

I nodded. He made a quick inspection of them, letting out a low whistle over the grenades.

"Changes things, don't it?"

"Hope so," I said.

"Question is, wot's the plan fer usin' 'em?" Otto stared at me, an eyebrow cocked questioningly over his good eye. "Don't s'pose ye got one?"

"Actually, I do." I'd been mulling over our strategy since the night before, and Guts and I had discussed it at length while we were wrestling the cannon down the hill. "As far as the soldiers know, all we've got is a handful of rifles—and your men aren't necessarily on our side. On top of that, the soldiers won't open fire unless they have to."

"How do ye know?"

"I just do." I looked back at Millicent, who was leaning against the door frame to the kitchen and listening. Pembroke wasn't going to risk accidentally shooting her if he could help it. "So their plan will be to frighten us into giving up without firing a shot. They won't sneak up on us, because that could cause panic, and panic could lead to a shootout. So my guess is they'll send their whole force straight up the road in a show of strength, and only take up battle positions if they run into resistance.

"Which means the thing to do," I continued, "is for most of your men, all but ten or so, to stay in the lower fields, gathering the harvest. Hide your guns in the fruit crates, look like you're busy working. Don't give them any reason to think you're a threat. They'll march right past you, up the road to the house. Once they've passed, get your guns and slip in behind them from the orchards on either side of the road.

"Guts and I will take up position on the porch with the rest of the men. Lure the soldiers in as close as we can. Then open fire with the cannon—"

"What?!" Millicent cried out.

"Shhh!" hissed Guts.

I did my best to ignore them. "As soon as we do, the rest of you open up in a crossfire."

Otto nodded. "Not bad."

"You can't be serious!" Millicent grabbed me by the arm. "Egg, that's murder!"

"It's them or us—"

"You *can't* fire first. You've got to do everything you can to avoid it!"

"We *have* to," I said. "It's the only way we can win."

"'E's right," said Guts.

"It's a decent plan, girlie," said Otto.

She stared at the three of us, her mouth tightening in anger. "You're pigs. Every one of you!"

She turned her back on us and clomped up the stairs. We heard a door slam.

"Might want to tie that one up in the mornin'," Otto suggested. "She could be trouble. Other'n that, nice work. Be up to fetch the guns at first light."

He left the way he came. Guts went over to the crates and started unpacking rifles. "Oughta load these."

I started toward the stairs. "I'll help in a minute. I've got to go talk to Millicent."

"Long's ye still can."

"What do you mean?"

"After tomorrow, she'll be done with ye."

"How do you figure?"

He shrugged. "One o' two things 'appens. Ye die . . . or 'e does. If it's 'im, she never forgives ye."

"But she knows now. What he's really like."

He shook his head. "Don't matter. Kill 'er dad, that's it for ye."

There was nothing to say to that, because I knew he was right.

IT WAS A LONG WALK down the upstairs hallway to Venus's bedroom, because I needed to solve the unsolvable before I got there.

How could I get rid of Millicent's father without losing Millicent?

I had no idea. I knocked on the door.

"It's me," I said. "Can I come in?"

I heard her sigh. "Yes."

She was lying on the bed, staring at the ceiling. I shut the door behind me.

"I'm sorry—"

"Stop." She sat up. "You've made your plan. And it's stupid, and you'll die—"

"I have to—"

"Just listen to me! I've got a better plan. We'll copy the map, scrub the original off the wall so they can't find it, and then run."

"I'm sick of running—"

"Better than dying."

"But it's pointless! Say we run. Say we can somehow get off Deadweather without a fight, which I doubt. The map's useless if we can't translate it. And the only Natives who can do that are in the silver mine back on Sunrise—"

"No," she said. "There're others."

"Where?"

"In the New Lands."

"Are you sure? I thought all the Okalu were wiped out."

"Not all. There're remnants of them. Somewhere in the north. Might even be some in Pella Nonna. Isn't that where the cargo ship's headed?"

I nodded. Pella Nonna was the closest Cartager port in the New Lands, backed up against hundreds of miles of wilderness. I didn't know much about it, other than it was strange and exotic and I didn't speak the language.

"I don't speak Cartager," I said.

"Well, I do," she said. "So we just have to avoid my father long enough to get on that ship. Then we'll be safe."

"Because he wouldn't follow us? He'd just give up?"

The look on her face said she knew he wouldn't.

"I can't spend the rest of my life running away from your father."

She squeezed her eyes shut, pursing her lips. She took a deep breath and held it for a long time before she exhaled sharply. "Then you and Guts go. I'll stay behind. When he comes here, I'll talk to him. I'm still his daughter, and he loves me—"

"He'll tell you what you want to hear, then he'll do what he wants."

"If I make him promise—"

"He'll break it."

"Egg, he's not a monster—"

"He killed my family, and he barely knew them!"

"He didn't—"

"Yes, he did! He murdered them! You can't deny it!"

She started to cry silently, her face wrinkled up and her body shaking.

"I'm sorry," I said. I don't know what I was apologizing for, but I hated to see her like that.

I sat down on the edge of the bed, and she buried her head in my chest. I put my arms around her and stroked her hair gently.

"Don't do it," she whispered. "It's suicide."

"No . . . it's going to be okay," I said, even though I knew it wouldn't be.

Finally, she stopped crying.

"I have to leave," she said. "If you're going to fight him, I can't stay."

I nodded. There was a hollow, heavy feeling in my stomach, and my whole body felt like it was getting sucked into it. I took a deep breath, trying to fight back against the heaviness.

"Do me a favor," I said.

"What?"

"Smile."

She let out a little half laugh and wiped her eyes. "Why?"

"So I can remember you like that. In case I never see you again."

"Oh, Egg . . ." She put a hand on my cheek and gazed into my eyes with a smile full of hurt.

I couldn't tell if the hurt was because we were doomed to be apart, or because I was a fool for liking her that way and she didn't know how to tell me.

I looked away. I had plenty of those pictures of her in my head—the ones that asked the question without answering it. I didn't want another one. They just made me confused.

What I wanted was something that gave me an answer. Like the very first one, that bright pure smile she gave me on the lawn when we were alone together for the first time.

If she gave me that again, just once, I could lock it away in my head and keep it forever. I could remember every detail of it.

That's what I was thinking when a different answer came to me.

I stood up.

"I'm going back to the tomb," I said.

"I'll come with you."

"No. I need to go alone."

I TOOK ALL the blank parchment we had and stuffed it in a sack along with an inkpot, a couple of quills, and a copy of *The Savages of Urluk,* because the cover was big and stiff enough to use as a writing surface, it had fat margins I could write on if I ran out of parchment, and it wouldn't be much of a loss to burn it when I was done.

Guts came into the kitchen as I was filling a lantern with oil and asked me what I was doing.

"I'll tell you later," I said. "Wait here in case Stumpy comes back. If he does, come get me at the tomb."

On the way up the hillside, I stopped at the woodpile behind the house and got the sledgehammer we kept there for splitting firewood with a wedge. It was heavy, and carrying the lantern and sack along with it was awkward because I had to keep both of them level so the oil and the ink wouldn't spill.

Managing all of that made for a slow trip up the mountain, and as I climbed through the moonlit orchards, I had plenty of time to think about whether what I was about to do made any sense.

My plan was to memorize the writing on the wall, copying and recopying every hieroglyph and squiggle until I could draw it all from memory.

Then I was going to smash the wall and burn the copies, so there was nothing left except what was in my head.

It wouldn't solve my problem, exactly. But it seemed to change the rules in a way that would help me. It bound the Fire King's treasure to me as tightly as if I'd swallowed it whole—Pembroke couldn't find it without me, and if he killed me, he'd never get it.

Which meant I'd have an advantage over him—and it felt like I should be able to use that advantage to get him to agree to quit trying to kill me. If I could do that, I wouldn't have to kill him after all.

Which meant I wouldn't have to lose Millicent.

And I might even be able to keep the treasure out of his hands for good—which, short of killing him, seemed like the best way to avenge my family.

I wasn't quite sure how to make it all work out in my head—in fact, the more I thought about it, the more confused I got.

But even though I couldn't figure out exactly how it was going to help me, something about memorizing the map just felt right. I wasn't spending the night lying around helpless, waiting for the soldiers to march on my home. I was taking action, seizing control of the situation, doing something bold and unpredictable.

There was a little part of it that felt cowardly—the part where, if push came to shove, I could use the map to bargain for my life—but mostly it just seemed clever. So clever, in fact, that I couldn't even really understand it.

But I'd figure it all out. I was sure of it.

When I got to the cave, I quit thinking about the plan, because I needed all my brain space to memorize the map. If I couldn't do it before Pembroke showed up with his soldiers, the whole plan was wrecked.

I didn't know how much time I had—I guessed it was about midnight when I finally got to the cave, but I could've been off by an hour or more on either side. And there was no telling how long it would be before Guts came up the mountain to get me.

Making the first copy was agonizingly slow, not only because I had to keep setting down the parchment to raise the lantern and study the wall, but because the markings seemed to have been drawn with a shaky finger, making the lines fat and indistinct. Add this to the fact that I'd never seen such writing before, and it meant that much of the time, I had no idea what I was looking at.

That feather might be a plant stalk . . . What seemed like a spear could just as easily be a shovel, or an arrow . . . Two squarish ovals on either side of an oblong one looked like a butterfly at first . . .

then turned into the eyes and nose of an owl . . . and then finally, one hopelessly confused minute later, turned back into a butterfly.

And the mess of squiggles, dotted lines, and random shapes in between the clumps of hieroglyphs—what seemed to be the map itself—was even harder to decipher. Was that fat dot actually a circle, drawn too tightly? Was that boxy circle actually a lazy square? That curved splotch at the end of a straight line, next to two nearly identical straight lines: was it a tail? Or a dot? Or just a mistake?

Halfway through the first copy, the uncertainty overwhelmed me, panic tightened my chest, and I had to step out of the cave and lie on the ground for a while, staring up at the stars.

I thought back to a book I'd read about the constellations, one that created absurdly detailed patterns of men and animals by connecting what to me looked like meaningless dots of light in the sky. That helped calm me down, because I realized I didn't have to choose between an owl's face and a butterfly's wings—I just had to memorize the figures well enough to recreate them so someone else could decide what they were.

Eventually, I got through the first copy. Then I made three more, straight from the wall itself, until I settled on what I thought was a fairly accurate version. Then I sat down with my back to the wall and just copied the copy, over and over again, giving whatever names to the figures would help me remember them, giving myself permission not to care if they were correct.

Dash dot feather, cup, two dash dot firebird. Spear, sun eye, jagged line stars, tree. Three dash four dot woman face rays. Arrow down line, skull, snakes circled . . .

Cornstalks, lightning fist, boat over water, cloud eye . . .

Three squiggles down left, four dashes up, side bird, three circles straight, X . . .

Sun eye, cloud eye, circle X. Man under circle. Man in circle.

Check the copy. Do it again.

Dash dot feather, cup, two dash dot firebird . . .

Check the copy. Do it again.

My hand cramped. A leg fell asleep. I stepped outside and hobbled around the lava field until the tingling stopped.

I wished I'd brought food. I should have. There was room in the sack. Stupid.

The stars were fading. It would be dawn soon. I wasn't ready yet.

I went back in and started again.

Dash dot feather, cup, two dash dot firebird . . .

Three copies later, I made a perfect one.

The one after that had two mistakes.

The one after that had six.

It was light outside now. I still wasn't close to finished.

I ran out of paper. I started on the margins of the book.

Three copies later, I made another perfect one.

The next one had two mistakes.

I heard the crunch of feet on the volcanic rocks outside.

It was Guts and Millicent.

"Stumpy's back," said Guts. "Boat landed at dawn. They're comin'."

"Do the pirates know?"

Guts nodded. "When we left, they was handin' out the guns."

I gathered the book and the parchment into a little pile in the corner. They watched me.

"Did you memorize it?" Millicent asked.

"Pretty much," I said. Then I lit a match to the paper. *The Savages of Urluk*'s cover peeled into sections as the flames consumed it.

I picked up the sledgehammer.

"It's in yer 'ead? All of it?" Guts asked.

"Hope so," I said, and swung hard at the wall.

It was strange how easily it all fell to dust. That map had stood undisturbed for a hundred years, and I shattered it beyond recognition in half a minute.

The little fire died out, and we left the cave. The bright morning sun made me blink.

I started down the mountain with Guts, but Millicent hung back at the cave entrance.

"I'm staying here," she said.

I stopped and looked back at her. She was leaning against the rock wall, arms crossed. Not angry, exactly. More sad. And frightened.

I wanted to tell her I loved her. But it was too big a risk. At that point, it was better to live with the question than press for an answer and get the wrong one.

"Wish us luck," I said.

She shook her head. "How can I?"

Guts and I walked away. When we got to the edge of the field of wildflowers, I looked back. She'd disappeared inside the cave.

"Don't worry," said Guts. "She'll be down in a few."

"How do you know?"

"Not gonna miss it. 'Ow could she?"

"Then why didn't she just come with us?"

"'Cause she don't know what side she's on."

CHAPTER 19

SHOWDOWN

T ook courage, memorizin' that map," said Guts. We were at the edge of the upper orchard, moving at a pretty good clip down the hill.

"It's not about courage," I said. "If anything, it's cowardly."

"Wot ye mean?"

"I mean, he can't kill me now. If he does, he'll lose the treasure."

"Nah. Just kill ye later. After he tortures ye."

"Why would he torture me?"

"Make ye draw the map."

I hadn't thought about that. *Why didn't I think about that?*

Guts looked back over his shoulder at me. "Why ye stoppin'? Gotta hurry."

"I'm thinking."

"Think and walk, then!"

I started moving again, slower than before. A little knot of worry was growing in my stomach.

"The point is . . . he can't kill me—"

"Not till he tortures ye."

"Stop saying that! Look . . . I memorized it because I want to avoid killing him—"

"No avoidin' that."

"There's got to be a way—"

"How?"

"I haven't figured it out yet."

"'Cause it's impossible."

The knot of worry was spreading through my entire body. I was starting to feel shaky.

"Oh, God . . . was I just incredibly stupid?"

"Not stupid! Genius!"

"How?"

"'Cause now ye *can't* run. He'll follow ye to the end of the earth. Can't surrender, or he tortures ye. Yer all in, man. Gotta fight him to the death." Guts finished the sentence with a jubilant-seeming twitch of his whole head. "Brave, that is."

"I wasn't trying to be brave," I said in a small voice. "I was trying to be clever."

"Stick with brave. Better at it."

I TRIED NOT TO THINK about the fact that my brilliant plan to salvage my future with Millicent had not only guaranteed its destruction, but probably my death as well.

Fortunately, I didn't have much time after that to think about anything. When we got back to the house, the last of the field pirates were disappearing into the lower orchard with their weapons. A dozen men, Mung and Quint included, had stayed behind to man the fortifications on the porch. Quint had brought out his stew pot and turned it upside down to use as a perch so he could shoot over the dirt-bushel fortifications.

Guts cursed when he realized the pirates had taken all the grenades into the fields. Then he cursed even more bitterly when he stepped onto the porch and saw that someone had pushed the cannon to one side to clear a path down the porch steps.

"I had her locked in on the middle of the road! Gotta aim her all over again!"

As he hauled the cannon back into position, I found Stumpy. After two days of shuttling back and forth from Port Scratch, there were baggy dark circles under his eyes.

"How many soldiers?" I asked.

"Hundred twenty. Plus a few what don't wear uniforms."

"Is Roger Pembroke one of them?"

"Dunno. What's he look like?"

"Tall. Handsome. Rich."

"Yeh, think it's him. Leadin' the pack."

Guts aimed the cannon as best he could, and we were about to fire it to test its range when we heard the drums. They were surprisingly close—probably no farther than the edge of the property line a couple hundred yards down the hill.

We all got into position, crouched behind the dirt-filled bushels along the length of the porch. Guts and I were in the middle on either side of the cannon, its barrel peeking out over the bushels at the top of the steps. Mung was to my right. Quint was on the other side of Guts. Everyone kept his head and rifle down.

The drums were getting louder. Their relentless, pounding rhythm must have been meant to scare us into giving up.

They didn't scare me exactly, but they did make my head hurt. I felt dizzy and weak, and I wished I'd eaten breakfast and gotten some sleep instead of staying up all night and memorizing the map like an idiot.

But Guts was right—there was no chance of my running now. I was going to defend my home to the death. And even if I failed, Pembroke wasn't going to get that treasure.

Maybe that was why memorizing the map had felt like the right thing to do.

Maybe it was brave after all. Stupid, but brave.

The drums rose to a wall of sound, overwhelming everything. They were close.

I got up on one knee, raised my rifle over the bushel in front of me, and sighted down the barrel to the point where the road first broke through the trees.

If Roger Pembroke was leading the pack, I was going to shoot him the moment he came into range.

The first line of troops appeared, in crisp blue uniforms criss-crossed with black ammunition belts. Ten men across, rifles at the ready, bayonets fixed. Pembroke was nowhere in sight.

The first line was followed by a second. Then a third. Then a fourth.

Within seconds, the lower road had filled with a sea of blue uniforms, bayonets glinting in the morning sun.

I searched the throng for Pembroke. All I could see were soldiers.

When the last of them came into view, someone must have barked an order, because they stopped in unison. Just as quickly, the drums stopped.

The silence that followed was much more unsettling than the drums themselves.

Then I heard his voice.

"My name is Roger Pembroke," he boomed from somewhere in the back of the sea of troops. "I am the lawful owner of this land. I've come to retrieve my daughter and bring a murderer to justice. To anyone who can hear me, I offer a warning and a promise. The warning is this: the penalty for harboring a fugitive is death."

He let that one echo through the orchard before he continued.

"The promise is as follows: if I leave here peacefully, with justice served and my daughter unharmed, as a token of my gratitude I will bestow on every employee of this plantation a bonus of one hundred pieces of silver."

I heard the low grumble of voices to either side of me. The pirates were mulling over the offer.

"He's lying!" I hissed at them.

"Let me repeat that!" Pembroke called out, still unseen. "A hundred silver for each of you! And all you need to earn it is to stay out of our way."

There was a sudden clatter on the porch, followed by a gurgling bark from Mung. I looked to my right to see him glaring down a line of abandoned rifles at the last of the pirates, hobbling out of sight around the corner of the porch.

Mung looked at me helplessly. The rest of them wouldn't be back until it was time to collect their money from Pembroke.

I turned to look at the other side of the porch. They'd all disappeared on that end, too—except for Quint, who was still standing on top of his stew pot but looked like he'd rather be anywhere else.

And Guts, who was crouched over the short cannon fuse with a match in his hand, ready to light it.

"Say the word," he said.

"Don't!" I held up a hand, begging him off.

Then I looked back at the sea of troops. It was hopeless. Pembroke's money had beaten me before we'd even fired a shot.

"Forward!" I heard a soldier yell.

The troops fanned out, spreading into skirmish lines as they began to march on the house.

"Guts, be smart," I whispered. "Get out of here. If you tell them you're a field pirate, there's a hundred silver in it for you."

"Nuts to that," he said, and lit the fuse.

The thunder of the cannon nearly burst my eardrums, and the smoke briefly obscured my view as I felt the earth shudder from the impact.

When the smoke lifted, the same array of troops was in front of us—all staring at a smoking crater two-thirds of the way between the house and the front line of soldiers.

The only thing Guts had killed was the front lawn.

"Nuts," he croaked.

Then he hurriedly dragged the cannon back to reload. But there wasn't any time. The soldiers had quickened their approach, and they'd be on us with their bayonets long before another round was ready.

I could shoot one of them, maybe even two or three, considering the loaded rifles abandoned all around me. But it was pointless.

Unless I could shoot Pembroke.

But I couldn't even see him.

And the soldiers were closing in. I had to draw him out quickly.

"I HAVE WHAT YOU WANT, AND IF YOU KILL ME YOU'LL NEVER GET IT!" I yelled at the top of my lungs.

Someone barked an order. The troops stopped advancing and went into a defensive crouch. A hundred guns pointed in my direction, the closest one less than thirty feet away.

"Is that you, Egg?" I heard Pembroke call out mildly. His voice was coming from the rear, where a cluster of soldiers stood together.

"It is."

"Where's Millicent?"

"Never mind that," I said. "I've got the thing you've been searching for."

"What might that be?"

"Come closer and we'll talk about it."

"Not unless you stop reloading that cannon."

I motioned for Guts to move away from the cannon. He gave it up reluctantly, moving back to the other side of Quint and picking up a pistol.

There were a dozen bushels of dirt at the top of the porch stairs, guarding the front of the cannon. Taking care not to stand up and present a target, I shoved the middle ones down the stairs with one hand, then swung my leg out, pressing my foot against the cannon's carriage and giving it a hard shove until it rolled forward and tumbled down the steps with a heavy crash.

Then I scurried back into cover.

"Show yourself!" I yelled.

A moment later, the cluster of soldiers at the back parted to reveal a small group of men in civilian dress. Pembroke stepped forward from the group.

"Satisfied?"

I crouched behind one of the bushels under the porch rail, sighting him down the rifle in the little open slot created by the space between the bushel and the top rail. From the other side, the rifle wouldn't be visible. He might guess I was aiming at him, but he wouldn't know for sure.

The problem was, he was still most of the way down the road, too far away for me to be confident I'd kill him with one shot. And I probably wouldn't get a second.

"Come closer," I called out. "I can barely see you."

He took a few steps forward. Still not close enough.

"Let's not play games. What do you have?"

"Come closer!"

"I'm close enough. Tell me what you have."

I wasn't going to get a better shot. My finger curled over the trigger.

"Here it is," I started to say—

"DADDY!"

She must have been watching from inside the house, because she burst out the front door and down the steps so fast that by the time I readjusted my aim after the startle her voice gave me, she was standing right in my line of fire, the only figure in the thirty feet of no-man's-land between the porch and the front line of soldiers.

"Millicent!" He started toward her.

"Stop! Not another step, Daddy!" He did as he was told.

"In fact, move back. All of you," she said, making a wide shooing motion at the soldiers.

They stared at her, bewildered, and held their ground.

She put her hands on her hips, her shoulders thrust back indignantly. "Seriously, Daddy, make them move. We've got a lot to discuss, and I really don't think all these guns are helpful."

Pembroke turned and muttered something to a soldier in the cluster at the rear. He must have been their commander, because he barked, "Fall back!" and the soldiers retreated a respectable distance to watch the situation unfold.

"Here's the thing, Daddy . . . Can you hear me all right?" She was speaking so loudly they could probably hear her in the lower orchards.

"Yes, darling," he said, more than a little impatiently.

"There's been a terrible series of misunderstandings. Absolutely dreadful. First Egg goes out with Mr. Birch on a perfectly pleasant excursion, they're getting along famously, when suddenly there's a horrible accident. Birch trips on a root, falls to his death, and somehow everyone gets it in their head that Egg pushed him.

"Which couldn't be farther from the truth. I mean, Daddy, you know Egg. He's the gentlest and sweetest of souls, and he'd never hurt anyone on purpose, LET ALONE KILL HIM . . ."

As she said this, she turned away from her father and threw a pointed stare in my direction, as if to say, *Put that gun down.*

"Shoot him," muttered Guts from the other side of the porch.

"She's blocking my shot!" I muttered back.

"And that's just the start of it, Daddy," continued Millicent. "There's been a whole series of absolutely fantastical rumors swirling around. Completely unbelievable, and so slanderous of you I ordinarily wouldn't even dignify them with a response. But they've gotten so widespread that I really must mention every single one so you can denounce them all, unequivocally, in front of all these people."

"Darling, I really don't think—"

"Here's the first one: that you intentionally rigged that balloon accident to send Egg's family to their death. That can't possibly be true, can it?"

"Of course not, darling."

"And the idea that you sent Birch to kill Egg—it's preposterous, isn't it?"

"Quite so, sweetheart."

"That's what I keep telling everyone! It's laughable! But they're quite stuck on the idea, probably because of the other rumor— that you created some phony adoption certificate and forged Egg's name to it so you could take control of the plantation. Surely *that's* false, right, Daddy?"

Even from a distance, I could see Pembroke's face begin to turn red.

"That's a bit less clear, darling—"

"Then let's clear it up straightaway! Egg, did you ever agree to be adopted by my father?"

"No, I didn't," I called out.

"You never signed any papers to that effect?"

"Definitely not."

"So if any papers did exist, they'd be forgeries, and completely illegal?"

"That's right," I said.

"Millicent—" There was a hard edge to Pembroke's voice. She'd pushed him to the limit.

"Don't get cross, Daddy. It's not your fault at all! I think I know what the problem is."

"Which is what?"

"Shoddy legal advice. Is Mr. Archibald with you?"

"No, dear. He's back on Sunrise."

"Well, I think you should have a *very* pointed conversation with him when we get home, because he's obviously served you quite poorly. Wouldn't you agree?"

"I suppose it's possible."

"It *must* be the case! Because I love you so *very* much, Daddy. You're the kindest, most honorable man in the world, and you'd *never* hurt an innocent person, or try to take what isn't yours. I mean, if you'd really done *any* of those things, my heart would simply break! I could never speak to you again."

Her voice wavered a little. She paused for a moment. When she started again, she was all brightness and good cheer.

"But that's *obviously* not what happened. So can we all just agree, on both sides, that this was completely silly, and with the possible exception of one incompetent lawyer, no one's done anything wrong? Egg?"

I looked at Guts. His eyes were scrunched together in a confused look, and a little disappointed, too, like he was sorry the morning might not end in a rain of bullets after all.

"Works for me," I called out.

"Daddy? Do you agree?"

"To what, now, darling?"

"Do you agree that Egg didn't kill Birch, he's not your adopted son, and the plantation is his property?"

Pembroke was silent.

"Please tell me you agree, Daddy. Because I love you so."

I saw his shoulders rise, then sag a bit. When he spoke, I could barely hear him.

"Of course, my love."

"Oh, that's *such* a relief!"

She raised her hands, addressing everyone like the director of a play. "Now, let's all put the guns away and go about our business! Daddy, Egg, come meet me in the middle so we can shake hands and part as friends."

It took some doing on both sides to make that happen. There was a long, muttered argument among the cluster of civilian men on Pembroke's side that Millicent had to horn in on, and it took me almost as long to convince Guts to set down the pistol he was holding and agree not to shoot anybody.

But within a few minutes, the soldiers' guns were strapped to their backs, they were facing downhill in formation for the march back to the port, and Pembroke and I were standing with Millicent in the middle of the lawn, near the fresh crater left by the cannonball. Pembroke's associates watched from a safe distance over by the soldiers, as Guts, Mung, and Quint stood on the porch.

"Now, let's shake hands so Daddy and I can sail away to Sunrise and forget this whole thing ever happened," said Millicent.

Pembroke's face was expressionless, but his eyes never left

mine. The firm grip of his handshake stopped just short of being painful.

"Terribly sorry about all these misunderstandings," he said.

"That's all right," I said.

"We certainly enjoyed having you as a houseguest those few weeks."

"Thank you for your hospitality," I said, trying to sound sincere.

"Wouldn't mind having you again. In fact, you're more than welcome to come back with us now if you'd like."

"Think I'll stay here," I said.

"Shame. Still, hope to you see you again soon." He smiled when he said it, but the look in his eyes made my blood run cold.

He turned away. "Come along, Millicent."

"Just a moment, Daddy. I need to say good-bye to Egg."

She stepped past him toward me, with a kind of smile on her face I'd never seen before.

"Thank you," I said. "For everything."

"Is this a good smile to remember?" It was sweet and tender, but less confident than usual. It almost seemed shy. Like a lot of things about her, it confused me.

But I liked it. I nodded.

She stepped closer, so close our chests were almost touching, and slipped her fingers through mine.

"Remember this too," she breathed, as her lips rose to kiss me.

I let my eyes fall shut as I leaned into her. When we finally separated and I opened my eyes again, I saw spots.

She laughed a little. I did too.

Then I saw the look on her father's face.

Someone was going to pay for that kiss.

It might have been me, right then—I wouldn't have been surprised if Pembroke had reached out to strangle me with his bare hands. But she tugged him on the arm, guiding him away from me.

"Good-bye, Egg!" she called.

"Good-bye," I said.

Pembroke gave me one last cold look.

"See you soon, boy."

Then he turned away, and they started off toward the others.

I turned around and began to walk back toward the house. I felt like I was floating, blissful and stupid.

Which was why it took me so long to register the look of alarm on Guts's face.

He shouted a warning as he started toward me, his eyes locked onto something over my shoulder.

I turned around. One of the men in civilian clothes—big and rough-looking—was sprinting straight at me. He was almost past Millicent and Pembroke, and they were shouting at him to stop.

But they didn't get in his way, for fear of the knife in his hand.

I might have been able to outrun him, back to the porch where I could pick up a gun and defend myself, if I'd focused on the knife and not his face. But the face froze me in place, baffled, unable to believe what I was looking at was real.

It was Birch. I was watching a ghost, risen from the dead to take his revenge on me.

I stood there like an idiot, motionless, just waiting for him to plunge the knife in my chest, until a low blur entered my line of sight and hit him at the knees just a couple of feet in front of me.

He went down hard, and Guts was on him like a wild animal,

thrashing and quick, and we were all converging on them—me, Mung, Millicent, Pembroke, a few of the other men—when we heard Birch scream.

The knife fell to the ground, and I saw it first and plucked it up as Millicent reached me. Birch was still screaming, and the others were pulling Guts off him, and there was bright red blood spurting from Birch's arm and smeared across Guts's face, and I realized he'd bitten Birch's arm right through the artery and down to the bone.

"Are you all right?" Millicent asked me.

I was fine. Birch's knife was in my hand. The other men were dragging him off, trying to calm him down and tamp the spurting of his bloody arm. But I still couldn't understand what I was seeing.

"That's Birch."

She nodded.

"Thought I killed him."

"You did. That's his brother."

He screamed curses at me as they took him away, and I knew then Roger Pembroke wasn't my only enemy in the world.

We stayed on the porch after that, close enough to the guns to be safe. Millicent waved one last time as she disappeared from view at the back of the procession.

I waved back. My arm was heavy as lead. I was exhausted.

Mung put a hand on my shoulder and gurgled something supportive. I smiled at him. He smiled back, then started down toward the lower orchard to help finish the harvest. The pirates who'd disappeared on me after Pembroke offered them money were slinking back into view as well, trying not to meet my eye as they limped back to work. A few of them were bold enough to pluck their abandoned guns from the porch before they left.

"Strange day," said Quint, vaulting toward the front door on his arms. "Biscuits inside if ye want 'em."

I turned to Guts, standing next to me. He'd tried to wipe Birch's blood off his face, but he'd missed a couple of spots.

"Thanks for saving my life," I said.

He looked at the knife in my hand. "Keep that. Learn to use it, maybe next time I won't 'ave to."

He started for the door. "Let's eat some biscuits."

CHAPTER 20

INTO THE SUNSET

Once we'd eaten, all I wanted to do was sleep. But I couldn't let myself nod off until I knew Pembroke and the soldiers had left the island, so Guts and I went down to the orchards to find Stumpy and ask if he'd make one more trip to town and report back to us when the ship sailed.

The orchards were worryingly empty, the harvesting hooks leaning abandoned against tree trunks and fruit crates. Halfway to the property line, we found out why. The first trickle of giddy pirates, still armed with Burn Healy's weapons, were hobbling up the road and jingling coins in their hands.

I stopped one of them and asked where everyone had gone.

"To get the money!" he cackled. "That richy was gonna leave without makin' good on his promise. So we stopped him and had a confab. First, he said he didn't owe us nothin', 'cause there weren't no justice to be done after all. Then the boys pointed out he got his daughter back. So we settled on half. Fifty silver for every man! Be drunk for weeks on this!"

Guts looked at me. "Might check this out."

"Go," I said. "You deserve it."

He came back half an hour later with fifty silver pieces and a smile on his face. By then, I'd found Stumpy, who'd begged off another trip down the mountain. So Mung went instead, happy for the chance to ride a horse and be helpful.

Guts and I watched him trot down the road, weaving past handfuls of boisterous, newly flush pirates who kept startling the horse by firing their guns in the air.

I was starting to worry that the combination of money, guns, and pirates was going to cause problems.

Guts agreed. "Least they ain't got rum. Yet."

Otto the foreman was concerned, too, enough that he threatened to kill any man who left the plantation for the taverns of Port Scratch before the harvest was loaded in. For the most part, the men obeyed him, but for the rest of the day, the work seemed to go much slower and get a lot more dangerous, especially once someone discovered that stuffing a live grenade inside an ugly fruit made for a fun practical joke.

Guts and I spent the afternoon around the house, trying to ignore the gunfire and explosions coming from the orchards as we planned our journey to Pella Nonna and the New Lands.

There wasn't much to plan. We each packed a knife and a pair of pistols from the Healy cache. Quint helped us wash our clothes, then got out his mending basket and sewed up some of the tears we'd accumulated in them. When I put it back on, I realized my itchy shirt had seen so much wear that it no longer itched, or if it did, I didn't notice it anymore.

I practiced drawing the map a few times, on title pages I tore out of some of my least favorite books. I burned the results over the stove when I was finished. I hoped I'd remembered it right, but there was no way of knowing if I hadn't.

There was nothing else to do except wait for Mung to come back so I could get some sleep. By the time he showed up in the late afternoon, I was pacing the house because I'd gotten so groggy I couldn't sit down anymore without my eyes falling shut.

With a combination of hand gestures and reassuring gurgles, he managed to communicate that the ship had sailed, with the Pembrokes, the soldiers, and the rest of their party aboard. I was so grateful I hugged him. Then I dragged myself to my bed and collapsed into such a heavy sleep that even the sound of the occasional grenade detonating in the orchards didn't disturb me.

I WOKE UP in the quiet just before morning and lay in bed for a while, thinking about Millicent. For the first time, I didn't have to argue with myself about her. The endless, maddening *does-she-or-doesn't-she?* was over. The answer was yes. She did.

Which made the next question all the more painful.

When will I see her again?

I didn't know. All I knew was it wouldn't be soon. I had to go to the New Lands, farther than I'd ever traveled in my life, and overcome who knew what to find a Native who could read Okalu and tell me where that map was pointing.

And then I had to follow it wherever it led. The treasure might be on Sunrise, or back here on Deadweather, or deep in the jungles of the New Lands. Or somewhere else.

Or there might not be any treasure at all.

Was that possible?

Anything was possible. The only thing I knew for sure was that Guts and I weren't the only ones who'd be searching for it. Thanks to Millicent, Roger Pembroke and I had both walked away from our last encounter, but it seemed even more true than ever that my troubles with him wouldn't end until one of us was dead.

And then there was Birch, the twin brother of the man I'd killed. I hadn't seen the last of him, either.

But there was nothing to do about any of that now, and no point in worrying about it.

I got up and padded out to the front porch. It was the best time of day on Deadweather—the only good time, actually, a sliver of an hour before dawn when the temperature and the humidity were low enough to be almost tolerable. The ugly fruit harvest was finally in and loaded onto a six-wagon train, waiting near the stable for the horses to be hitched to it for the trip down to the cargo ship at the docks.

I'd made that trip with the loaded wagon train a dozen or more times, but I'd always stopped at the water's edge and turned around again to come back home behind an empty wagon.

This time was different. I'd be following the harvest to the end of the line. And I didn't know when I'd be back. Or if I ever would.

And my family was gone. No matter what, *they* weren't coming back here. Thinking about them put a lump in my throat. I even got a little choked up over my brother—maybe not so much over Adonis himself, because he was so vile, but over the idea of a brother, and the loss of what we might have had if my mother hadn't died having me and things had turned out differently.

I heard the creak of the front door. Guts stepped out. He smiled at me, his bad arm hidden behind his back.

"What are you smiling about?"

"Went shoppin' last night. Bought a little somethin' from one o' the pirates."

He pulled his arm out to show me. There was a steel hook strapped to his wrist over a worn leather cowl.

"Congratulations! You always wanted one of those."

"Yeh," he said, admiring it. "Think I'll call her Lucy. Can't wait to see how she does in a scrap . . . An' I took a trip back up the mountain—"

He reached into his baggy pants pocket and pulled out an unwieldy clump of something that unfurled into a string of dirt-crusted gems and raggedy shafts of decomposed feathers, culminating in the three-inch firebird pendant.

"The Fire King's necklace."

He nodded. "Only thing up there worth hangin' on to."

Something about it made me uneasy. "You sure it's okay?" I asked.

"What?"

"Taking it from a dead man."

"He ain't usin' it."

"I don't know . . . I mean, what if it's cursed or something?"

Guts snorted. "Only curse on this is the smell." He gave it a sniff, then twitched and stuffed it back in his pocket. "'Sides, might do us good with the Natives."

I nodded. Then I took a step back to get a good look at my house.

"Feels strange to be leaving again so soon."

There was a distant whoop from the direction of the pirates' barracks, followed by the boom of a grenade. Then a scream, and then a sprinkle of laughter.

"Good time for it, tho'," said Guts.

"Yeah. At least until they're out of grenades."

EVERY LAST ONE of the field pirates went down the mountain with the harvest, clinging to the sides of the wagons or hobbling alongside them. The ones with two hands carried their money in one and their guns in the other, their good eyes blazing with anticipation for the hell they were about to raise.

We must have made a fearsome sight, because even the drunks on the street in Port Scratch got out of the way as we lurched through town.

Guts and I were in the lead wagon with Otto. He'd spent some time around Cartagers, and on the way down, he gave us a lesson in speaking the language.

"Tell ye all ye need to know," he said. "*Weh.*"

"*Weh,*" I repeated.

"Means yes. *Neh.*"

"*Neh.*"

"Means no. And *Perfa neha ma graw.*"

"*Perfa neha ma graw?*"

"Means 'please don't kill me.'" He clapped me on the back. "Ye'll do fine."

THE CARGO SHIP, a creaky-looking schooner named the *Thrush,* was waiting at the dock. The sight of so many armed pirates, and the manic speed with which they started heaving the fruit crates into the hold, clearly spooked the captain, a lanky, weather-beaten man whom Otto introduced to us as Racker.

"These two need passage to Pella Nonna," he said.

Captain Racker eyed me and Guts with concern. "Can't bring you back," he said. "Headed down to the Barkers after that."

"That's all right," I said. "One way is fine."

He shrugged. "Climb aboard, then."

Guts checked the waterline on the dock pilings. "Tide's fallin'. Gonna wait to ship out?"

Racker looked down the dock and across the street, where a throng of field pirates were pounding on the door of the closest tavern, yelling for the proprietor to get out of bed and open his taps.

"Think we'd better go now," he said.

WE NEARLY RAN aground rushing out of the harbor against the tide, but Captain Racker put oars in the hands of every man on board, Guts and me included, and we managed to row out of the shallows before the field pirates got drunk enough to start real trouble.

The farther out we got, the more frequent the sound of gunfire became, and by the time we were under sail and Port Scratch was slipping out of view, I thought I saw flames rising from one of the buildings. God only knew what shape the place would be in when I got back to it.

If I ever got back.

I took one last, good look at the black lump of the volcano, smoldering in the sun. Then I turned away from Deadweather and looked ahead, to the western horizon and the New Lands beyond.